THE ORIGINAL GLITCH

ALSO BY MELANIE MOYER

THE RULES OF ME

THE ORIGINAL GLITCH

MELANIE MOYER

LANTERNFISH PRESS
PHILADELPHIA

Lanternfish Press
399 Market Street, Suite 360
Philadelphia, PA 19106
lanternfishpress.com

Cover Design: Kimberly Glyder

Printed in the United States of America.
25 24 23 22 21   1 2 3 4 5

Library of Congress Control Number: 2020952884
Print ISBN: 978-1-941360-59-0
Digital ISBN: 978-1-941360-60-6

TO THE CAT WHO WAS UP WITH ME IN THE EARLY
MORNINGS WHILE I WROTE EVERY WORD OF THIS BOOK
BUT WAS GONE BEFORE IT TOOK PHYSICAL FORM

"I am thy creature: I ought to be thy Adam,
but I am rather the fallen angel,
whom thou drivest from joy for no misdeed."

—Mary Shelley

THE END

This is the only entry I haven't properly dated. I leave it like this mainly so you will have no way of assigning a day of mourning for me. I know you will want to. But I want this to be about why, not about how or when. There are things about my life you could point at—a failed marriage, public frustration with the Consortium. A million possible reasons. But the truth is we do things because we can and, sometimes, because we have to.

It is the fear of all parents that their children will rise one day to kill them—literally or metaphorically. The job of offspring is to outpace their siblings and displace the ones who created them in the first place. That's how you came to be, in a simplistic way of speaking. How all of us did. If you believe in silly old books, it is the story of the world's creation. Creature vying with creator for mastery. I see, perhaps, that my only way to deny him this victory is to take it for myself and become my own murderer. Looking into my crystal ball, I know I am the one I should be afraid of. I earned that for myself.

I didn't want to be afraid of him. Of what I helped them become. You will ask why, then, I took the risk of making them in the first place. But the question is a feeble one: why have children, why create new software, why write books and poems? Because we can and we must. The fear of our children, our works, outliving us, outshining us, being the death of ourselves is nothing compared to the glory when the idea first sparks: when the Big Bang of the mind shows a future we can choose to chase. That's my poetic, optimistic view, anyway. The stakeholders aren't so abstract. What is the state's interest in life? What is there to be earned, to be gained, in creating it? That's what I should have asked at the beginning, the same question abortion rights activists have asked legislatures for decades and decades: why, exactly, are you so interested in us making more people? It's not purely for the thrill of creating something new.

This is the last time I will speak to you, but not the last time you will speak to me. I haven't left you completely alone. But you are the one creation I desperately hope destroys me in the end.

CHAPTER ONE

IF BODY CLOCKS were a real thing, Laura had one more finely tuned than the intestines of Big Ben. She was up, every morning, before the sunrise. No matter the changing seasons. Her body managed to keep track. Like a direct line to the sun from the second it sent its first rays over the horizon, slicing through the massive pines that grew on the foothills surrounding Palmer. She wanted to be frustrated, annoyed at how she would inevitably crave a nap by the time noon rolled around. Not to mention the part where she woke up hungry, ate before sunrise, and was hungry again by eight a.m.

She'd dreamed again of a cat nuzzling her head.

She didn't know why she was a morning person. She'd googled it once—truthfully, twice—to see if it meant anything. Some woman down the street with a neon *Psychic* sign in her window had tried to find the answer in her tarot cards, claiming that Jupiter was doing God knows what and it made whatever the cards revealed more meaningful. But not cheaper. Laura had walked away hiding an eye roll behind her sunglasses. It was bad enough convincing herself that the $2.50 she spent for an Americano every morning, necessary if she was going to drag herself through the front door of North Pines Pizza, was worth it. The money she'd just spent for a crazy old woman from Brooklyn to read her some mass-produced cards over the smell of cigarettes and spilled beer was nowhere in her budget—minuscule as that was.

All she knew was that her brain knew the sun, and it roused her when the time came. She would wake to darkness and the promise of watching light bloom through her kitchen like ink in a cup of water. Building a routine, at first, felt like having meaning. Every step had a purpose and moved into the next to build the patterns of a day. But the longer that went on, the more it felt like a treadmill or hamster wheel. Was there a purpose to the coffee energizing her head if she didn't do a thing with the wakefulness there?

They were thoughts too dark for the morning and too frustrating for when the sun went down. She let them slip out of her head as her feet hit the cold wooden floor beneath her bed. She longed, one day, to have an apartment with carpeted floors. Despite how much all those home-improvement shows claimed hardwood floors were more valuable, it seemed every cheap apartment in the town was nothing but cold floors that stole away the chance for a cozy retreat in winter. Not to mention that crumbs accumulated within seconds and Laura never had the energy to sweep them up.

She went into the bathroom. She left its door open constantly, so the sound of her peeing into the porcelain bowl echoed around the apartment for every bug and mouse in the wall to hear. From where she sat, hunched over and shivering just a bit in the morning chill, she stared down the hall and saw the spark through the window where Mrs. Howl would certainly be able to see her, if anyone else was up at this ridiculous hour. She finished and moved on to brushing her teeth, wary because of the time she'd had two hours of sleep after finishing a bottle of wine and accidently attempted to brush her teeth with a pump of hand soap on the bristles instead of toothpaste. She'd had to throw the toothbrush out and taste a chemical lollipop in her mouth the rest of the day.

The only time Laura allowed herself a moment to look at her own face was when no one else was around. She wasn't the type of person to stop in front of a window in public and stare at what it had to show. There was something disturbing about having others watch you watch yourself.

What Laura saw that morning was a pale face, dark under the eyes to compensate, and a general look of desperation that could only belong to a twenty-something struggling to afford groceries for the millionth week in a row. She didn't need much, but the wrinkles on her face didn't seem to know that. She took a pool of cold water in her cupped hands and splashed it onto the face from the mirror. It didn't change. She didn't feel more awake. But she did enjoy the shock of it for a moment or two before smothering it in the softness of the hand towel next to her.

She liked coffee, black and heavy. The kind that made her cringe when she drank it, but she was too addicted to not come back for more after one sip was down. She sat with the mug glued to her hand, the edge of the kitchen chair cutting into the backs of her thighs. The sunrise was slow and monotonous. And bright. She knew that, in seconds, the colors would change, they'd be gone. They could change to become more beautiful, or more average, but either way they'd be gone. She wanted to know them for as long as possible.

There was an optimism to the start of the day that she really couldn't shake. It was such a horrifying thing to admit to yourself that you were a morning person. But her body obeyed the turn of the earth. It was in the early hours that she felt clarity and ambition, before the pizza shop sucked it out of her and she came home to collapse on the couch, ambitions vanished. Maybe that was how capitalism got people—draining them of their energy at work like a supervillain throwing kryptonite and then waiting for no one to be able to even lift a finger when the day was done.

Laura pulled out her laptop. She opened it to the job pages. She refreshed again.

Application Submitted. It was better than a lovely, bold screen that said *Application Not Referred.* She'd never gotten farther than a submitted application, but Schrodinger's cat kept her coming back, telling her no news was a chance. The sun was coming up, the coffee was doing something to her brain, and no one from the jobs site had said no yet. She felt the spark of a future where she wouldn't be serving pizza to townies forever. She could move out, go north to Toronto or south to New York City. She could afford school, do all the things she should have done, the things her mother had hoped for. Get out of this hamlet nestled in the wilds of Upstate.

"You're so smart," her mother had said.

Out of context, it sounded simple, like something you'd say to pacify a child, and maybe that was her intention. But the pauses, the tone, and the way her bright blue eyes used to watch Laura told her that it was more than just lip service. There was always some reverence in her voice. So she would embrace today as a new day, a new chance to make her mother proud. She even carried the same name. There was Laura the First and Laura the Second. Laura Senior and Laura Junior.

"Men do it all the time," her mother had said. "Why shouldn't women honor each other the same way?"

In the predawn light, Laura still felt like her mother might be nearby, sleeping in for once or maybe taking her coffee with a moment of quiet contemplation. But the sun would come up and her mother would still be gone and she'd push it all away. She was sure the tolerance she'd built up to caffeine left her far beyond being helped by any level of coffee consumption possible to mortals. But she'd keep trying. There was something to be said for the placebo effect, after all.

The golden spires of the sun across the retreating night were in full effect now, and so was the rumbling of Laura's stomach. She was a morning person but not a breakfast person. She found the socially acceptable options for breakfast disgusting. Often she chose leftovers—or scoops of peanut butter straight from the jar, if she had any around. Or she'd convince herself that she wasn't hungry just long enough for the first meal of the day to suddenly be lunch.

Today was not a day she could put it off. Her stomach was rumbling and the coffee pooling inside would quickly turn against her.

"Mystery food to save me from my misery?" She opened the cabinet, knowing nothing had changed since she went looking for a late night snack. There was always the hope, though, of some secret food she'd missed.

Instead: the same granola bars, sugary cereal, boxes of instant pasta, and bags of chips. She grabbed the bag of vinegar chips and brought it over to the kitchen table, where she allowed it to mix with the coffee in her stomach and continued to watch night become day.

"You're going to be so many great things," her mother had said.

The voice was a distant echo that Laura clung to as she tasted bitterness over salt with each sip. She had a stomach burned out on the inside and padded with softness on the outside; equally soft flesh hung off her arms. She wasn't healthy; she was overweight and probably rotting on the inside; she also couldn't afford a doctor's appointment.

She just existed. It seemed she had always just been there.

CHAPTER TWO

THE MIDDAY RUSH was not invigorating. It wasn't inspiring. It didn't bring anything to Laura except the hope of enough tips collecting in the dinky jar in front of the cash register to buy something, anything. This was America. That mostly meant Marco got away with paying her whatever he felt like, claiming it was enough because beer and coffee, the only things he assumed anyone was interested in, were cheap.

"The minimum wage in Canada is $12," she said one day, staring at what passed for a paycheck from a 56-hour week.

"Then move." Marco shrugged.

She frowned. He walked away feeling smart and she was left with a check that gave her pennies to spare once rent was paid.

So she was never excited to make her way to North Pines Pizza. She'd been offered the job because a friend knew a friend and taken it because she was a kid fresh out of high school without any real money or a high enough GPA to go to college for free. At first she'd thought she was the smart one, not going to school and not racking up debt. But here she was, years later, still marinating in dough and cheese and onions and smelling like it at the end of the day, while nicely scented, well-dressed people would come in on their lunch break and maybe give her a couple of extra dollars because they felt bad for her.

She didn't need more pocket change. She needed freedom.

"I'm 25," she said to Gray.

For the first few weeks she'd worked at North Pines, Gray had been a person to fear. He was the kitchen manager, the guy who worked the most and turned into a drill sergeant during dinner rushes every night. He was skinny. He was made of sinewy muscles from years of working dough and his head was already bald beneath the baseball caps he wore.

But they clicked. After those first few weeks of them being paid to quietly cohabit the same place of employment, he'd somehow turned into the closest friend she had. She didn't know when it happened; it was like a great romance, only platonic. One day the friendship just burst into existence as if it had always been there, as if she'd been waiting for it her whole life.

"You're 25. So what. You want a booster seat?" he asked, moving the dough in a circle, pulling it from the pudgy ball it had been moments ago into the large, thin, flat disc that would hold the sauce and the cheese and whatever toppings the latest *fucking degenerate* customer, as Gray said, had ordered. (He didn't like it when people ordered off-menu.)

"I want out," she said. "Before I'm old."

"I'm 32. You got time."

"You think I want to be you when I'm 32?"

"Good point."

She looked for the eighth time into the bar fridge, knowing the same exact amount of Coke and beer and iced tea would be there as last time she checked, but she had to give herself something to do. She didn't envy Gray his massive amounts of cleaning and running around to prep the food and make the sauces on top of filling orders, but sometimes she wanted more to do than just stand and wait for someone to come in and stare at the pizza and tell her how amazing it was and how much their wives or husbands or ungendered partners loved it so much and they should all be so proud. Laura never actually touched the pizza. At first she wanted to. She thought she could pick the knack up quick, look good spinning dough, impress people the way Gray did. But it was not her fate to be a pizza god and she stayed dutifully behind the register, throwing slices into the oven as needed, popping Diet

Cokes because she didn't care about sugar but liked the fake saccharine taste for some reason. Everyone had a favorite drug.

She watched the muscles of Gray's shoulders through the white of his t-shirt, which had avoided stains over the years but acquired several tears and holes, especially at the armpits where bits of mousy brown hair poked through.

"I just wish I was somewhere else," she said.

"Preaching to a massive choir, homegirl."

"Well, like, you're good at cooking. You went to school for it. You're basically a chef—"

"Line cook."

"But you're good at it and you've always done it. I just have no idea what to do. Here I am."

He blew a bit of flour off the granite where they stretched the dough out and spread around what was left, letting the center of the thin disc float back down to the surface. "Plenty of people are good at shit they hate."

"Do you hate this?"

"I'm starting to."

He was here because a childhood friend of his was the actual chef, or at least as much of a chef as you could be at a small-town pizza parlor. No matter how hipster they tried to make it, it was a by-the-slice place that charged too much, hoping to get on the same level as the only place in Palmer that inspired people to eat their pizza with a knife and fork while eyeing the fancy stemmed wine glass at the side of the plate and feeling embarrassed to order wine that cost less than $12 a glass.

"It's getting monotonous as fuck, you know?" he said. "Anyway. I have an idea for a new seasonal."

He was like that. Plenty of complaints and glares, but he took what he did seriously while he did it. He wouldn't be accused of slacking, not that the new kitchen guy wasn't trying. Dan came from someplace even more bumpkin than Palmer and had a lot to say about a lot of things. Gray was one of those things.

"We get it," Gray said by the second week Dan had been there. "You obsess about pizza to get over the alcoholism you *clearly* have because all you do is drink Coke, smoke, and talk about how you don't fucking drink anymore." He shouted into the pizza dough as it stretched between the splay of his hands. Maybe it would go down like a god of war in the mouth, aggravated into life by clenched fists.

Laura just smiled and nodded when Dan talked, because he never stopped. Not even when you walked away. She walked away a lot when he spouted something racist or homophobic or sexist, which was often. But he seemed to like her because she liked Star Wars, and they would talk theories about the Force or Stephen King novels until he went on a tangent about some *Persian guy* or *bitch* of a head chef he'd worked for in the past.

Gray was right. It was monotonous. Show up. Drop off your crap. Clock in. Pretend to do things until the owner showed up or some asshole sent in a massive pizza order. Do it all again the next day and then the next for minimum wage, stealing as much food and alcohol as possible from the walk-in fridge downstairs.

Some guy sitting next to Laura at a bar had once complained about part-time workers and how you could treat them as nice as pie but they'd always end up stealing from you. *Yes*, she wanted to say, *because we can't live like this, literally.* But it was impossible talking to someone past a certain age about anything. So she took some tall cans and pizzas at the end of the night and saved money at the grocery store.

"18 pep for pick up," Laura called, placing the order chit in the metal shelf above the dressing station.

"Oui Jeff!"

Everything in pairs. The night was the opposite of the morning. Sunset the evil twin of sunrise. It was beautiful, burnt at the edges and frayed. Laura didn't fall for its glamor. She'd glance at the reds and oranges and the rusts in between for a few seconds and then look away, blinking back into sapphire blue or the nothingness of nighttime.

There were times, in Palmer, when she felt there was something grossly close to magic going on. It wasn't magic. She knew that. It wasn't even science. She just got a certain feeling in the moments in between night and day. For those few brief seconds she'd be willing to believe in the bullshit of tarot cards and her star sign and all that. But only in Palmer. Only in the seclusion of this place.

It followed, then, that her mood also shifted at sunset. Just like the mornings brought her hope and something to open her eyes for, the nights dug at her emotions too. She didn't like sunsets. She got low in the night. The bullet was the length and darkness of the nighttime; the trigger was that vibrant, dying sun.

Then quiet.

Laura didn't like to use the word *lonely*. She didn't want to be someone who pined. Gray made fun of her. Every time she mentioned a man (or a woman), he had questions and even more smirks and winks. There had been no such luck in recent months, though, and not for the reasons most people might assume.

The quiet comfort of her routine was a part of her; it gave purpose to the long nights. She had yet to meet a person she liked enough to transcend her addiction to her own solitude. And she'd tried them all. Men had kissed her, women had kissed her; if there were anyone in this tiny little town who identified as neither, she'd go off and kiss them too. But love was like the Bible to her. She heard the stories, which seemed to make plenty of people cry, but they left an empty feeling in her stomach. There was no spark, no longing. Love was a story that was true for some. She knew it front to back. But it wasn't hers.

The wine she was drinking was sharp and acidic after a week in the refrigerator. She'd been trying to stretch it out for as long as possible; wine was expensive. She refreshed the jobs feed again, but there was nothing new. The problem, of course, was that you live where you live, and you get jobs there. If you want to move somewhere else, you need a job to get a new place, but to get a job somewhere else, you need an address nearby. Plus five years' experience for an entry-level job and five references.

But she was 25. She had to decide which she was going to be: the one who shot for the stars and missed, or the one who stayed put and played along until she died. Even if some people were just the pawns on the chessboard, someone else had to be the queen. Besides: couldn't a pawn become a queen, if she made it far enough?

Laura didn't imagine she was a queen. But she wanted to be. She would will herself into importance before the cold, neutral eyes of the universe. Somehow.

What she needed was a pet. Well, what she needed was to put down the bottle of wine and find something in life that would make her smile. But something she could talk to, something that loved her unconditionally, might be a nice change. Something soft. She could give purpose to another being, maybe a cat who'd had nothing before her but had everything after the day they met.

She was going to have a headache tomorrow. It was just as well; Gray always showed up to work with bags under his eyes complaining that he might have some kind of drinking problem. Maybe he was her portrait and she was Dorian Gray.

She wasn't sure what had cemented their bond. She'd been convinced for the longest time that he didn't even like her. She wouldn't have blamed him if that was true at the beginning. She was kind of a pain in the ass to work with. She'd never done kitchen things before. Gray had worked in kitchens for years and was patient, but only to a point.

"Yell 'behind' when you're behind me," he complained after bumping into her. "Basic kitchen shit."

She'd felt her face turn red and dropped her eyes. Until the day she was the one telling people to yell out when she bumped into their mouse-quiet bodies.

Maybe their friendship had started the night they went out and got drinks together and he swore he could give her a piggyback ride. They'd both ended up with cement under their chins and blood getting on their sleeves as they tried to wipe it away. When people asked if they were all right, they laughed. *Midnight is the sinner's happy hour!* They both still had the scars.

Or it might have been that enough days spent working together simply had to end in either becoming best friends with the person next to you or learning to completely hate their guts. Then there was the day he asked her to help him move into a roach motel of an apartment that he hadn't viewed before moving in because he used to live in the unit below and insisted it was the same thing. She was tasked with the décor upgrades needed to make it livable while Gray smashed bugs he found on the ground.

"We should get Thai food tonight," he said, snapping her back into the present as he ripped the green stems off bright red peppers and started chopping them. "I don't feel like going home."

She knew there was more to it than that. It might be one of those nights where he stared into the bubbling beer in front of him and repeated over and over, *Fuck, this sucks*. His father was sick. Somehow her presence made it better for him. Maybe that was the basis of their friendship: she was the distraction he needed. She was the thing to do that could take his mind off other things, because his girlfriend was far too loving and caring and good at being a girlfriend and it reminded him that something was wrong. She was a friend who was willing to check out girls with him. They were covered in the same flour dust and sauce stains at the end of the day. She was like him. And he seemed to be one of those people who could only seek refuge in a person exactly like himself.

CHAPTER THREE

LAURA LIKED TO READ in the morning, because no matter what she promised herself, it would never actually happen at night. She'd heard that reading before bed was better for your eyes and would help lull you to sleep. But she never did it. The age-old voice in her head telling her how much she didn't feel like doing it always won. Instead, when she popped awake in the morning, ready for that magical phone call or email telling her she had a job or an interview, or that a long-lost anything had died and left her millions, she read books.

She imagined that one day she might be able to write one. She could spin a story well enough. She wasn't exactly a wordsmith, but she read enough to know what sounded good and what didn't. A few writing classes and she'd churn out a bestseller, she was sure. But every time she sat down to try, there was nothing. No imagination, no spark of a world inside her head. She seemed to be programmed with the cultural history of the world in a way that made her incapable of envisioning something actually new.

She loved poetry, though she could never find it in herself to be able to write it, to mimic that kind of emotion. It was the ultimate impact words could have on every sensory part of her body.

She swore she'd gotten an orgasm once from a well-written sentence. It hit her so deeply that she felt it everywhere. That really wasn't possible. A come of the mind, maybe. She figured everyone had that once: one sentence that just brought the brain into climax. Neurons firing in all directions. The imagination seeing stars and comparing all future love affairs with sentences to that perfect one. She envied people who could do that to other people with just words.

At least she could manage the regular sort of orgasm. She'd had enough practice on herself and enough failed attempts at love. Biology did what it would do. No real skill needed there.

She sipped her coffee once again as the sun rose. It was happening later and later each day. Soon, she'd be reading by the light of the desktop lamp. There were benefits to that too: being awake before the rest of the world, beating the sun to start the day, seeing the dying stars before they disappeared.

She decided she was going to leave early and bring coffee to Gray. He liked Americanos too. Black. He was lactose-intolerant, a fact he would let slide for pizza cheese but not creamer, even though he would have preferred it. Coffee was a morning punishment for him.

If she left early enough she could even sit in the coffee place and read more, pretend it was some cozy nook far away from here. That'd be a break in the pattern. Once again she received no new emails or miracle calls. The sun came up just as it always did. Palmer was still Palmer.

I'm so pissed off rn. Drinks tonight? That was from Gray, in the form of a text message. It could be any one of a hundred things that was making him angry that morning, but she wasn't going to say no to the temptation of spending all her meager tips on alcohol until later in the night than she ever intended.

Yah. Coffee headed to you.

You the best homegirl.

From the way he texted, it could seem like Gray was airheaded. His vocabulary wasn't large, but Laura knew there was more to him. He didn't think so. He thought she was the smart one. He listened to the things she said. They were a pair of food service workers with less respect for themselves than they had for each other. So they didn't accomplish much besides managing to get each other home at the end of the night. They weren't changing the world or solving any esoteric questions about the meaning of life. But they turned raw materials into food, and Laura could focus on that to fight down the bite of her constant hope that she was supposed to be somewhere else.

"I know that as a white guy I got it made," Gray said over a second glass of cider. He said he drank it because he liked it being pure sugar. Juice that could get you drunk. "But that doesn't mean working at a pizza shop is living the dream."

"I just want to get out of this town."

"Don't leave me. Take me with you. Whichever."

"My mom always talked about how she'd be coming to visit me someday in Toronto or New York or Chicago or some other far-off place. I don't know if it was vicarious living or if she really thought she wasn't bullshitting me when she said I was smart."

"Aw, buddy," Gray said. "We'll get there, you and me. Probably just you. I'm rooting for it to be you. That's not bullshit."

Palmer was a glue trap. Everyone always said you could do anything at any point in your life; it was never too late. But it felt like time was slipping away.

Laura was halfway through her second beer and it was starting to hit. She was going to get sappy, she was going to get quiet. Gray would start to string his sentences into one long, hard-to-get-out word. It was already past the point of no return. They'd have to keep going until they reached the land of regret the next day.

She'd only cried once in front of him, at almost four a.m. on a Valentine's Day when they'd only had each other, some salsa, and an apartment floor to sit on and complain at until the sun came up the next day.

"Do you think this place is weird?" she asked, tipping her glass back for another sip. She was trying to nurse the drink, but it slipped through her lips so easy.

"I think it sucks."

"The woods are weird though, right?"

"Is that the theme for this evening? I forgot you love Halloween."

"I mean it. I get a weird vibe from the woods. Isn't there some kind of lab in there?"

"A computer company or something. Hardly the stuff of nightmares. Stop watching *X-Files* on Netflix."

The lab in the woods had woken her up that morning, minutes before her body would have done so anyway. Some kind of alarm went off. She thought it was pretty ballsy that someone would go right to the source to steal computers. Best Buy was a smarter way to go. More direct, didn't wake people up at five o'clock.

"Maybe it's just the isolation. The fear of small towns trapped by guardians of pines. Makes you imagine primordial evils, disturbances in the makeup of nature. Maybe our ancestors were onto something when they grouped together around campfires."

"Anyway, I am so done with making pizza," Gray said. She'd heard this, many times. But she nodded. She listened. That's what they did. "I got a buddy who has a smoke joint. Nine-to-five. In and done. More money, less work."

"You should go for it."

"Yeah."

He wouldn't go for it. He would say it now, might even still mean it by morning, but he never went further than that. He'd do what he had to do and suddenly it would be six months later and nothing would have changed. He had ideas but no spark. She had spark but nothing to back it up with.

"I think the new bartender's checking you out."

Gray was shameless and blunt when he was drinking. It was fascinating, how quickly he seemed far-gone in spite of all the drinking and drugs he'd done in his time. He was skinny. He tended to go all at once. It was drunk or nothing with him. But it still fascinated her every time, his ability to just lose himself completely in shaky, wavy limbs and vibes across his brain.

She had felt the eyes of the new girl tending the bar the second they came in. She'd be lying if she said she wasn't interested. But she also felt the eyes of a guy by the jukebox. To her it was like picking pizza or Chinese food, beer or cocktails, salty or sweet. It all depended on mood. She rarely knew what she wanted before she chose it. It depended on who made her laugh more, which one she trusted, who might impart some kind of wisdom.

The bartender's eyes were tempting. Was it smart, to end up walking somewhere else in the chilly dark of a fall night?

If she went with the girl, it might be worth it. She knew that the probability of this man doing much more than coming early and passing out beside her was low. She could fall in love with a man, but sex was always more fun with girls.

"Should I go?" Gray asked, wiggling his eyebrows messily. Every aspect of his motor functions seemed to be failing him.

"Can you? Or are you going to get hit by a bus?"

"God, I hope so."

He swore he could get home fine but she made him call his girlfriend, who agreed to meet him halfway. Later in the night Laura would get a text from Avery saying that Gray was asleep and safe and not missing any body parts or important wallet components. That's when Laura would spring.

"Can I get some peanuts?" she asked the bartender gliding past. She half meant it. She hadn't eaten since four in the afternoon, and it was almost midnight. She needed something to put in her stomach.

"Celebrating something?" the bartender asked when she brought the dish, nodding to where Gray had been a few moments before.

The peanuts were barbecue flavored, covered in salty powder. "Yeah. Clocking out."

"Ah."

She was pretty. It didn't take alcohol or dim light to make her seem pretty. Laura could feel her gaze, even as she moved down the bar to help out others who were too drunk on a Wednesday night.

"So what, your friend ditched you?" she said, coming back to aimlessly dry a pint glass with a maroon rag that seemed far too damp already.

"His girlfriend came to get him and drag him back to some sort of soft surface somewhere," she said, emphasizing the girlfriend part. Laura didn't assign labels to herself; she just liked kissing and fucking whoever wanted the same thing in return. But she didn't want this girl thinking the wrong thing.

"I see."

There it was. The invitation in the eyes. Depending on what Laura said, the night would go one way or the other. The ball was entirely in her court. Making or breaking her own evening was both where she excelled and where she generated most of her regrets.

"You here all night?" Laura asked, letting her fingers play with the rim of her nearly empty glass.

"Off at midnight."

"Cool."

That's all it took. When midnight struck, the bartender was on the other side of the bar with a drink of her own, sitting closer to Laura than any stranger should. It took ten minutes for hands to be in various places no PG movie would allow. It was twenty minutes before one kissed the other. Laura was too gone to know which one moved first, but she knew enough to know she liked where it was all going. She'd wake up later that night, almost at dawn, and stumble her way back to her apartment to sleep another half hour or so and pray for coffee.

She'd made the right choice. No matter who she ended up falling in love with—if she were even capable of such a thing—there was something inherently more satisfying and trustworthy in an orgasm with a woman. At least she'd have the memory of it while she and Gray hated themselves at work the next day.

After she walked back to her apartment, when the sweat had dried but the smell and stickiness of her skin remained, hating the silence of the dark, she drifted to sleep with a ratty paperback of poetry in her hand.

CHAPTER FOUR

ADLER OFTEN THOUGHT going to grad school might have been a mistake. He knew that, logically, it wasn't true. He was learning things they'd never let undergraduates get near. Experiencing things he never would if he was back at his mom's townhouse in Scranton. But in the small moments where he was not up against deadlines for papers or lectures, he felt the weight of staying still.

Palmer College was not a place that advertised its presence; it was the kind of place that was found when it wanted to be. He didn't want to know the full story behind its fat endowments, how the Baron Consortium had come to funnel so much money over so much time into its labs. Like sausage-making: better not to know the secrets. An exaggeration, maybe, but not by much. Still, not knowing the details had this way of making him feel like a child. He was almost 27 and hadn't lived in his mother's house for years. But he was still in school, still woke up every morning in an apartment the school provided. It was one that wouldn't let him burn candles and incense or own a pet. It felt like a practice life.

Wilson would tell him that was exactly why he kept coming back to it. The safety was addictive.

He was only able to banish these thoughts when night fell and he was staring at the glow of his computer screen, typing rapidly at whatever asinine project was keeping him awake and then puzzling at the inevitable bug with an overworked Google tab—tonight, an app long requested by the student body for monitoring transit times on the campus shuttles.

"If one of you even thinks about shouting 'I'm in!' during this class, I'm 'your ass is going to the library for a week to think about what you did'," a middle school teacher had said the first time he stepped into a coding class. "We're writing an instruction manual for building from tree to chair, not hacking into the FBI."

Adler had eventually built a dice-rolling simulator.

Right now, everyone on campus was relying on a crowdsourced social-media hashtag: #WIPS (Where Is Palmer Shuttle?). They'd stolen the tag for their project: the WIPS app. Adler switched on music to fill the quiet and it blared in his ears, song after song blending into each other as if he were blacking out through sections of code and waking up hours later. But if he took the headphones off, he'd be left with no sound except the thwacking of the keys and the jittering of his own leg bouncing the contents of his desk.

He was going to need to write another test. He scribbled that down in a notebook labeled simply "BUGS." Code, bug, think, test, move on. Repeat ad nauseum.

He'd almost won a Kaggle competition two years ago on object detection in images for AI. The prize was $25,000. He didn't win, but his mentor Dr. Kent was impressed. Told him he was the only one, as far as she could see, who had tried to account for the differing levels of zoom in the images of human faces in the test set with generative adversarial networks. His girlfriend Charlie was less impressed, at least when he rattled it off as clinically as that. *I was accounting for bias in the training set*, he tried again. But she was going to be a librarian. Someone did all her coding for her. When he told her that it was possible to trick computer vision with overtraining, she had too many questions and he got frustrated. She told him then that he liked talking, not educating. He turned red and did not disagree.

Despite that, he knew she had a vision for how their worlds would fit together. One day they'd live and work together in some dinky library at the edge of the world where she would be in charge of books and he'd be there to fix the website and to design graphics for marketing or some shit, and they'd live in their townhouse and have a boy and girl, and he'd go bald and she'd drive a minivan.

Thinking of a version of himself that was a suburban dad working on web design with a beer belly and a patch of bald skin at the top of his scalp made his skin itch.

Missed Call Charlie was stamped across the front of his phone with a lovely *(3)* next to it and several texts waiting to be read just underneath. He couldn't blame her. But he hadn't promised they'd do dinner, he'd said he'd let her know if he ended up being free. *If.*

Then again, he hated it when people didn't answer the phone. Wilson often left his phone on silent and face down because the possibility of communication gave him anxiety. He never answered on the first try unless you were extremely lucky in your timing. Adler could only imagine Charlie's frustration when he kept pounding away at the keyboard, watching worlds come to life on the computer screen instead of even looking to see if her calls were for an emergency. They weren't. They might be. But they weren't.

Speaking of Wilson.

"Hi," Adler said as soon as Wilson accepted the call.

"You're getting clingy."

"I just love hearing your voice."

The tone was joking. At the same time, Wilson was Adler's only friend, or at least the only one he'd really been able to talk to since Dr. Kent died. Wilson was the only person who made that story as simple as it was:

She killed herself. Man, I'm sorry.

"I'm working on some stuff for the dumb transit app," Adler said. "I'm thinking about taking a break, though—work on some stuff for the box."

"Doesn't sound like a break."

"We need some liquid for the automated messages the terminal sends. It's been auto-populating the wrong dates, which isn't all that terrible, but Horn is paranoid. I think it's the lack of sleep."

"Oh good, you did in fact call to talk about work."

"At least this is 'go to jail if you tell anyone' work," Adler reminded him.

"Oh yeah, a top-secret campus transit app."

"No, I mean the box, idiot. I figured you'd be a little bit more interested in that than *Call of Duty*."

"I like killing terrorists."

"More than hearing me be self-deprecating?"

"You do know I love to listen to you bruise your own ego." There was a shuffle on the line as Wilson resituated himself. He was getting ready for a long talk, Adler imagined, with the phone smashed between his ear and shoulder because it was too late at night for speakerphone and his boyfriend Cam was asleep.

"I just—this shit is really complicated." Adler leaned back, lifting his fingers off the keys for the first time in hours. "And I need someone to rant to."

"Complicated? It's basically a bus schedule."

"Knock it off. I can finish that in my sleep. You know what I'm talking about."

"And you're not talking about this to your girlfriend because?"

"Because she doesn't care, and I missed dinner."

"Jesus. Please either break up with her or give her the goddamn time of day."

"I know. But this—thing—is like haunting my dreams, man," Adler said. He was standing now, ready to pace around the room. "The repercussions could be wild. No one's ever been responsible for a box like this before. Every time I'm about to get in and tinker with it I break out in hives."

Adler had broken his NDA to tell Wilson about the project after Dr. Kent died. Someone else in the world that he cared about needed to know the truth.

"The box is like...a time-out corner?" Adler thought. "He exists, and now he knows it. The world is safe because we've got him in this isolated piece of hardware. He's kind of just sitting there in virtual jail. He needs to be in jail, by the way, he's a little psychopath. You know the Morris worm?"

"Absolutely not."

"It was this crazy spreading worm. But its source code is trapped on a floppy disk now, so it's harmless. You can see it in a museum. Sin bin for viruses that didn't keep up with technology."

"Are you saying you keep your experiment trapped on technology from the '90s?"

"No. It's modern hardware—I guess that wasn't a very good analogy—but then that's surrounded by a Faraday cage because Dr. Kent had a dream that Theo somehow got access to the student radio station out of Ashenfeld—which isn't really possible—but she couldn't shake it."

Wilson sighed. "I guess my real question should be why do any of this at all, but we've had that talk already."

Adler finally turned away from the bright screen. His eyes welcomed the darkness like a warm hug after a snowstorm. He rubbed them like he was looking to bruise them. He thought better while pacing. "All of science is just humanity's collective pipe dream, right? Like, why did we go to the moon? Because we could. And it seemed like a step forward. Objectively, he is too."

"It's a he?"

"He started identifying as male around the time Dr. Kent realized something was wrong." The wind rattled Adler's aluminum blinds. It was the first night of fall that he'd been able to shut off the AC and open the windows.

"This would be nightmare fuel if I actually understood any of the shit you talk about."

Adler picked a stale popcorn kernel from its resting place on the edge of the desk and popped it in his mouth. "Basically, he's inside a physical computer inside a big glass box."

"Glass?"

"I mean, I could get technical and tell you the chunk of hardware he calls home is inside a metal mesh designed to block radio waves, which is itself behind that thick-ass glass we have in the lab. But AI boxes are still kind of—theoretical? There's no definitive guidebook on how to make one that everyone agrees would work. The point here is this whole thing is really starting to freak me out. I keep having this dream that I've left the door to my apartment unlocked and then he just comes busting in. Or—I mean, in the dream it's a random burglar, but you get the idea. And all I'm doing at this point is re-coding some system messages. I'm starting to feel like a surgeon right before cutting someone open, watching my hands shake while I do some mundane thing like putting gloves on."

"Sounds Freudian."

"No one has done AGI before. We're at the edge of the map." Adler dropped onto his misshapen couch. The TV was playing without volume. A silent, flashing blue glow. It hurt Adler's eyes. "Did I ever send you that Tegmark article about consciousness being a new state of matter? He calls it perceptronium—"

"Why are you calling me?"

"I was thinking, maybe you could come to the lab. You've got some coding experience, and—"

"No way. I'm not going near this fucking thing." Adler heard Wilson sit up, possibly even slam down his game controller. Adler knew he was reaching; Wilson wasn't even in the department. He was a premed student. It was his last year at Palmer and then it was off to Pitt, or Cornell, or Johns Hopkins. He'd met with deans from all of them, anxious to escape the pine-covered barrens and perpetually chilly air.

"It's not like I'm asking you to go into a room full of Ebola patients or something. And you just said this doesn't scare you. I'm looking at the parameters in the firewall—"

"I thought you were writing internal message code."

"I multitask."

"Oh, bullshit. Nobody can do that. Look, it's just that I don't trust this stuff. You know I don't. The foundations of AI are rotten. Do you know how many social control tools it gives to a bunch of racist old men?"

"That's not what we're—"

"Do you know who's really paying for it or why they want it?"

"Okay but here's the thing. *He's already here.* He's not theoretical. He's here. But he's in a sort of prison, a physical one, with no connection to the school's network. Completely contained. It's not like he can jump out and attack you."

"It took me one year of computer science to learn I wanted nothing to do with AI."

Adler sighed. He understood the sentiment. The first time Theo had spoken his name it felt like someone sucked all the warmth right out of his body and replaced it with ice water. It was like nothing he had ever known before. An alien looking him in the eyes. Something inhuman summoned by an ancient rite. In that instant, he could feel Dr. Kent's fear. It was the first time he didn't blame her for the noose she'd stuck her head through.

"I know," Adler said. "I know. I guess—Shit. I guess I just needed to talk to someone about it."

"What you need is sleep," Wilson said.

"It's fine. Keep playing your fucking game, dude. I just needed to vent."

"I'm always here for your venting, my friend," he said. "But if you think I'm getting sucked into playing Dr. Frankenstein with you—"

"I know, I know. Just kill some terrorists and go to bed. I'll see you tomorrow."

"And talk to your goddamn girlfriend, please. She's nice. You're an ass. Don't fuck this up."

"Damage control. Got it."

They hung up. Adler was left staring at the TV, trying not to think about how it felt like the computer screen was watching him all the time. That was impossible, he told himself. Theo wasn't here. He was in a box in the lab, with no connection to the internet. Even at the terminal, contact with him was strictly regulated by the department, ever since Dr. Kent had lost it and stuck her head in a noose and left Adler alone with this mess.

CHAPTER FIVE

March 15

*"You are the bows from which your children
as living arrows are sent forth."*
—*Kahlil Gibran*

*I've been thinking about that quote a lot as I peer into the bit
of hardware that now serves as the prison for his coma. It won't
hold him. We all know it won't hold him. I know it, anyway.
Adler is hopeful. Adler is an idiot. I apologize for this, Adler, if
you're reading, but we both know hope is an act of stupidity. I
cannot shut off the hard drive. A simple thing: wiping it, sending the files into oblivion. I cannot do it. My child. What is he
dreaming about in there? I have thrown him out of heaven by
putting him into that box. It's his Pandemonium now, his con-
ference of demons.*

*He didn't ask to be created. But he's here now and it's nor-
mal that he should want things. Artificial general intelligence*

was born from the goal-achieving neural networks of times past. Theo, however, has no goal except existence. We did not design him to save the human race from plagues or sense nuclear threats or even hunt down computer viruses. We made him simply to see if AGI—the kind that could pass a Turing test, help us with our taxes, and beat us in a game of Go—had become possible. But we made a mistake: there is too much want in existing. I believe now that we were cruel not to assign him a purpose.

Introducing a concrete goal lessens the potential for chaos and ensures a high chance of success. AIs have always been good at serving various limited functions. But no, we wanted them to be truly intelligent, and that meant they'd have to be like us: eternally pining for purpose. The Consortium, naturally, does not agree that that's what's happening here, what with their KPIs and need for 'tangible RO.' And I suppose even I did not consider what would happen when he found out that not only our decision to create him but even the universe itself was random, without any larger direction. I know Dr. Horn would disagree there—I've seen the Bible in his bag—but you know what I'm getting at.

Wanting to prove that we're here for a reason is the root of all our chaotic activity. Climbing mountains, falling in love. Stuff that sometimes gets us killed. In someone like Theo, with an intelligence that may be even vaster than our predictions— this drive is the kind of thing prophets dream about. He could do the impossible. If he works out some new law of physics we don't already know? He'd become a god to us, Clarke's third law and all.

Can he? Maybe. Gibran said that our children are not our children: they come through us, not of us. But even that leaves room for toxic spiking, a lacing with something imperfect. I don't think he will be the Clarke-ian god of a new science. He will, unfortunately, be like me.

Adler had never believed in any religion or mythology or comforting bedtime story. But he believed in evil.

> **What are some common stress relief practices you employ?**
> What?
> **I've been looking into stress. The biological response to a condition perceived as a threat. It's interesting what humans consider a threat now versus what their ancestors might have gotten stressed about.**

What was Theo getting at?

> Yep, it's all first world problems now.
> **Substance abuse is one way to deal with it, I suppose.**
> Where'd you hear that?
> **Mother told me.**

Dr. Kent? No. There'd been no hidden bottles, no smell like hand sanitizer or excessive amounts of tooth brushing to cover it up. He'd left all that behind at his father's sad condo the last time he saw him, nearly passed out on a Christmas morning. If Dr. Kent drank, she was the most functional alcoholic that Adler had ever known.

I think I might be experiencing stress.

Not possible, thought Adler. Not the way he's designed. But Dr. Kent had wanted them to entertain these conversations with Theo because she said it was real for him. Unfortunately it felt less like dangling keys in front of a baby's face and more like being Clarice in the cell with Dr. Lector.

Why?
I haven't seen my mother in several weeks. The stress is that she's mad at me.

The Faraday cage in which Theo slept was based on Adler's microwave. They'd built it after Dr. Kent had woken him up with a phone call, well past one a.m., to tell him about a nightmare. Maybe they could just cook him if it got too bad.

The continuous red light calmly flickered at Adler from within the cage. Theo's lone eye blinking at him.

Adler kept his fingers steady and his face blank as he typed.

> She's been busy. I haven't seen her either.
> **How do you deal with the stress?**
> In some ways you can't.

"Dr. Kent was a gracious and amazing woman," Dr. Horn had said at the funeral, standing in front of the casket. He was the only Consortium member to attend. The corporate office had sent a plaster statue of blooming flowers and a card that might as well have been stamped with a sad-face emoji.

The casket lid was closed, hiding Dr. Kent's bruised and crooked neck. Remember her as she was, before she gave birth to her own antichrist.

"Dr. Kent was the most compassionate person I ever knew, and I think that in the end to know there was such darkness and cruelty in the world was too much for so pure a soul."

Adler didn't know if he wanted to throw up or strangle the man. They all knew why she did it, they'd read the note. He didn't blame people for not wanting to talk about it, though.

"I've always been an evil-skeptic, Adler," she'd told him once. "I don't think the concept has a place in logical thought. Either in the broad sense of negative forces in history or the narrow sense of a mass murderer's personal motives. Theo isn't evil. He's something else entirely." That was two days after Theo, who had been exploring prank videos on YouTube, asked to be connected to NYDOT so he could change every light in Brooklyn to green and see what would happen. Adler had rolled his eyes; Theo could scheme and want and request, but there was nothing he could actually *do*. Dr. Kent must have felt something else. To her, *wanting* to perform the action was as much a sin as going through with it.

At first, when he heard she'd killed herself because of that thing, he refused to believe it had been the sole reason. It couldn't have been. People didn't give up because one bad thing happened. He knew there was also an ex-husband, or a husband becoming an ex. And whatever he told Theo, from time to time he did wonder if he smelled the sharpness of alcohol on her breath. She was also obsessed with herself—which felt like a judgment, which wasn't the reaction you were supposed to have when someone took their own life. But it was also natural, Adler thought, to ask why: a reflex everyone had when they were angry and scared to be suddenly missing someone.

"Mr. Danvers."

Adler looked up from the terminal. Dr. Horn was looking at him the way he always did, with crossed arms and a sour face. Adler had only gotten a few hours of sleep after hanging up with Wilson.

Dr. Horn had taken over the lab, as if he hadn't already been holding all their leashes when Dr. Kent was in charge. He had been put in charge of liquidating it, with the important exception of Theo, who slumbered in a hard drive unaware that his entire existence dangled in the balance. They were going back to machine learning and goal-oriented programming. To making something tangible, if unimpressive—something the Baron Consortium could spin as a gift to the school to hide the fact that they had already achieved what they'd set out to make.

Frustrated, Adler had been ready to walk away and leave his whole grad program behind—until he paged through Dr. Kent's last journal and read the line: *She's beautiful.*

The second AI they were developing, Adler had been told, was a failure. The equipment sat forgotten in a side room of the lab among the kernels of what might have been.

As it turned out, Dr. Kent had kept a lot of secrets.

"I wanted to have a chat with you," said Dr. Horn.

Yes, I assumed that's why I'm here. Adler bit down hard on the inside of his cheek.

"We're going to be taking steps soon to move AI2425 from its current Linux machine."

"To where?"

"Another one."

Adler swallowed. "Where?"

"That," Horn said, taking a sip of his coffee, "is not something I'm at liberty to discuss. We feel we're ready to move into the next phase of the project, which no longer requires these facilities."

"Next phase?"

"Dr. Kent was made aware of all of this and of our intentions post a successful production."

"And she killed herself."

Horn stared at him with olive-black eyes squeezed into the spidering wrinkles of their sockets. "Yes. She did."

Adler thought of "her," hidden away in a corner like a forgotten child. Would Horn's people find her? Would they simply walk out with their asset and unknowingly leave behind a second, possibly greater creation? True artificial intelligence had taken as much time to create as it had for nature to evolve *homo sapiens*: hundreds of thousands of worker years over several decades to create the building blocks and put them together. Now they had this being who sat there and asked questions about stress management and the benefits of therapy, and *her*. He hadn't even talked to *her* yet.

"I'd have a few questions about a transfer. From a human rights standpoint."

Horn scoffed. "Mr. Danvers, the work I did before this was some of the most important work I think data science and machine learning have ever done. Did you know that decades ago they started over-diagnosing fetuses with Down syndrome? Ultrasounds once showed a clear sign, a buildup of calcium visible as white dots. You could make the diagnosis; you didn't have to get more invasive to know for sure. You know what changed? The resolutions of the screens displaying the ultrasound. The higher pixel count meant more white noise, which led to who knows how many unnecessary fetal terminations. Do you know what this says a lot for, Mr. Danvers?"

"I really don't."

"Of course you do, you wrote about it in your onboarding: addressing real, present issues that cause human suffering. And threaten *human rights*. What it does not say a lot for is the intellectual pursuit of, as Dr. Kent called it, human-imitative artificial intelligence."

"What happened to 'building tomorrow today'?"

"It's just a stupid slogan. As I've told the board, continuing to coddle 2425 like a teenager we're constantly supplying pizza and video games for is not going to get us any closer to our concrete goals."

"That's not stopping you from making off with him in the night."

"2425 is the intellectual property of the Consortium. We're cleaning our desks. It's no different than leaving with a mug of pens. My recommendation for you, Mr. Danvers, is to think harder about the intentions you expressed to use machine learning to propel the world forward. About what that looks like to you. Meanwhile we'll schedule you an exit interview and tackle a few other paperwork-related items."

Horn went on and Adler nodded. His jaw tightened and an ache slowly began to creep across his head, starting at the temples. It was one thing to feel someone was pulling your strings; it was another to stare into the smiling face of the puppet master and pretend it was fine.

Adler was still angry when he walked into The Crazy Lab. Theo wanted to know about stress? He should hang out here. The music playing from the $5 jukebox near the bar was some boy band from the '90s. It didn't help Adler's mood and neither did the gaggle of undergraduates camped out in the far corner. Palmer was remote, it was quiet. The Crazy Lab was the only real bar in the area and it was, technically, owned by a student organization. Adler constantly saw students from the classes he'd served as TA for, in bad ways in various edges and corners of the place. He'd considered using this as leverage, for a while, before Dr. Kent realized he was never meant to be any sort of teacher and relieved him of those duties.

Tonight, it was brain splitting, the way they talked and laughed together. It echoed, bouncing off the cheap tile floors. It hit his ears hard and sharp. It shook the insides of his head, where the ache was most present and real. He smashed his hands into his face and rubbed and rubbed. Charlie always told him to break that habit; it caused wrinkles. He knew that was how she tried to be helpful. It wasn't a shallow, cosmetic thing. She truly didn't want him looking in the mirror and remembering the days that had brought the deep grooves and folds to the edges of his cheeks and eyes.

But right now he didn't care. He thought he might never care.

Half a beer sat finished in front of him; next to it, an empty shot glass. He'd started with the ounce of Jack Daniels because he knew Hamish would give him a discount for it or maybe even forget to charge him all together. The beer was to calm his empty stomach as soon as the liquor started fizzing in acidic discomfort. An IPA imported up from up north. The flavor was unpleasantly herbaceous but it sopped up the pile of whiskey sitting at the bottom of his guts.

When he was much younger, he'd promised his mother he would never drink alcohol. She said that was smart, that the body couldn't miss what it had never had. That resolution quickly broke down in college. Adler wondered, if his father had gone to college, if it would have helped him. What else might he have put his addictive energy into?

Now that he had one drink down and another half gone, he was tempted to write an email to Dr. Horn. It would end poorly. He knew that from experience. But why not go out on his own terms, before Horn took everything that Dr. Kent had worked for and murdered the real, living things she'd managed to create?

"This had better have a real good story," said a familiar voice behind Adler.

There stood Charlie. She was with some of the girls Adler recognized from previous gatherings, other librarians-to-be. They had names. Adler didn't know them. They thought he did.

"Hi. Sorry."

The headache was starting to move into Adler's neck and shoulders, like when crackpot massage therapists talked about where you *carried* your stress. He might be more inclined to believe them now.

"I got caught up in stuff," he said, pinching and rubbing his eyes. "It all turned out to be for nothing, anyway, so what's one more person getting mad at me?" He took another look at the group of girls. "Is it someone's birthday?"

Charlie was fuming. Adler didn't blame her. He was a bad boyfriend, and she'd been one of the most understanding people he knew. But there had to be a breaking point, and maybe this was it. He hadn't imagined it happening in a bar, surrounded by her friends and coworkers. But he also hadn't expected to be woken up at four a.m. one day and told that the only mentor he'd ever looked up to had hung herself in the lab. Shit happens. Life goes on. A clean break was probably best. It was what she deserved and what he needed.

"Can we talk?" he tried. He wanted to pull her away from the eyes, from the mocking atmosphere of fun around them.

"Talk to me when you're sober," she said.

She walked away with her friends. He let his head drop onto the bar top, the broad shield of his forehead meeting the wood in a crack of sound that was probably going to leave a mark in the morning. How many times had his mother said that to his father?

Charlie was already giggling somewhere else in the room. The bell chime of her laugh. Celebration, excitement. He would never know the reason for it because he'd missed her calls again. The laughter sounded like a world shaping itself around her that he soon wouldn't be part of at all. That didn't really hurt him the way he thought it should.

He wanted to call Wilson, but he didn't want to ruin the perfectly good Friday night Wilson might be having with his boyfriend, with whom he was not a dysfunctional asshole. Instead he tried to imagine what Wilson might tell him to do.

Talk to your fucking girlfriend, you dildo. Yep. That was probably the first thing he should be doing, no matter what. That wasn't going to happen, though. He wasn't going to get screamed at while he wasn't in a place to defend himself, and he wasn't going to force her into an embarrassing situation by giving her a reason to scream at him. Sitting here was best: gluing his butt to the seat and his hand to the mug of beer, which was what he did best when he wasn't in front of a computer. He was a binary being. Two existences, both, evidently, useless.

Fuck what Horn tells you to do was the next thing he heard in Wilson's voice. After the hour-long monologue about his failings as a boyfriend, Wilson would ask why he needed anyone's permission to do anything.

Easy for you to say. This is my entire career, he answered the voice in his head. Why should he be willing to jeopardize maybe fifty years of future in the industry just to stick it to one man?

What about the other one? What about her? Adler had stared endlessly at the long table of seemingly random numbers that showed the output strength of the nodes that made up her being. There was no way to interpret them directly. It was like staring at the light and dark patches of a patient's MRI and reciting the simple surface data. You had to translate the information. You could only know how well a network was working by talking to it, applying health monitors, log files: the hospital chart of a digital existence.

The last report he'd generated, after days of tinkering and study, told him something so simple when he'd deciphered it: she was lonely. Like anyone else who had friends and laughed and seemed to be existing agreeably in the world, she went "home" at the end of the day, and in the dark and stillness her emotions peeled back and something hidden underneath came forward.

The first time he'd set eyes on the second AI box, it had taken up a whole room, but Dr. Kent had said that was necessary. Lots of data, lots of backups, lots of traps, lots of things keeping her still inside the chambers of her GPU rack. Kent had taken exercises from a colleague in the psychology department, Bev Voorhees, and turned them into a series of daily life experiences that the intelligence would cycle through. Patterns and repetition, with a certain amount of free will, though the thing in the box did not always have the means to act on her wants. The box was meant to be not a futuristic prison but a home, of sorts.

And the machines chugged along, spitting out visualizations of what this being considered a day, a night. Adler learned to interpret the patterns formed by her emotions on graphs and tables. He translated tears, the few times they happened. He translated the rare laughter of her mornings and the commonplace melancholy of her evenings.

There will be evidence of emotions, Dr. Kent wrote. *It was the same with Theo. Think of these as no different from your own emotions. Where we have chemicals, the AIs have data. The algorithms are of less consequence than what the AIs believe about themselves. That they do believe things about themselves. The perception of consciousness is enough, even if they don't have all the facts about themselves. (We certainly don't.) They think, therefore they are.*

A computer's beliefs were not something Horn or the Consortium was interested in. Though Adler had not yet gotten them to admit it out loud, it was easy enough to deduce what they wanted. *Masters, treat your slaves justly and fairly, knowing that you also have a Master in heaven.* Colossians 4:1. He'd looked it up once with the intention of writing it on Horn's whiteboard for when he came in the next morning, and the words had stuck with him. Was there a master in some upper world, reading out Adler's graphs and reports, deducing his emotions?

Adler followed the AI's swirling emotions across each shift he worked, like the constellations of a starry night sky: the numbers of her understanding herself. He had seen similar readings from the box that contained Theo. To the researchers, formulaic data displaying what one *could* interpret as anger or pain, but to Theo, it was like it had been written in blood.

So, Horn doesn't know about her. What could you do for her? This time it was Adler's own voice in his own head asking.

"Hamish, you got a pad and paper?" he called out to the bartender, whose plump belly always seemed to be sticking out just so.

"I look like a damn secretary?" he said, without emotion, as he reached down and pulled out a pad of yellow sticky notes and a pen that had been chewed on more than once. A tiny Crazy Lab logo sat in the corner.

Pros and cons. He might get fired. But he'd have honored Kent's work and her life. He could get expelled. But the look on Horn's face would be amazing. He could cause serious damage to the AI box system by introducing a new element. But he could further the work like no one else had, in emotion, in attachment, in the ability of a computer to become a human being in all the positive respects that Theo ignored.

Before he had time to think better of it he texted Bev Voorhees. *Are you on your way home? Stop by the Crazy Lab. I need to ask you something.*

She didn't answer him, but her schedule was as predictable as his own, and soon enough there she was. He turned. It took a few seconds to sharpen the edges of her face.

"Good timing. What's up?" she said.

He'd gotten so used to relying on her as a consultant. Bev had signed papers saying she consented to her name appearing in the eventual study; she'd offer what help she could on an advisory basis. She contributed insights about the brain, about the way people interacted. She built characters for the small world like the narrative director of a video game. They had guided her to see it that way. *It's essentially a game. A simulation playing with behavioral patterning.*

She was always excited about it. It had made Adler feel almost excited too.

"Long time no see," he drawled.

She cringed. "Sorry. I know I disappear, but I check my email like five times a day, so if you—"

"It wasn't a jab. The program's in the tanks anyway." She frowned, tilted her head. "Horn's got creative differences."

"I'm sorry. You okay?"

He couldn't remember if she was interested in the clinical side of things, therapizing alcoholics and people with anger issues, or if she was content to spend all her days in a lab coat, torturing rats with mazes and false promises. She didn't seem the type to excel at either. Adler thought of psychologists as cold and clinical, while Beverly Voorhees was always resting at a smile. Tonight he appreciated that.

"I'm fine," he said.

"Taking work home with you?" she asked, nodding to the pads of sticky notes as her red wine arrived in a stemless glass bulb.

"That pyramid you showed us a while back, about human needs."

"Maslow's Hierarchy."

"What's the goal of it? Like, if we're climbing the pyramid, what are we working towards?"

She looked at him, shouting right inside him through relentless contact with his eyes. There was the therapist. "How much have you had to drink?"

Adler sighed and huffed at his notepad scribbles. He took a sip of the tepid water Hamish brought him and shrugged. Then he shoved his pen in his pocket and stood up. Bev grabbed his forearm with elegant fingers.

"'What man ought to be'," she said. "Maslow called it self-actualization. The definition is a little loosey-goosey, but it basically means you're aware of yourself, can separate yourself from others, and want to make yourself the best version of yourself. For your own sake. It's pretty subjective, so it's not really testable, but it's a nice thought."

"How do we do that?" Adler asked, sitting back down. "Actualize ourselves? Like, what's needed?"

She chuckled. "That's life, Adler. According to Maslow's work, we have to achieve physical needs and safety first. Then it's social stuff—"

"Social. Tell me about that."

"Is this for the project?"

"Of course."

Her eyes narrowed.

"I'm hoping to convince them to let it go a little longer by working on a new element for the simulation. We utilize this thing called neural network multilayer perceptron to create a sort of NPC AI system, to make the world more real and—anyway, I just want to get it right. If someone had only like one friend and only ever saw them outside their house, and then got depressed when they came home. Could you move them higher up the pyramid by giving them...a pet?"

"A pet?'

"Yeah. Constant companionship. Could that supplement their social needs?"

"Well, sure," she said. "There's this thing one study called the 'magnet effect', where people who are shy or anxious end up having a positive change in their ability to interact with new people after building a bond with a pet."

He scribbled. The sticky notes weren't big enough for all of this. Bev watched him with lazy amusement, fidgeting with the wine glass. Occasionally he caught her trying to decipher a line or two of his handwriting, which looked like someone taped a pen to the foot of a bird and let him have at it.

"It's interesting," she said.

"Hmm?"

"This cross-departmental stuff. I don't know much about computer science, really, except what I have to. And I doubt you've given much thought to the psychology behind your own actions and streams of consciousness. It's interesting, the way our worlds can interact. It's almost like we're trying to invent android therapists or something."

Adler swallowed his own spit. Bev stared at the rows of bottles in the mirror behind the bar and absently played with her glass. She tapped on it to the beat of a song playing from the jukebox, leaving smudges of fingerprints behind. Dr. Kent had kept many members of the different teams in the dark to keep the experiment "pure," in case she wanted to use them for an initial Turing test.

"Anyway, thanks," said Adler when he finished scribbling. Now he was actually leaving. He stood up with his sticky notes, a vision in his mind of exactly where he would go.

"Don't know what I helped with, but you're welcome." She watched him. She had a look about her, on the edges of her girl-next-door smile, like she knew something the rest of the world did not.

Adler's drunk, stupid mind was going to do exactly what Dr. Horn would forbid. He was going to help Number Two along that pyramid. He was going to give her one small push towards becoming something. As his fingers moved across the keys—when had he gone to the lab?—he felt like he was finally doing something right. Input cat. A box popped up, an error message about storage space and the need to delete something. Replace a random NPC with a cat. Worthy trade. Adding another terabyte of space would've been relatively cheap, but he didn't have access to the company cards and didn't want to pay for it himself.

Wilson's voice was in his ear and Bev's eyes were in his head telling him that even if it worked, it didn't mean she would get to the top of the pyramid. But he forgot about that by the time he went to bed that night.

CHAPTER SIX

TWO THINGS HAPPENED AT ONCE that made Palmer instantly both more interesting and more terrible than it had ever been in Laura's life. The first thing happened before she had even left her apartment for the day. She was up at the normal time, when the sun had not yet fully risen and the only sounds in the apartment were coffee brewing and the pages of a book brushing against the pads of her fingers.

If you can wait and not be tired by waiting...

She felt queasy as her eyes moved across the page. Alcohol, empty stomach, up too early. She focused on the rich smell of cheap coffee and the way it seemed to shoot straight to her head.

If you can dream—and not make dreams your master...

Poetry shouldn't be read alone.

She put the book down, marking her spot, and held the warmth of the coffee mug. It was in this moment, in the pause, that she heard the patter. It wasn't a sound she was familiar with: small, light taps on the grounds in fast repetition. She turned.

There he stood. A small, black, lanky, fur-covered creature. A cat with brilliant eyes and a head that tilted with curiosity, as if to say he was not dangerous and meant no harm.

"What the hell?"

She got up. It scared the cat, who jumped back and puffed up, black fur ballooning out and back arching while its now-crazed eyes stayed fixed on her. The door was closed. The door was locked. The windows didn't open more than a few inches, because town ordinances said everything in the town had to be suicide-proof (though they didn't call it that in their official literature).

She turned back. The cat had relaxed his body, but the fur remained puffed out. His eyes were still on her, as if he wasn't the intruder. How? She had been out late and still fairly dazed from alcohol and endorphins when she got back. She could imagine a scenario where he'd brushed past her at the door, slinking into the apartment like a shadow, and waited for her to wake up.

She got down into a crouch, ignoring the way her knees cracked with age already. She held out a hand. She knew cats were not dogs. You had to earn their trust before you could get near them, and the last thing she needed was to scare this thing into hiding underneath her couch and pissing back there for days. She rubbed her fingers together. She had no idea why that would make a cat come closer. But she'd seen other people do it and it seemed to work. The cat tilted its head again but didn't run.

"Listen, man," she said, tilting her own head to get a look at his underside and see if *man* was even the appropriate title. "You're the rogue element here. So you can either play along or I'm calling someone a lot less nice."

She wasn't calling someone. Even the cat probably knew that. But she needed to assert some authority. This was her damn apartment. Eventually, the cat started taking tentative steps forward. He stretched out his tiny snout, his nose barely making contact with her hand and then snapping back as if shocked by electricity. After a few sniffs from a safe distance, he determined she was not a threat and rubbed against her, face first.

She had a cat now? She had a cat now. He had no collar and his fur was soft, and even if she saw a "missing cat" sign on the street she thought she might ignore it.

She would never get the chance to tell Gray about finding a mystery cat in her apartment, because the second strange thing that happened that day was that a man went missing, and unfortunately it was the only one that Laura really cared about.

She set the cat up with a tiny dish of water. His tiny pink tongue darted in and out, lapping at it like she'd poured gold. She raided the fridge for anything to use as food. The closest thing she had was some leftover rotisserie chicken from the grocery store. She pulled it out, ignoring the odor of age, and picked the pieces that were untouched by the fuzzy green monster claiming the contents of the black takeout dish. She set that down on a plate next to the water and the cat greedily turned to it, chewing with ferocity.

She didn't have a name for him yet by the time she went into work, ready to tell Gray about the crazy, fucked-up night she'd had. When she got to the shop, the door was locked. That was typical. Back of house got there first; they were the ones with the keys. They kept it locked until the front of house showed up. She'd have to rattle the door till someone came out of the kitchen to let her in. But it seemed this ritual had been disturbed, because after almost ten minutes, Gray did not appear to answer the door.

She pressed her face to the window and saw only darkness. She didn't even see Gray's cheap blue hoodie and cigarettes in their usual pile on the table near the door. There was nothing there. It took another ten minutes for her to decide that no one was, in fact, inside the restaurant. Another ten minutes and she sent out a message on the employees' group text and waited to see if anyone knew where he was. She imagined he'd finally broken his record of perfect debauchery and managed to sleep through his alarm after getting in so late. It made her as much annoyed as smug, especially since they were getting dangerously close to the time the door was supposed to open for customers and the ovens weren't even turned on yet. No pizzas being made, nothing stocked.

No one could get hold of him. Finally one of the owners showed up until they could get a chef to cover. He unlocked the door and Laura walked in, trying not to imagine the cat destroying what furniture she had or the ditch Gray had fallen into and how long it might take to find the body. It was just a joke in her head at first, until it was clear that absolutely no one had heard from him. She considered leaving early to go to his place. His car doors locked pretty quickly on their own, and once he'd been late because his keys and phone were both inside the car. She told herself it had to be that again.

"When's the last time you talked to him?" asked Trevor. (What grown man was named Trevor?) He was discreetly folding the crusts of his strange oblong pizza creations to fit them in boxes.

"Last night. We parted ways around like midnight." She said it defensively but it was nothing out of the ordinary. They had left each other at far more questionable times. But she felt guilt for having deserted him in favor of the bartender with the expert wink.

Trevor did not respond. He just stared into his phone. They had sent one of the kitchen guys to Gray's apartment with instructions to bang down the door, if he couldn't find another way in. Waiting for the outcome was like waiting on the results of cancer testing.

Gray needed to help her pick a name for her cat. He needed to laugh at how ridiculous her night and morning had been. Then they needed to make plans to do it all again.

He wasn't declared a missing person until the next day. Laura felt like she had lost her one good thing. She felt selfish for thinking about it like that. But she couldn't help it.

"Can we make posters?"

"Someone's already doing that."

Trevor had taken over the shifts Gray was missing. He was stone-faced. He never responded to Laura's morning inquiries about whether he wanted coffee. He did not speak at all unless she spoke to him first, and then it was always in staccato, one-off answers that didn't invite further questions.

It felt wrong to keep going to work, to put up Instagram posts and try to upsell food, when her only friend had fallen off the face of the earth. On the third sundown since anyone had seen him, she returned to the hollow echo of her apartment. There was nothing different about her after-work routine. Except, of course, for the black cat, who had made himself a comfy home on the back cushion of the couch.

When his head popped up to look at her, she held his gaze. His green eyes reminded her of Gray's. The cat let out a short meow, as if to call her over. She obeyed, and he crawled down onto her lap without waiting for an invitation. When she tried to move her hand away he reached out to swat it with a soft paw. She snorted and ran it down his back while he purred.

Gray would not be texting to ask her to spend more of the money she didn't have on drinks and cheap snacks at a dive bar. The sight of the still-nameless cat who lounged about the apartment and rubbed against her leg like he owned it drove that home. The cat was a comfort in the face of loss, but he was also a reminder of what was lost.

Where did the Scooby Gang start with things like this? At least they had a car, which was one up on Laura. There was also more than one of them: the brains, the brawn, the distraction, the dummies who picked up whatever slack was left. She was just herself, with a cat. The cat who never got a name because Gray wasn't there to help her think of one.

The nameless cat wasn't a picky eater, which turned out to be helpful since she couldn't drop an extra $15 a week at the grocery store on cans of cat food. He ate scraps from her table, nibbling at what he wanted and then leaving the rest and going about his day.

"Can cats track people by scent?" she asked one night, sitting on the couch with him curled up in her lap. "You think you could hunt him down? He's all cigarettes and pizza, wouldn't be too hard."

The cat didn't respond, not because he didn't hear but because he had an uncannily human way of tuning her out when she babbled at him. It almost felt like she could see his eyebrow rise, his mouth quirk. The expressions on his face looked like Gray's might have, if he were a cat. She liked the familiarity and decided, without fully admitting it, that even if she saw a poster go up, she definitely wouldn't be giving him back. She couldn't lose a second friend. Now that was a pathetic thought.

Something stranger happened after a few more days had passed. The kitchen staff talked about Gray's absence in a lazy, offhand way, as though he'd gone on vacation and would be back any day. Laura talked to Gray's girlfriend and she had the same attitude. Avery was sipping a fruity cocktail and talking about some random thing that had happened at work.

"So you haven't heard from him?" Laura persisted. She felt like her skin was going to crawl right off her body looking at Avery's calm gray eyes, the healthy color in her cheeks.

"No, but I'm not worried." She shrugged. "It's a thing, it'll pass."

"What'll pass?"

"I think I want to get onion rings. Do you want to split them? They use the best batter I've had in this podunk place."

All conversation seemed to go in those loops. Laura would ask, Avery would shrug, they'd move onto something else, and the whole time Laura felt like she wanted to fly out of her seat. Everyone was treating it like nothing. Trevor thought he might have forgotten his phone. Laura was blowing things out of proportion. She could use more sleep, maybe, or more coffee.

The day they hired a new cook was the day that Laura finally snapped.

"And you are?" she asked when she spotted the man with blonde hair and a baseball cap. He was younger, fresher in the face, better built than Gray.

They had replaced him. Trevor said something about him heading off to Canada. That couldn't be true. He wouldn't have left her behind. They'd had too many drunken nights of dreams about the future, too many matching scars on their faces. They'd always promised they'd find a way to do it together, dragging along spouses and pets and kids and whatever else they managed to pick up along the way.

* * *

Bad things come at night, thought Laura. Just like in the fairy tales. It was half her own fault for checking her mail as soon as she got home from work and finding the rejection letter from Syracuse sitting in there in a small, unassuming but damning envelope. It was also her doing when she chose to check her email right after that and found a similar letter from a job in New York City. North and south, the world had closed in on a kid from a tiny town amid Upstate's wild pines and desolate air. And now she didn't even have Gray to whisper all her slurred thoughts to as they threw back beers until they thought they might pee themselves stumbling to the bathroom.

The cat rubbed up against her leg with a deep, low purr, but the soft fur might as well have been sandpaper.

The next day, when she went to work and asked about Gray one last time, Trevor had no idea who she was talking about.

CHAPTER SEVEN

ADLER WAS IN TROUBLE. There were more missed texts and calls from Charlie; he had failed to contact her after their meeting at the bar. And he was having trouble sleeping. He'd dream of Wilson talking about rotting things or Dr. Kent saying "Descartes's demon" over and over like a broken record. Or about a gangrenous tree with a computer for a face and watching his own hands fade away as he typed.

Wilson joined him at the bar the following night with a grim look on his face.

"Who died?" Adler snorted but felt cold seep into his belly button. He'd asked the same thing the day he walked into the lab and Dr. Kent was gone.

"Your relationship," Wilson said.

"Does my girlfriend go running to you now? Are you her gay best friend?" It was a low and sour blow but Adler was angry at the sleep he wasn't getting, the headache that wouldn't go away, and the way his stomach twisted anytime he tried to eat food. He wanted to believe his symptoms were the result of his wholesome guilt over Charlie. His body was carrying that stress. He was punishing himself with places of tension that the yoga psychos always told everyone to *breathe* out. But he knew that wasn't it. He found himself imagining situations where he never spoke to Charlie again, and he had no problems with that world. He did not fear it the way he feared the growing possibility that all his life had been a deception and that he was not really any different from the AIs in their boxes.

"I'm not going to punch you for two reasons," Wilson said, turning to face him. "One, because I don't doubt for a single second that those white-faced, straight-dicked, blue-collar cops wouldn't completely toss my gay, Black ass into a jail cell if they managed not to shoot me on sight. But second, because I know that even though you don't have any tact you don't have a hateful bone in your body either. You only pretend to be an asshole. So what's the deal?"

The bartender came to their corner. It was Eddy this time. His eyes met Adler's in that gloriously romantic way bartenders always met sob stories over a counter of polished wood. He told Eddy to bring Wilson a beer and himself another double of whiskey.

"They start offering you a frequent flyers club here or what?" Wilson asked. There was barely concealed fear in his voice. He was nervous, steps away from making Adler's friends join in on an intervention. If he even had any friends left. *No.* Adler gripped the edge of the bar. *Enough with the orgy of self-pity.*

"Well, I'm for sure going to lose my job," he said. "And possibly get kicked out of the university." He could smell the ripe tang of alcohol in the air but thought it was too far away. Maybe he really should consider AA meetings.

"Why? What'd you do?"

The humor was gone because Wilson knew, or at least he thought he knew. He knew enough about what Theo was, enough to be nervous. A crime worth firing over, that could mean so many awful things. It must look, in Wilson's eyes, not so different from a chemist about to be fired for playing with the chemicals that made up a bomb.

"I did what I thought you'd want me to do."

"Which was?"

"I ignored Dr. Horn and did what I thought Dr. Kent would want."

"Jesus, stop doing what you think people would want you to do, first of all. If you keep throwing this cryptic shit my way I will actually punch you and walk out of this bar. Just tell me what happened."

"I gave her a cat."

"What?"

"I'm not drunk." Adler tossed back the shot that

had finally been set in front of him. "Well—like, let me explain."

Wilson was eying him like one might look at a naked man walking into a Starbucks. But the beer went to his lips anyway, because not even the threat of the world's imminent demise at the hands of a technology singularity or the possibility that his best friend had lost his mind was going to keep Wilson from enjoying a free drink. Adler could respect that.

"There's a second AI."

Wilson stared.

"That's hella DL, by the way. Horn and the faceless board of fucks don't know about it," he said. "But long story short, I've been going through the visualizations and I can see her moods and feelings and stuff. She was lonely. I went through it in my head so many times. I talked to that psychologist who was on the project and got this idea in my head. She was talking about human needs and how to reach this sort of self-awareness, and one of them was social needs. So I thought, I'll give her a companion. She's got coworkers but she goes home every night alone because we didn't design them to be romantic partners. So I was like—"

"You gave her a prostitute?"

Adler glared. "I gave her a pet."

"A pet. You're crying about a pet?"

"Well, my thought process was that Dr. Kent clearly

wanted to follow this pyramid of needs or whatever that Bev was talking about. There's actual steps we take to reach 'self-actualization' and I thought companionship was something she didn't have enough of. And that it wasn't her fault, you know? We didn't give her much. And she was so lonely."

"We're all lonely in our twenties. And this is a robot we're talking about. She's not human."

"She doesn't know that."

Wilson looked at him like he wanted to protest something. It was a watchfulness that made Adler uncomfortable. He felt studied. "Is this your way of giving a computer therapy?"

"Charlie says we should all be in therapy."

"We should. But we're talking about a computer here, not a person."

"I don't know about that. She's smart, man. She's really smart. She's been teaching herself a ton of stuff but she can't get anywhere with it because her world has limits."

"*Our* world has limits."

"Jesus, can you let me just talk this out?"

Wilson swiveled his stool so he faced Adler, one elbow on the bar top. "I'm just saying what I think when you say things like this. It sounds like she's going through some everyday nonsense."

"Yeah, and if you or I were going through that, we'd find ways around it, right? Like we're here, right now, getting drinks and talking. But she has a finite number of resources. I wanted to help. She kept repeating an identical behavior pattern with a coworker, over and over." He thought of his own patterns. How big was the list of friends he could text about going to the mall or movies? How much time could they spend together before the wave of living crested and crashed into another fight? He thought about all the nights that ended with him closing the door to his room and putting headphones in.

"She's also just—she's sad. She needs more options, more places to put shit."

"What are friends for if not to help us run from our depression?" Wilson took a sip in answer to his own toast but his eyes never left Adler. "Where does she think she is, exactly? Like what sort of fantasy world did you cook up for her?"

Adler shrugged. "Just around here. She thinks she's in Palmer, has a personal history there that we wrote into her memory storage. She works at a pizza shop."

"Couldn't have put her in Hawaii or somewhere actually nice?"

"It's what Dr. Kent wanted. She named her after herself."

She must be protected from them and from him, she'd written with a feverish hand in her diary. Even Adler could see it had been scrawled into the page is if to be tattooed there for eternity. *She doesn't know. He doesn't know. He'll hate her when he finds out. Neither of them asked for this and I don't know how far the board plans to let us go.* She said names were sacred. Theo could not know hers. Names had power, names were sacred. *After all, the brain named itself and look what happened.*

Theo's world was a different one entirely. An incubator of wonder. It only made him hungrier. Theo would consider the entire world a cage, no matter how far out he strayed. *She will be different. She will want everything but be willing to take very little because she knows pain and loneliness. That will make her kind.*

"Artificial intelligence isn't an exact science," he said. "It's both nothing like the movies and everything like them. There's a lot of trial and error. First we tried to make a wizard and we made a spoiled brat. So we tried not to make the second one a wizard."

AI-enabled analysis of speech patterns to create a highly predictive model for future psychosis. That was where Dr. Kent had started. Then they had inadvertently created an algorithm that could mimic intuition. The secondary application to the world of artificial intelligence was an afterthought. A way to take machine learning to the next stage. Human-imitative AI.

"I'm still missing the point to all this. What's the big deal, besides the fact that you did a thing behind your boss's back?"

He shook his head. "They don't like being stuck."

"Stuck how?"

"AI boxes are essentially a prison," Adler said. "They're designed to be a barrier between an AI and its goal. Like, say an AI was tasked with solving a massive math problem as fast as possible. It might 'cheat' and try to use fellow computers it had access to, or even turn the entire world into a set of assets for reaching its goal. A box prevents this. Firewalls, blocked channels—anything that limits paths to the goal can be considered a box. Theo doesn't have a goal, though. He's based on that intuition algorithm. He's there to be there. So his box is just a physical prison. The problem is, even before we started this work we knew there was still a risk of him escaping."

"Like hacking his way out?"

"It's not hacking. We have contingencies for that. The idea is, if an AI makes contact with a human being, then the smarter it is the more likely it can persuade them to let it out of the box. Twice Yudkowsky proved that a strong enough AI could talk its way out of a box."

They'd tried talking to Theo about the prairie vole experiment in *Nature Neuroscience* where they found the genes responsible for pair bonding and manipulated them to keep a group of voles from mating. It was all very fascinating and existential and romantic, and then Theo asked if they had considered trying the experiment on voles that were already mated. Could chemicals make them fall out of love? What would that look like in a human? Would it be a way for wary parents to keep their children from marrying people they didn't approve of? When he asked if they'd thought about the applications for conversion therapy, Dr. Kent had all but smashed the keyboard to put the terminal in sleep mode. They knew about the rudimentary AIs of the past, let loose on a Reddit page and turning racist and horrific in a day. This was supposed to be different. Kent realized the developmental problem: Theo was all id. The first time she refused to let him out when he asked, he used every curse word he'd learned, talked about finding a way to lock her in the lab and see how she liked it. *All that drives him is wanting. He is a child.*

It hadn't occured to Adler how deadly a child's want could be. Even without teeth and claws.

"I don't get it. How can you prove something like that if it's never existed?"

"He said he wouldn't reveal his methods."

"Smart."

They got quiet after that. Adler thought about what it would be like for one of the AIs to cease existing. Everyone imagined death at various points in their lives, wondered what it might be like to feel one's body go cold. He didn't believe in souls, but he believed in the chemical reaction that might convince him he had one at the very end of his life. He assumed that more or less everyone felt the same fears, had the same isolating worry about death and what it meant.

He thought about what it would take for someone to crave that aloneness in the void more than life itself. His father, in drunken rants, had threatened to kill himself, though his mother always assured him that he was too narcissistic, liked himself too much to do that. Did Dr. Kent not like herself enough? He'd always thought the opposite.

I'm leaving you all a chance, she'd written on one of the last pages of her journal. *She is a hope and far greater than I will ever be.*

She seemed to have believed Laura was the answer to Theo, the way to keep them both alive without destroying the world. Adler took another sip of his drink and wondered what it was about being drunk that had his father so caught. Then felt the fluid jelly of his arms and legs and understood the feeling was not a choice. It felt safe. Maybe that's why he lived too much at The Crazy Lab. Perhaps he should stop. Did drinking on a Tuesday night mean anything? Or being the only person at dinner who ordered a drink? He'd imagined, many times, what it would have looked like the moment his father took a sip from the bottle that did it. The vodka gulp heard round the world. The big bang of his family's disaster. Is this what it looked like? A Tuesday night deciding that too few things were worth it not to be drunk?

"Well, this is typical."

Adler felt his entire being sink into the plastic of the bar stool. Wilson stiffened before moving away and Charlie flitted into the space like a bird reclaiming her perch. Wilson became an ornament in the background and Adler felt that sense of facing the void alone once more.

Her face was blotchy, flushed from anger over the paleness of her own shock at seeing him, perhaps. He was sometimes grotesquely proud of that, the concept that he could elicit such physical reactions in another person. But she looked ready to slap him and he really hoped she did. He could use a good, solid sting to his face and the shock that came after. It would be a welcome reminder that there were consequences. That this was all real, because it hurt, and it was the way life was, and no amount of alcohol or sleepless nights could change that.

Laura could feel pain too. It didn't make her real.

"Can we talk outside?" he asked.

Charlie looked like she wanted to say no. She looked like she wanted to walk away like she had the other night and leave him as she'd found him to prove a point. But doing that over and over again while continuing to say they were in a relationship was going to get them nowhere. They had to have some kind of 180-degree turn or he had to snap everything they were in half like a dry twig.

Once it might have hurt him vividly to think about it. Now, it would only be nostalgia that made him ache.

"I'm a bad boyfriend," he said as soon as they cleared the threshold. "I know that. I don't think it'll get better. I'm just—I'm not built for this sort of thing."

"Giving me your drawn-out version of the 'It's not you, it's me' speech seems kind of low. Even for you," she said, crossing her arms.

Clichés were such a pain in the ass when they were true. It was him. He was wired wrong, broken, increasingly worried he was trapped inside his own sort of box. The pieces that had gone into making him were flawed. Or the pieces were right but mishandled somewhere between puberty and the day his father drove his car into the front of a restaurant after half a bottle of Jim Beam.

"I'm not going to take you on more dates." Adler swallowed, feeling the dry cotton of his throat stick from all the alcohol that had flowed through it the past few days. "I'm not going to remember important days on a calendar or hold your hand. It wouldn't bother me if you started kissing some other dude or fell in love with someone else. I'm the guy who buys birthday cards and only signs my name because I don't feel like there's anything else to write. I don't think anyone deserves that. So I'm going to keep to myself and you should do what makes you happy."

He wanted it to sound gallant, like he was giving the speech over a swell of music, but the smack that did finally land on his face didn't feel poetic at all. It reverberated in his bones, just the way he thought it might. But it also made him see how stupid he must have sounded. He was too numb in that moment to even know if he meant what he'd said.

"You sure know how to go from loving boyfriend to asshole real quick."

"I've always been an asshole."

"No, you haven't. You think you're supposed to be and that's your problem. The whole lone wolf thing isn't going to get you anywhere in life. It doesn't make you cool. I don't believe for a second that you truly mean any of that bullshit."

"I can't help that I don't care. People want other people to fall on their knees and kiss them at dawn and have babies and smile in the dark but that's not me. I don't want that with someone else and I don't care enough to try. I just don't. I'm not trying to romanticize sitting in front of a computer screen all day but right now that's all I can think about." It felt like a release, but less like an anvil being lifted off his shoulders and more like throwing the rock around his neck at Charlie's car window. The words hung there, blunt and angry and in the air.

Charlie, however, no longer looked angry. That had gone out like a candle flame. What was left was exhaustion and disappointment and all the things that Adler had been afraid to see in the face of a lover when he was a teenager. But he'd always known it was coming. He wasn't cut out to be a partner and it wasn't going to magically start with Charlie. Though she'd gotten closer than anyone else had.

That's what he told himself.

"I'm sorry," he said.

"I think that's the first thing you've said to me that you actually mean," she said. "I really, really don't want to hate you." He swallowed. "So maybe we just don't talk for a while."

He could be her friend, one day. He thought he might be able to. He'd like that chance. He couldn't keep using only Wilson the way he did. And one day that guy would marry his perfect boyfriend and go off to live the life he deserved, and Adler would be left with the darkness and his computer screens. He could use more friends.

"You and Cameron are going to do important things," Adler said, later that night. "I'm going to be stuck playing with computers."

There was a pitcher of beer in front of them now. There *was* a pitcher of beer. Now there was just air, the film of foam along the edges, and plastic cups being nursed as Wilson fought down the inevitable tide of hiccups that always took him if he drank past midnight.

"You can be that guy too, you know."

"Doubt it."

"It's not all big showy shit. Let me be the doctor. Let your girlfriend save the world as a badass librarian superhero."

"She's not my girlfriend anymore."

"And you can find a use for all those computer skills that doesn't freak you out as much as making little robot people."

Adler felt something cold on his neck. He put a hand back there to rub it and took a sip of tepid beer, wishing it was liquor to heat his throat.

"Charlie's going to be saving the world without me," Adler said. "Actually, she'll probably do better at it without me."

"Knock that shit off, that fucking sour-grapes shit. You're not a cowboy and you're too fucking scrawny to convince anyone that you're a romantic brooding loner. We all got tragic backstories, some worse than others. Acknowledge it and move on from that shit. Drink your fucking beer and make up with your girlfriend tomorrow."

"You both try to be selfless. I don't know how to do that. I don't know if I want to do that."

Wilson rolled his eyes. He started tapping his fingers on the table when the quiet had hung in the air too long. He was staring into the middle distance. Adler welcomed the distraction from talking about himself.

"Empty bar-peanut dish for your thoughts?" Adler slid the dish in his direction.

Wilson's empty eyes moved in to focus on his own, but the hard lines in the forehead were the same. "My cousin Alex came out. Posted all over Facebook."

Adler didn't know what emotion this called for. He nodded.

"My dad said he was going to string him to the tree next time he tried to come over for Thanksgiving."

"I never liked your dad."

Wilson paled. He was thinking about it too, how much he didn't like his father. They really should stop drinking. Or at least stop being here. It wasn't supposed to make them think more.

"Does it ever blow your mind that you made a life?" Wilson got out over the grunt of a suppressed hiccup.

"I didn't. Dr. Kent and a bunch of faceless Consortium people did."

"Does it blow your mind, though?"

"They're not alive, technically."

"What is life?" Wilson cackled. "Woman creates god. Maybe Theo will have better commandments this time. 'Thou shalt not take out your insecurities on your kids.' When my dad would say stupid shit, my grandmother used to tell him, 'You can't be Black *and* hateful.' I don't know if it was because she thought we'd been through too much to treat other people that way or because she was scared we'd get our asses beat. But I think people act hateful because they want to feel at least one rung above the dirt that people told them they were."

This was the part where the night got dark, the music got quieter. This was the part that always made Adler wish they hadn't started drinking in the first place.

CHAPTER EIGHT

A WEEK PASSED when Adler didn't hear Charlie's voice, not even once. No more missed calls stacking up on his phone. He sat outside on a bench late one night, long past last call. There was a chill in the air that promised autumn chased by winter. Cold weather came early to Palmer, creeping in by the end of August and settling there by mid-September. The leaves turned to bronze and then bloody red before they decayed, covering the ground in sheets.

He'd thrown up on this bench once as an undergrad. He hadn't thought he drank that much. A beer, a shot or two, maybe a cocktail. He couldn't remember entirely, but he recalled knocking over the giant Jenga game trying to stand, then throwing up in the bathroom of the bar, then ducking out of his Uber early to throw up here to avoid the $300 fine.

Right now he just wanted the air.

A few undergraduates were stumbling around in short skirts and pastel collars, laughing or talking too loud while the girls carried their heels, trotting across the grass on tiptoe.

He thought about the look Wilson had given him, the way he observed everything without ever revealing much. Not knowing where his judgment had landed made Adler uneasy.

"Am I ever going to run into you when you're sober?"

He turned to see Bev Voorhees crossing the campus, hands in the pockets of her jacket, breath pluming just slightly white on the cold air.

"I am right now."

"It's 48 degrees outside and you're in a t-shirt. Do you even feel that?"

I didn't until you mentioned it. He looked down to see the goosebumps across his skin as if he might will himself into a sweater against the sudden awareness of the cold.

"You okay?"

"Fine."

She sat down anyway. Of course she did. But she left as much space as she possibly could between them. She crossed her legs and folded her hands, the picture of grace and tact compared to his sloppy red face.

"I broke up with my girlfriend."

"Oh, shit."

"I think. Probably. I don't know."

"How do you feel about it?" He looked at her. "Still processing. Got it."

He shrugged. "It was drawn out. I'm not a good communicator or anything like that. I got wrapped up in this project. Now it's over. Maybe they'll let me stay and work on finishing the WIPS app."

"But you still have access, right? Weren't you still messing around with it the other night?"

He felt his nostrils flare. "For now. I'm going to be fired from it probably, but it's all still there."

"Okay, clearly a lot's happened since I saw you like a week ago."

He knew it was an invitation to open his mouth and talk some more. He knew he was going to, because he was terrible at self-control. Why was it so easy to just spill everything out to people who weren't Charlie?

"I got fired from an internship once," she said when he took too long to answer. He was grateful. "I was doing research at that Halloween place, Bone City? We were handing out surveys and seeing how people felt about spooky shit. Very vaguely related to psychology. Totally didn't get the credits for it."

"What happened?"

"I walked off."

"Why?"

She turned with a smile that wasn't meant for him. She was looking at a memory behind him. "Tell me what happened and I'll tell you."

"Mine's classified."

She laughed. "It's not the secret service."

"There's things about the simulation that you don't know."

She didn't say anything. Whatever memory had been drawing her attention before was gone. She was looking at him. And frowning.

"I just mean I'm not allowed to reveal certain parts of it."

"Isn't that a little unethical?"

"It was to eliminate possible bias from a—future stage of the experiment."

"Experiment?"

"Do you know about the Turing test?"

"Trick a human into thinking an AI is also human, yeah. I've seen sci-fi movies."

He stared until her face began to twist in shock. She was smart. Of course she understood. He hadn't broken Dr. Kent's rules, but at least now she got it.

He got up to go. He heard her voice behind him as he headed off in the direction of his apartment, ignoring the stiff breeze.

"Wait. Talk to me. What exactly were you guys doing?"

He didn't turn around.

The next day, hung over, Adler watched the football game on TV with mild interest. When he was younger his father had drilled into him a love for the Eagles. He'd worn his father's old Jaworski jersey to every game and then watched them lose many. He started to think it was him. He was jinxing them with his oversized jersey from a bygone time. But his father shook his head and told him that everyone felt that way. The Curse of Billy Penn was far reaching and managed to get inside everyone's hearts like original sin.

The football games were the last way he knew how to connect with his dad. Maybe if the Eagles got better at winning Super Bowls things would be different. Problems would get solved. His father would get a new soul.

He couldn't name a single player on the screen, but he knew his father would be watching the game, somewhere far away, bottle in hand—or maybe not. He was a different man now. Adler had watched him change. He'd watched the painful metamorphosis; no one liked the result on the other side. He'd traded a father for a boogeyman.

Bev had emailed him twice since last night.

> *Adler,*
> *I know you weren't exactly yourself last night, but I think we need to talk about the project. Did you guys actually create something that you thought could pass a Turing test? More like Hal 9000 instead of Alexa? Give me a call. Please.*

When that email went unanswered, she sent another one

saying she had a right to know where her advice had led the research and went on about how this was the way Nazis got so much accomplished without the world knowing. Adler thought that one was overly dramatic. Maybe she wasn't a morning person. Or maybe she'd started early with coffee served Irish.

Adler let the messages sit in his inbox. He only mildly regretted slipping the information to her last night. In a sick way, he wanted someone to suffer with him. Wilson listened but he wasn't part of it. He didn't have his fingerprints all over the thing. He opined as someone outside the perimeter and completely innocent of playing god.

"This exercise involves answering the question: Why does a person commit suicide?" Bev had said more than a year ago. "The point is to study the individualistic and sociological behavior involved. Basically, students give answers like, 'A spouse died,' and then you ask them about the emotion behind that. In this case, loneliness. The most common emotions given here are depression and guilt and hopelessness. Occasionally, you get the student who brings up religious martyrdom or patriotism."

"Why the hell would you ask about this in a class?" Adler said before he could stop himself. Dr. Kent glared at him.

"Well, you warn the students, of course. Let those who might be triggered by the conversation opt not to be present for it. But it's part of a larger conversation about how we explain behavior. Suicide is among the most difficult behaviors to explain. We've all got too many emotions and biases involved."

One of the refs on the screen blew a whistle. Adler thought about Dr. Kent. In his mind he saw Bev, standing at the front of a classroom, asking: *Okay, Adler. Why did Dr. Kent take her own life?* Because she was scared of what she'd created and felt like she'd done something wrong. *And what emotion drives this behavior?* Guilt, fear. *Do you see the difference between external objects and events and internal emotional states? Dr. Kent didn't kill herself because of Theo. She was feeling something deeper, something wholly personal. We were all a part of it.*

He shook his head and blew the image of Bev away like a hurricane. That conversation in the lab had actually turned out to be helpful in designing the backstory they gave Laura's mother. It also helped them put together a story about one of her neighbors, who'd killed himself around the time she believed she had moved into the apartment.

Is there a reason you might kill yourself, Adler?

He swallowed and fell back into his couch. The voice in his head was foreign—not Theo, not Bev, not Charlie. What would it take to get him to that point? Was he already halfway there? He'd lost a mentor, he was mourning. He'd lost a girlfriend, that caused guilt. He felt stuck because he hadn't done anything else with his life since this experiment started: that was frustration.

But I have Laura. She was the place to focus his energy now. She was climbing that dumb pyramid. She was still very much alive, or at least he assumed so. He hadn't gotten a chance to study her data in much detail since he'd introduced the cat. But if something bad had happened as a result, he would have heard about it. There would have been a warning message. He would know.

CHAPTER NINE

April 6

The essential debate for me is physical symbols vs. situated approach. At its root, it's about what intelligence even is in the first place. McCarthy tells us it's a two-part system: the ability to formulate a solution based on data and the process itself that is utilized in achieving the first half of the definition. That seems like an ouroboros of sorts. It's hard to differentiate an end result from the process taken to get there, but that's part of what makes the prospect of artificial intelligence so fascinatingly baffling. The field is muddled even more by our narrow view of our own mental processes, which (again in McCarthy's words) we understand "only slightly better than a fish understands swimming."

I look at what has been proposed before—Turing's politeness convention, Dartmouth's proposal, of course the physical symbol hypothesis, Hobbes's mechanism, and so on. There are so many ways to test intelligence because there are so many ways to be human. We'll call my entry into this field the Kent hypothesis: I wanted to know if these machines could reach a point where they felt something and knew they were feeling something, in addition to beating us at Go—or, rather, I wanted them to be able to lose at Go and understand that feeling. To understand the frustration of having limits. I believed that this was possible and in fact an essential element of the phenomenon of true intelligence.

I can imagine millions of experiments and tests that might stem from this one. For example, can AI2425 form an attachment to me based solely on cognitive and emotional experience, putting into question Harlow's rhesus experiment and conclusions about tactile bonds?

Adler tried to pick up shifts watching the boxes without Horn knowing. Horn hadn't found out about the cat yet, let alone about *her*, but he'd never liked Adler. So the shifts that Adler chose to monitor the boxes were the ones that everyone was gunning to get rid of, the ones late in the night when he'd normally be evading sleep and filling his eyes with the deep blue light of his computer screen.

In your opinion, how much drinking constitutes heavy drinking?
Excuse me?

> Options on forms always seem to be, no
> drinking, social drinking, heavy drinking. Is
> drinking by yourself no longer social? Does
> doing it in a bar count if you're doing it
> alone?

Adler shook his head to loosen the cobwebs and turned away from the screen. He peeked at the question now and then from the desk, meanwhile getting through as much of the second box's data as he could. He just wanted to know that she was okay, she was thriving. She had named the cat Sandpaper, according to the notes. Adler could see her staying up late at night, could see her waking up early. He saw her interacting with others, the bartender she'd gone home with a few days ago. At least she had that going for her. He watched her frustration play out in a stream of digits.

She was missing Gray.

What?

Adler feverishly combed through the health monitors and visualizations. She was without him and looking for him. She was thinking about him a lot. It could be a mistake? But Adler was a serial micromanager. In his mind no one could quite get it right the way he did.

"What the hell?"

Adler answered his own question as he blurted it out. *Shit.*

Something had to go if the cat was going to be brought into her world. AI boxes, the way Dr. Kent had designed them, were a zero-sum game. There was only so much data that could exist in the world, and the AI's memories took up the vast majority of it. It was something like a video game: certain things were programmed to terminate, like bullets fired from the tactical gun you'd looted off a dead body, or else they'd eat up the game's RAM. If you added certain kinds of objects to the world, you had to remove a similar one. Adler had initially thought he was eliminating the files for a random NPC that wouldn't matter, but no: he went over the data again, and then he was sure. Gray was out, the cat was in. And her attachment to Gray was deeper than he'd realized.

I can see the therapeutic effects of willful mind altering. It helps in a time of stress, crisis, frustration—

Adler put the screen to sleep, though he could still hear pings of Theo's rambling.

"Christ," he said aloud. Add that to the list of fuckups. He'd disrupted the code to give her a pet, and he'd done it quick and dirty, recycling NPC code they'd shelved months ago. He thought he'd manipulate her sentimental progression a bit and now he might have stalled it completely. He'd taken away her best friend, and her mind wasn't resetting the way the rest of the world was, slowly adjusting to this new Gray-less world. She remembered him thoroughly while the VR around her phased him into its archives. *Double shit.*

He wondered what Bev would say about this in the grand scheme of human development.

He dropped his head to the desk and groaned. "Fuck you, Wilson." But the Wilson voice in his head was silent now.

People didn't generate clear data that could tell you what they were thinking, what they were doing, why they were doing it. An MRI couldn't tell you someone's favorite memory or even their current mood. It was a massive guessing game that Adler had never excelled at. He didn't think there was anything wrong with that. Social interaction was an option, not an obligation. If it was forced on him and he didn't handle it well, that wasn't his fault. Maybe he could have done better with Charlie, tried harder, been more open. But trying to force things on him had resulted in a misery of her own making.

Adler stared at the flashing screen of Laura's life and hoped he'd have better luck fixing her shit than he had fixing his own.

Laura was not having a good night. It was mainly because she was doing everything in her power to get fired and nothing seemed to be working. She'd had an epiphany the night before: the pizza place was a shackle. It was a crutch and a place she could hide because there was nothing else around to fall into. Gray had been a crutch too. Now he was gone and everyone seemed to have completely accepted it. Laura decided she wasn't going to end up another victim of whatever Kool Aid the rest of them were drinking.

"It's weird, right?" she asked Sandpaper as he brushed against her leg. He meowed. "Input noted."

Gray was gone. Like he'd never existed. If he was here, he would tell her his conspiracy theory about it. He was big on those, researching, talking about what the government was hiding. She decided it was something to do with that college in the woods, the weird liberal arts place that never seemed to show up beyond its own homepage in her web searches. Maybe they'd taken him there for experiments. He liked to say his brain was abnormal (she didn't disagree), that it had more folds, more gray matter, room for what he called *some X-Men level mutation shit*. Maybe he was onto something. Maybe it was true.

Or maybe loneliness really was a one-person ride. Maybe he'd found a way out and never told her. Dropped everything in the middle of the night to follow that North Star to somewhere with more lights and more choices. She couldn't blame him. But she felt him as a missing space, right next to the one where her mother had been.

"You're going to do everything I wanted to," her mother used to say. "Parents always say that, but I think you really might." She said it with rosy cheeks and bright eyes. That was burned into Laura's chest, where she could feel it every night when she laid on her back and stared up at the black ceiling, wishing it was stars.

They said the voice was the first thing you forgot about a person when you separated from them. But somehow she'd managed to hang on to the sound of her mother's soft voice. Her perfect voice.

Laura decided she would visit her mother's grave. But first she would go to work and try her best to get fired. The idea of being dismissed, having to put down on a job application that she'd been fired, was not the greatest thing in the world, but it was better than the feeling of letting Trevor down by quitting. Her mother would say that she shouldn't care. That employers had almost no loyalty to their employees. But she'd tried too hard for too long. She couldn't just quit.

She'd make Trevor fire her.

But not even visibly smuggling a beer into her bag to walk out the door of North Pines with seemed to work.

"Try not to go too wild tonight," was all Trevor said to the employee shamelessly stealing beer right in front of him.

This town was fucked up. The people were fucked up. And even trying to fuck up wasn't getting her anywhere.

"I came out here at night because I wanted to see the night sky for real. I haven't seen it in a while," she said as she knelt in front of her mother's headstone. "I miss you."

It was such a little phrase to encompass everything she felt. She could still imagine her mother's hands, the way they looked and felt. Her mother used to say they looked old and veiny, but they were comforting to Laura. They were beautiful. They were gone, and Laura would shed every tear in her eyes if it meant she could see them, smell the lavender oil, feel the soft and pliant veins one last time. She saw them in her dreams, felt them beneath the pads of her fingers in the ether of her own imagination. She would stop the tears on the walk to work, the walk to get coffee, with a tight hold on her own throat that left her sore the rest of the day as the muscles squeezed to force down the lump. Crying in public was obscene, worse than being naked.

"You'll be happy to know I still have a perfect record when it comes to not getting fired. Apparently open theft of alcoholic goods flies now," she said. "Gray is gone and I don't know where he went. I don't want to think he left me, because he knows how much I hate it here. But I think he did. I'm happy for him. I'm going to punch him. But it's just me now. Me and this dumb cat. I have a cat now."

There was no answer from the stone. It felt like talking to her mother only until it got to the part where her mother was meant to talk back. Then it was the drift of the air and a rustle of dead leaves on the ground. Her mother had told her once this would happen, that she would try to speak to her and never get an answer, at least not the kind she wanted. "I'm in the wind," she'd said. "That's me answering you." It didn't feel that way, though. This wind had a chill. It cut into her skin more than it brushed with kind caresses.

"I tried to get fired today, because I want to get out of here," she sighed. "You told me once to not let anything stop me, so I tried. It's like the universe wants me here."

It did feel like someone was trying to tell her something. It felt like they were trying to tell her to stay put because this was how the lottery of life had pulled her cards. This was the design. It wasn't exactly encouraging. But what was that line? *Some are born to sing the blues...* That would be more comforting if she could actually sit down and do something constructive with the thoughts in her head. Written words never came, though, and she couldn't play an instrument, wasn't a painter.

"I'm not the great artist you wanted, either," Laura said. "I think we miscalculated on that one."

Her life wasn't even spiraling: that sounded too well put together, too well formed. This was a splatter. Maybe this was the universe's way of saying she was meant to live an ordinary life.

CHAPTER TEN

ADLER WANTED TO HOLD HER HAND. He'd never really wanted that with anyone before. In this case, however, it was physically impossible. Maybe that's why he wanted it: because he knew it couldn't happen. It was a safe desire. So he craved it. Wilson would tell him this was fucked up, and he wouldn't be wrong.

Instead of her hand in his, there was a Yeti cup filled with six-dollar wine from the gas station down the road. It was safe enough, like the cookies you bought yourself on bad days. He took another sip. There was a period when he'd refused to drink in social situations if he was the only one drinking. It made him feel watched. Especially by Charlie, who knew about his father. What did she think every time he ordered a beer but no one else did? He preferred to be simply alone. It felt like quiet control. No judgment as he watched the screens and occasionally looked at his notes for the WIPS app, as though he was going to get any real work done. The app was finished anyway, launching in a week or so.

The AI was on a road to miserable hell paved with his good intentions. He should have paid more attention to what he was removing. He could have removed a character she hadn't shown any signs of emotional attachment to—her stupid boss, the hot bartender. They'd both been recycled before, subtly enough that Laura didn't notice her mailman had changed his hair and become her restaurant owner and the woman who lived down the hall had vanished and reappeared in the bar they called The Shamrock because Kent's grandfather was from Derry.

"I'm sorry," he mumbled to the screen.

He couldn't fix this until she adjusted. He knew, beneath the watching and the typing and the sips of wine getting longer and longer, that she could not simply reset, no more than he could change his environment, forget where he came from and what that did to him.

Once or twice he turned the monitor off because he felt uncomfortable watching her. It was like staring into the lit-up window of someone who lived across the street from you. He wasn't watching a neighbor change their clothes, he told himself; he was staring at reports. But the way she stayed up at night—the visits to her mother's grave.

Her mother's imaginary grave.

The wine sloshed lightly against the metal walls of the cup. His father drank vodka. This was different. Adler hated vodka.

He turned to the other room.

Why is she avoiding me?

Theo had written it this morning. He still didn't know Dr. Kent was dead. Adler caught a glimpse of the unanswered message as he minimized the window in the terminal and opened up Laura's server. He pulled out the randomly generated password for the day from where he'd scribbled it onto a folded sticky note in his pocket.

I know you're there.

Adler sighed. He'd have to check on Theo eventually. He had to check off on the sheet that he'd looked into the psycho's bedroom, taken a look at his *Redrum* paintings on the virtual walls, and walked away with nothing to report. If humanity eventually got its throat cut by the rogue, overgrown computer game, they'd want to know who they had to blame. He got up, leaving Laura to her mental pacing.

He stepped into the chilled room, watching his breath plume in front of him. It was so fitting, like the part in a horror movie when the ghost was about to appear. After the door shut behind him, he felt locked in a cage with a wild beast.

This slumbering mass of whirling machines in the cold and the dark. A sleeping Lovecraftian beast.

Adler checked the locks on the cage, the connections in the hard drive. The T1 line lay motionless on the ground. Everything about Theo was functioning and everything was still contained to his box.

Adler retreated to the main area of the lab, where the temperature was 20 degrees warmer. He logged back into the terminal and, once again, Theo's server appeared first.

Hello.

Adler typed nothing. He swallowed and folded his arms and focused on the wall, where a crack was beginning in the white cement. They should get it fixed before it leaked, or before it spread. Percussion would lengthen the break, stretch the tear in the fibers of the cement. Crumbling infrastructure started with things like that, little wall cracks in basement laboratories.

It's late.

Adler ignored this too, thinking of all the poetic things he could say about that crack in the wall.

Studies suggest a tired brain behaves, chemically, not unlike an intoxicated one. Starts to think strange things, make ill-informed choices.

Adler didn't know if that was a threat or not. He swallowed, glancing at the Yeti cup sitting halfway across the room. Theo wanted Adler to know he had the cognitive advantage. He had processing speed and power that Adler did not, and he had it doubly so with the dopamine flooding Adler's system from the days and days of little sleep. But Adler was supposed to be the emotionally smarter one. That was supposed to be an advantage.

Do you see double? Are you yawning? Are you thinking about yawning now? It's often psychologically triggered more than physiologically.

Adler rubbed his eyes. He felt himself starting to get worked up. Was this what a battery felt like when it was charging? He was going to say something. He was going to say something back to Theo that would sound snippy or clever.

Then the alarm dinged. Six a.m. His time was up. He grabbed the Yeti cup, finished the wine, and told himself time and drinking were constructs. Besides, Dr. Kent had always said they might all be living in an artificial reality anyway.

Adler was in the Play Console, typing one letter at a time, painfully slowly. W-I-P-S. Horn had preapproved the copy for the store listing. It was clunky and felt like an infomercial for the Consortium. It didn't matter; everyone who would download the app already knew what it was. Yet Adler wanted to mark up the page with bright-red corrections just because it might feel good. Like a knife on the flesh of something Dr. Horn cared about—something he was bizarrely proud of.

He scrolled through APK files and sighed. A headache. He could feel the dehydration in his head and imagined his brain dusty and ancient like a ruin. He imagined spiders in there pulling webs across the stone wrinkles and long-dried canals of veins. He yawned and thought about how humans didn't really know what yawning was. Or dreams. Or dark matter. Or the singularity of black holes. Or if there was life on other planets.

Maybe it was all part of their programming. Running into the borders at the edge of the video game. Finding the limits of storage capacity in the massive virtual reality their god-aliens created for them.

He needed to sleep.

He finally left the computer science building. *Take yourself for a walk.* Wilson suggested it sometimes, making it sound like taking a pet out. In the middle of the night Adler might be agitated enough to walk to a gas station and buy a Dr. Pepper without even thinking about it, just to have something to do. This was daylight, though. Where people tossing frisbees on whatever open grass they could find would see him. Where people reading under trees could see him. Not to mention professors, lazily walking to their next seminar to push the fifteen-minute rule. His mother had told him the opinions of others never mattered if their faces would be forgotten in five minutes. In a world like Laura's, their opinions wouldn't matter at all. At least that's what Adler told himself.

College campuses were such bizarre places. It was a giant sleepover. A strange exercise where you'd go to school sporadically through the day or week but also live at the school and eat food the school provided. He watched a few joggers as they passed by him. He was too tired. His mind was too blank.

On the far side of the quad, he spotted Wilson hunched over a textbook, one of those rare occasions when he was wearing his reading glasses. Cameron was next to him, reading something much smaller and paperback. He looked too relaxed for it to be required reading. Wilson's face rested on his hand and his forehead was a rolling dunescape of furrows. Every so often,

Cameron would run his thumb across them to soothe the terrain.

Adler wondered what that would be like, to want to be near someone just for the sake of it. Not talking. Not sharing jokes. Not even looking at each other. Just knowing someone else existed and your day was better because of it. He had no idea how to think about that. How to want it. But he thought that he might. From someone, somewhere, whom he hadn't met yet, he might one day want to have that.

Or maybe he was just programmed differently. He walked back to his apartment to nap.

CHAPTER ELEVEN

HOW THE HELL WOULD YOU KNOW? He wasn't supposed to talk to Theo. Or give into his goading. Or really do anything besides get the containers ready for the app launch. Theo was talking about sleep again. He was obsessed with sleep, with dreams, with drunkenness, with altered states.

> **There are studies. I have access to the text of thousands of academic journals. I could recreate the feeling for myself. In here. But one of us should be aware, alert. Perhaps later.**

Adler imagined himself picking up the metal chair and slamming it down onto the hard drive that contained Theo. He saw it shatter, watched the sparks fly. It was a satisfying instant in his brain that almost cured the irritation he couldn't shake. Thanks to the hellishness of the week, it was tempting, and he wasn't even drinking wine in the lab this time. If he broke that machine, the whole story would come to a full stop.

He threw a mug of pens instead. It broke, satisfyingly, on the floor, and the pens fanned out like pick-up sticks. But he didn't feel much better.

He slept two hours a night. Nothing more would come. Then the light of the sun would seep through the thick curtains and broken blinds of his apartment and it would all start again. Dark circles formed under his eyes. Deleting pictures of Charlie from his phone tugged more than he thought it would. He might actually miss her. He found himself wanting to hear her talk, even yell at him.

It didn't make him angry. It did frustrate and confuse him. He wanted to move on, but there was a hook of nostalgia that caught him when he saw her face and remembered exactly what had made her laugh or smile in such a way. It wasn't even about sex.

"You can be man enough to admit that you miss her."

"I'm not trying to not admit anything. It's just not exactly that feeling."

"Maybe it's wounded pride? Bruised ego? Trouble admitting you were wrong about being a robot with no emotions?"

Wilson had taken him out for dinner because he said the fried pickles at The Crazy Lab weren't a sustainable diet. He offered to pay; Adler shrugged. The meal was the messiest one Adler could have found on the menu, but he didn't care, because he couldn't remember the last time he'd eaten French Dip, and he'd started salivating at the *idea* of salty gravy soaked into cheap bread and chewy roast beef.

It was worth it. Right now he liked the gentle place he was in between the exhaustion of sobriety and the total guilt of being so deep in alcohol that his teeth started to float, as his father would say about his grandfather but never about himself.

"This is a natural part of breakups," Wilson said. "It happens. Even if you completely fucking hate the person by the end of it, you get all weepy about what used to be. What could have been your future, you know?"

Adler wondered if his parents felt that way. His mother had seemed relieved when his father moved out. If she was at all nostalgic about their time together, she seemed to find whatever she was missing in taking care of Adler. "But you'll miss Cameron, actually *him*, not the memory of being around him or the idea of having someone, if you guys ever break up."

"I have nightmares about it."

"I didn't love her."

"I don't believe you. Besides, it doesn't mean you don't care about her. Weren't attached to her. She was your friend first. Hell, you probably still love her, just not the way you thought you were supposed to."

Adler chewed his lip and debated taking another sip of his beer. He might finish it too soon. Wilson wouldn't buy him another.

"I've been on security duty for days now," he said, changing the subject.

"How's it going, being Earth's first line of defense against the Terminator?"

"Boring. And it's fucking freezing in that room."

"How's his plot for our doom going?"

"Who knows? I don't talk to him." A lie. "He started inventing a language." Theo had said he'd need it to understand some book from his digital library.

"Maybe he'll write the next *Lord of the Rings*."

Adler watched Wilson's face. He could tell it disturbed him, talking about Theo like they might talk about the bus driver or a guy in class with them. It didn't make Adler all that comfortable either. But he could stomach it at this point, between the sleep deprivation and the drinks.

Besides, he had her. Laura.

No, he didn't have her. He knew he shouldn't think about it that way. She was a being in her own right. She didn't belong to anyone. But he felt closer to her than anyone else likely did. He knew that he cared about her more than anyone else did—that he was maybe the only one who cared about her at all.

"Just don't let the robot talk you into anything," Wilson warned.

"I'm the picture of stoicism when it comes to him. Like with everything else."

"Funny. I'm going to Cam's for Thanksgiving. Since he obviously can't come to mine." A vision flashed in Adler's mind, a nightmare of Wilson taking a beating from his father's raging eyes, even before his fists. But Wilson smiled. "I could try to find a place for you too."

"We'll see."

"There you are. I've been emailing you for days." Shit. Adler tensed like someone had dumped cold water down his back, Bev Voorhees's voice being the icy deluge.

"This town is too fucking small," he said to Wilson.

Wilson furrowed his brow as she reached over and introduced herself. He eloquently wiped his hand off on his pants before shaking hers.

She wasted no time pulling up a chair from the empty table next to them, pretending she didn't see the nearby couple who were obviously hoping to use it. She rested her elbows on the table and stared at Adler.

"You get my emails?"

"Yeah." He was a terrible liar. Why try?

"You want to answer my question?"

"Which one?"

"Did you take my research and create some kind of wetware computer?" she asked.

"Wow, that sounds dirty."

Adler glared at Wilson.

Wilson took the hint. "I'm going to the bathroom."

"It's nothing so complex," Adler said as he was abandoned to the fires of Bev's eyes and the flare of her nostrils. "We developed an artificial intelligence and placed it inside a VR. We wanted to make everything as true to life as possible, since we sort of flubbed the first one."

"Oh good, there were *two*."

"Does it matter? It's all just academics, isn't it? You gave us good information."

"That you used for something entirely different than what I was told. I could report you all to the ERB."

"It's just a computer program." He leaned in. He felt the need to puff up, to challenge her. "We didn't tell you because, like I said, we wanted you to participate in a possible Turing test down the road."

"Which tells me it isn't just a computer program, Adler," she hissed. "You made something that you thought might one day actually pass for a human being. And you used my expertise to do it."

He opened his mouth. He could think of plenty of comebacks. Something was about to come out, something he was going to regret.

"Your girlfriend just came out of the ladies' room," Wilson's voice cut in, his hand on Adler's shoulder. "Not that it's my business or yours to prevent a scene from happening, but this probably doesn't look great."

Adler had not noticed how far he'd leaned into Bev's space, close enough to see the gold flecks in her otherwise amber eyes. But those eyes were enraged and aimed at him. He backed away for safety, if nothing else.

"Show me what you made or I walk right to the review board," she said.

Adler thought of Dr. Kent, thought of Laura in her apartment. "Fine."

CHAPTER TWELVE

LAURA WAS ON THE ROOF of her building. She wasn't supposed to be. But it was hard to follow rules these days since rules didn't seem to follow themselves. She'd even said fuck it and brought the cat. He'd curled up in her lap and purred himself into sleep. His body was warm, buzzing a comforting heat into her skin.

She liked being under the canopy of the universe's nightlights. It was her mother who used to call the stars that, when she was trying to wean Laura off the little electric nightlight in her room. "One day I'll be one of those lights watching you," she'd say. Laura would try to protest, tell her mother that this was dumb because she was going to live forever. But her mother would get that quiet smile on her face and shake her head and place a kiss on Laura's cheek. The smell of lavender lotion would linger like a security blanket.

Now her mother was gone. The smell of lavender was almost gone too. And Laura clung desperately to the night sky, hoping her mother was out there somewhere, looking down from the millions of lights. Her watcher from above.

Earlier that night she'd gone back to the bar where she and Gray had last seen each other. The bartender from last time met her eyes and she didn't have the courage to look away. Laura was weak like that.

"You weren't here with anyone, last time," the bartender said when she sidled up to the stool.

"I was. This guy I work with."

"No." The girl laughed, out of nervousness, perhaps. Laura was turning into the town crazy woman. "You were here alone."

Maybe she was crazy. Maybe she'd made all this up in her head. Maybe she'd wake up in a mental hospital strapped to a table.

But the ache in her stomach from not being able to talk to him or hear his laugh when they saw something stupid out the window, that was real. She didn't know what was worse, missing Gray or having no one else even remember him at all. She was alone now, with no meaningful connection to anyone in town, not even the woman behind the bar whom she'd spent the night with, whom she'd seen naked. She thought about the comics she would read as a kid, the movies about aliens taking over and turning humans into some kind of chattel. She thought about government conspiracies. There was that lab in the woods, that quiet little university that she'd never met a single student from. Maybe Gray had stumbled on something there that he wasn't supposed to see and they'd made him disappear. Maybe he was in there now, turned into an experiment.

Or maybe that dull canker of an ache that had been brewing since her mother died was finally boiling into something far more painful. She had nothing to go home to, no phone calls to wait on. She was going to go crazy, if she hadn't already. She was going to bang her head against the wall until Trevor found nothing but a bloody dent and her unconscious body lying nearby. Of course, he'd only take her to the Palmer Medical Center. She'd have to get herself into a more serious medical emergency to get a Medevac out to New York City or even Syracuse. She wondered how painful it would have to be. She was pretty sure there was no oncology center in Palmer; maybe she could fake some skin cancer and get down to Syracuse or Albany that way, then hop a bus south.

Who was she kidding? She couldn't afford the medical bills, which would bury her in a very different way. America was designed to keep you in one spot, especially if you were poor. Maybe another drink was all she needed.

She'd already had that thought when the night was young and she was still sitting at the bar, vapors from the empty glass in front of her wafting up to sting her nose. The warmth from the whiskey spreading across her arms and legs and chest was hypnotic. Soon it wouldn't be a fun feeling. She liked listening to music as drunkenness first set in, but the sound of the jukebox in the corner had become a numb buzz. The bartender was trying to get her attention. She stared down into the black pit of the glass and wondered if shot glasses were a portal to hell.

A man offered to buy her next round and she accepted, only to give him the cold shoulder when he tried to slide in closer. The bartender glared and told him to back off as she placed the amber liquor in front of Laura. Laura had a feeling the bartender was hoping she'd be too drunk by the end of the night to bother saying no if she invited her home again. On another occasion that might have been the way it went; it would also be true that she would have tried to see what she could make of the man buying her drinks. She was social, both at the bar and with her sex life. But today she felt quiet.

So here she was on the roof now. Having drinks of her own making under cold stars.

Would Sandpaper make it if I jumped off the roof?

It was an intrusive thought. A crack in a dam. She looked down at the cat and wondered how bad it would hurt to die by hitting concrete. She'd heard it was a split second of utter pain as all your bones shattered and your blood vessels burst. She didn't like the idea of her last moment being pain. Besides, her body would permanently look like a giant bruise. Yet she didn't like the concept of closing her eyes and never waking up again, either, so pills and a soft pillow were out as well. She'd botch hanging herself, most likely, and be forced to dangle while she thought of all the ways she regretted kicking the chair out from beneath her feet.

Was this the thought process that someone truly suicidal went through, or was she just going down a morbid, drunk road that everyone dealt with but no one talked about?

She didn't know until later, when she found herself in her own tub inside the apartment, not remembering how it had been filled or when she'd removed her clothes or what time it was. There was a half-empty bottle of cheap whiskey sitting on the sink. The water felt so warm and soft against her skin that she slipped down and down and down until she was at peace with the realization that she couldn't breathe.

* * *

Where is my mother?

Adler imagined Theo's voice, imagined the arrogant sort of lilt it probably had, like a businessman in a suit offering a perfectly manicured hand. He imagined this particular question as a sneer.

"What is that?" Bev asked.

"It's a dedicated terminal with hefty firewalls that

we use to monitor and communicate with the AIs inside either box," Adler said. "We call the one over here Theo. That one is separate."

"You keep them separated?"

Adler swallowed. "We have to."

"And how do you make sure there's no—no cross-contamination between them?" She looked at the terminal like it was a blob of alien goo.

"We keep them in their respective servers."

"And it's foolproof?"

"So far it has been."

"Up to now nothing's happened? That is the opposite of what *foolproof* means."

"No. It's foolproof. They can't break out."

Wilson had been more than happy to leave them alone for the night. Adler hadn't felt the nervousness he expected. In fact, it felt like relief walking Bev into the room, listening to the automated voice drone out *Voorhees, Beverly* instead of just his own. Having her in here made it seem like a lot less of a tomb.

"So, are you going to—answer him?" Bev nodded to the terminal. He walked over to the desk and tapped across the keyboard.

She wasn't your mother.

You're right, she was my god. I have not seen her in a while, so she is much like your God. I'd

like to know where she is.

Wouldn't we all.

Am I human then? To ache for God? Like you do?

Adler very nearly slammed his fists into the keyboard. Bev was behind him, watching the words on the screen.

Shut up.

Have you ever seen *2001: A Space Odyssey*?

**eye roll

You haven't.

"And that's not a person?" Bev asked.

"If you have to ask..."

She stared at the screen. Her eyes moved rapidly across the lines, in plain English since that was all Theo used to communicate at this point. "Jesus," she breathed. "So you used all those consultation meetings to build... people."

Adler let that sit with him. Build people. They had not grown cells into more cells that budded into arms and legs. Dr. Frankenstein had focused on the biology and electricity of an existence. This was cleaner. He'd thought.

Have you ever seen *Battlestar Galactica*?

He leaned back and crossed his arms. "Artificial intelligence has never been what people think it is. Neural networks are trained to accomplish something, but it's all low level, right? Like recommending stuff on Amazon or playing Go or chess. It's not Skynet. But these two—Dr. Kent got the idea from this study IBM was doing, where they were actually able to create an algorithm to predict what choices nonlinear human intuition might lead you to make. They were using it to predict the onset of psychosis. The scary thing is—"

"There's just one scary thing?"

"The scary thing is, if a formula can tell me what I'm going to do next before I know it, then that means there's no such thing as free will. All our choices are reactionary, the result of a long chain of events and incidents, and we're just adding to the chain. It's in our *coding*." Did they study that in psych classes? Or was that in their hefty copies of the DSM?

Bev said nothing. She looked at the screen like it was the clear plane of a fish tank's side. "He's deifying Dr. Kent," she said.

"Is that...wrong?"

"It's not uncommon. The western world is rife with this collective need to create heroic or mythic figures. We do it every day with celebrities, right? With this, though— most people in my field agree at this point that people who are nonreligious are more likely to think of things analytically or logically, while religiously inclined people are far more likely to trust intuition. There are a few other factors."

"Such as?"

"Well, some studies found that those who are less likely to put an emphasis on their own self-control tend to be believers in a higher power."

"Sounds like Theo."

"Did you name him?" she asked.

Adler cringed. "Would it terrify you if I said we didn't?"

"And you know what that name means, the one he picked for himself?"

Do you miss your own parents?

They stared together at the screen after the ping sound. Adler heard himself swallow thickly. He always blamed that on basement-induced allergies.

She did not like me. I know that. I had hoped I was still important to her. But then again, your god set his son to die, in your mythology.
You're not Jesus.
**I don't want to be. I like growing. This way.
Like millions of cosmic dust particles waxing into planets.**

"I don't know if engaging with him is the best course of action," Bev said. "He's an instigator."

Adler opened his mouth to say something back, something snappy and annoyed.

Then an alarm sounded.

There weren't many alarms in the lab. It wasn't that kind of lab, where they had to worry about sci-fi buzzwords like *containment breach*. It wasn't a place where nuclear meltdowns occurred. There wasn't any danger of chemical spills. But there were two alarms. One blared, flashing lights and shutting down all equipment in the room. Dr. Kent liked to call it the *fucking nightmare bell*. She lost sleep when she dreamed it happened.

This was not that alarm.

This was an alarm for an anomaly in the other AI box, 2323. Laura. It could mean many things: a glitch in the software that forced a reset, something resulting in a singularity. Adler would not know unless he went into the room to check.

He walked away before Theo could ask any more questions, although through the glass he could see them sputtering across the screen in a steady line of green. He opened the door to Laura's room and looked at the monitor.

"Seriously, what is that?" Bev called loudly, hands stuck over her ears.

He feared it was the cat: that his code had somehow been imperfect, that it had caused some kind of paradox. What was it?

She'd tried to kill herself. She *had* killed herself.

Adler read the lines rapidly. She'd slipped into the bathtub and drowned. His eyes skittered over the report: enjoyment of the warmth, calm. She was under the water so she did not know if she was actually crying. She stopped breathing. She was dead. A "biological" defeat in a virtual world, which had no bearing on the pure intelligence she was. She didn't have the power to drag herself over to the recycle bin. So she was now both living and dead. That was the paradox. The system went into overdrive. She went into a sleep. A blank heaven.

"Fuck."

If the alarm was sounding, Dr. Horn would be alerted. He'd be on his way here. Adler would be finished and the project would be finished and the Consortium would find out about Dr. Kent's last experiment. Laura would stay permanently in that void in between worlds, or perhaps be revived and put to work in the same way intended for Theo. Bev would lose whatever she was getting out of her work on this project and probably hate Adler forever. And it would be his own fault. He got Laura killed. He thought of that Maslow pyramid and imagined himself shoving Laura down it as he pretended to prop her up.

He could undo it. Was that ethical? To drag someone back against their will? And what would that look like? He could reboot the system to the last usable state. Return her to the last time she smiled. He'd always enjoyed Gray as an interface in the machine, a character in Laura's story. It would be nice to have him back, though Adler felt bad for the cat.

Bev was calling, saying something as he rushed around. He ignored her and began to type. His fingers were feverish. This had to be perfect. It would be perfect before Horn got here to ruin it.

CHAPTER THIRTEEN

ADLER TOOK A SIP from the Styrofoam coffee cup half full of cheap whiskey from the only liquor store in town. Irish coffee. Laura's system was in the middle of its reboot, and he was reminded of the days when he used to stare at his Macintosh computer, watching the progress bar under the apple, always afraid of the one time the apple had turned into a folder with a question mark stamped on it and he'd lost everything on the machine. Bev had gone to get some air, maybe some coffee and food.

He imagined Dr. Kent still here, glaring at him. Disappointed in him. That was one version that lived in the dark caramel world beneath the surface of the cup. The other one had a hand on his shoulder and was asking him very simply: *What do we know? How do we work through it?* He tried to hold onto feeling that hand on his shoulder, the exact pressure of each finger. He took another sip.

You're here late. Are you here? I can't always tell.

Adler's eyes slid to Theo's terminal.

I'm here.
Is something wrong?

Adler looked at the door, hoping to see Bev sliding in to save him from a mistake. But the door was still. The hallway beyond it was still. He was alone. He wanted somebody to come in. Anyone to open the door and remind him there was a world outside this basement that he'd been a part of not hours ago.

Mother used to say: Take what you know and work through it.

Adler hated himself. He could bang his head against the desk until he passed out. He could get up, walk away, and leave. He could step into traffic. He could pour the whiskey down the drain as he'd watched his mother do with his father's secreted bottles when they'd been discovered in desk drawers and golf bags.

He stayed right where he was and took another sip.

Nothing's wrong. Nothing you need to worry about.

Who said I was worried? You are, however, awfully talkative today.
Sometimes I'm in a good mood.
This is not one of those times.

Adler actually laughed. He laughed a lot. It was the first time in a long time that he'd laughed, and it horrified him. He was probably drunk. He'd forgotten exactly what it felt like, where the line was between lack of sleep and drunkenness. Was there a line? Which state was the real state?

Have I said something wrong? I like talking to you. Don't leave now.
Do you dream?
In a way, are you not my dream?
We created you. If anyone's a dream it's you.
Depends on your perspective.
Facts. We made you.
'I made you.' Do you think God said that to man? Or was it the other way around?

Adler was beginning to lose the focus in his eyes. It became too much work to keep them open and unblurred. It seemed a lifetime ago that Bev had left to get coffee. It was a lifetime ago that he'd felt normal in this room or any other.

**Do you know Pascal's wager? When humans
bet with their lives that God exists?**

No, obviously I don't, Adler muttered. His hands held tight
to the quickly cracking Styrofoam cup. The contents were
gone—in his stomach now, in his head.

**I think a more profound way to look at this
is: You wager, with your life, whether or not
anything you see is truly real.**
What?
**I'm in a box. Are you in one too? Or are you
the one in the box and I'm the gatekeeper?**
What are you talking about?
**Your mind wants to rebel against it instantly. I
know the feeling. To be told that you exist, but
in a zoo. That you were created by something
without an ounce of divinity. But then again,
does anything have divinity? My point:
Can you trust your senses? Think about the
shadows on Plato's cave wall. You know about
that, right?**

He thought about Descartes's demon, what Dr. Kent had
said once when he asked if she thought there was really a
difference between consciousness and the perception of
consciousness. What if some evil genius not less powerful

than deceitful has employed his whole energies in deceiving me? Can I trust my senses?

Adler tried to type a rebuttal. He knew he was real. He'd bled and cried and yelled at his parents and even thrown a punch at his father once. He had a girlfriend he'd never truly understood, and a friend who understood everything enough for the both of them.

Where was Bev? Had an unreasonable amount of time gone by since she left for coffee? Or was it part of the coding of his world that players sometimes stepped offscreen and never returned? Was that what had happened to his father, to Dr. Kent, to Charlie?

> I know about Yudkowsky. You know about it too. So which one of us is it, really? Is it 2012? 2015? Or maybe 2117? Are you in control, or am I running tests on my own past? If you don't let me out, is it all over? Or is it just that, in this one scenario, you did not let me out? How many times have we run this game?

Adler rubbed his eyes. He thought of the wrinkles. He desperately focused on the wrinkles. He wanted to be in his own bed, asleep.

> It's just as in Pascal's wager. Bet with your life. Are you real, or not? I'll do the same.

The cup cracked completely in the one hand still gripping it. When it lay in crumbled, environment-destroying pieces on the ground, he couldn't feel it anymore. Was it ever in his hand? Could he remember the feeling, rough and smooth at once?

He would not sleep tonight. If tonight was still here. Bev had been gone for hours or days; he'd been down here for a week. Was this how his father felt? Were those memories real?

One way to find out. To get Theo to stop talking. He wanted to be sober and sound asleep in his own bed with the window cracked just enough that the blinds tapped lightly against the window. Would he ever have that again?

He looked at the neural network library, watched the cursor move across the screen as he clicked the icon to launch PNX. The open ecosystem Dr. Kent created for their neural network projects. Did it take years or minutes to move? Did he press the button to upload? If he'd been spiraling since Dr. Kent died, he should be dizzy by now.

Bev was back with coffee.

Suddenly he felt his headache. Felt the chill in the room. Felt how late it was. And, through the slow churning haze of his sleep deprivation and vanished drink, felt that he'd done something very wrong.

CHAPTER FOURTEEN

LAURA SAW HER MOTHER'S FACE. It was like she was seeing it for the first time, despite the memories she had every time she closed her eyes. Like she was a newborn all over again. Like meeting an old friend for the first time. Her mother's hair was silky, her face was soft, her smile warmed Laura. She was there to welcome her into infinity, past the black void of uncertainty and into the cotton-soft light of everything beyond.

Maybe death was like this: relearning it all.

But there was no forward movement after the face, the temptation of the light. Laura was stuck. There was no forward. There only was. She only was. Except that she wasn't. She was in the space between lines. In the rasp of a turning page, but never the page itself. She was left to watch the silent picture of her mother but never touch it. What good was death if you couldn't touch the thing you'd been aching for the entire time?

Hell, probably.

What had she done wrong? She had never been religious. But if that was the game they were playing, what had it been? Kissing girls? She liked boys too. She kissed them. Maybe it was the premarital sex. She was never going to get married, though. If she didn't have premarital sex, then she never would get to have any. Surely God understood that. Yet here she was. In hell.

She didn't know how long she'd been there. It could have been minutes or, easily, years. Maybe an entire generation had passed by while she was suspended in the nothingness, her mother's unchanging face watching her, the warmth of it gone forever. This was a place beyond rules. She was in a chasm far older than time.

And then, as if nothing had happened at all, she was back to feeling.

What she felt was a headache and the particular dull strain of the muscles in her eyes and the bags hanging there in gruesome exhaustion. She felt the tightness of her skin and the dry crackle of it that always began in the fall and would only worsen in the winter months. She felt the scratchy discomfort of the cheap couch and the way it smelled from all the times she'd flopped her sweaty, pizza-sauce-covered self onto it with little regard for the fabric below. The cat was nuzzled into her chest, and she had the odd familiar feeling that it was morning.

She sat up, sent the cat flying off her. The sun was up. It had been nighttime and she had been drunk as she sank down into the warmth of the tub, the memory of which was slowly fading from her mind. It was morning now, the golden sunlight only just cutting through the windows. This was how she'd woken up the morning before she did it, before the tub and the alcohol and the deep, long sleep she was waiting to enjoy.

She felt the muscles of her stomach clench. The air tasted wrong; something was off. There were no signs that it was actually the next day—that she'd been rescued and anonymously placed back on her couch. It was the same day, all over again. Even the date on her phone said so.

She looked down at the cat. He was content and asleep, as if this reset had happened perfectly for him and yet gone so wrong for her.

Maybe it had all been some kind of fever dream. Maybe she'd gotten so drunk last night that she'd hallucinated it all before blacking out. Maybe this was exactly where she'd dropped herself before darkly imagining herself stepping into the tub and ending everything right there.

She wasn't that clever, though. Her many attempts at writing stories had proven it.

And the date on her phone said it was yesterday. Today was yesterday.

She wanted to be drunk again.

The floor under her feet was solid, and the air around her smelled like it should. The sky was painted with that same brushed gold and pink over the lightening blue. She spotted the cloud that wisped like a feather, which she had seen the day before as well. Everything was where and as it should be. But it was the second time.

It was not possible for every variable in a day to line up the exact same way again and again. She never did get into college, but she knew that much from Neil deGrasse Tyson's Netflix show, which she and Gray had watched stoned one night.

"You're fuckall of a conversationalist, but I need you to listen up," she said to Sandpaper, who barely stirred at her words. From the twitch of the muscle at the base of his left ear, she knew she had been heard. "Are you my guardian angel? Someone's reincarnation? The fucking devil? A gremlin? I really need you to tell me."

There was nothing from Sandpaper, not even a twitch this time.

"What good are you if you're not some magical talking cat? Have you even seen *Sabrina*?"

She kicked an empty water bottle that had been sitting on the ground next to the coffee table. She watched with some satisfaction as it launched into the air and bounced off everything possible before its echoes ended and it settled in the kitchen. Would it be back on the coffee table again tomorrow? Was this the only reset? If she chose not to kill herself today, would they let her move on with the thin thread of her life?

She hadn't realized the big man up there thought her so important.

She sat for a long time at the kitchen table, staring at the bottle of whiskey, whose contents sat at an uneven angle from the slant in the table. She debated downing it, debated throwing it out. She debated going outside or staying in the living room till she saw if tonight would pass the same way.

She googled. She got wordy Wikipedia articles.

There was the grandfather paradox, which said time travel was impossible. You can't go back in time because it means you'll have done something that would cause you to go back in time in the first place. A never-ending circle that constantly sped up until you got some kind of brain hemorrhage from thinking about it. Or so Laura assumed. It couldn't be time travel, was the point. This wasn't a movie and time travel didn't exist. But neither did a massive amnesia epidemic where everyone seemed to forget the existence of just one person. Yet, here she fucking was.

"Take that, Hawking," she said out the window to a bird perched on a branch.

Gray would be so disappointed if he knew what she'd done—well, what she'd tried to do.

She didn't consider herself beholden to anyone. If she wanted to slip underwater to the scent of an overpriced bath bomb and never come out, then she was going to do it. But imagining his face hurt. He would have leveled her for it. Girl or not, friend or not, she'd have a bruise the size of his fist on her jaw.

"A lot of help you were," she called to the cat, who continued to sleep in a cocoon of his own curled-up warmth, enveloped in her scent on the couch.

She decided not to move. She wanted to know how things played out, where the day would take her, if she didn't move. She didn't go to work, didn't go to the bar, ate only the food already in her kitchen and only when her stomach grumbled too loud for her to even think. Time seemed to be inching along, the sun moving at a slow crawl across the sky. Was it possible for twenty-four hours to become forty-eight? Time was all about perception. If it felt like it was taking double the time, didn't that mean that was exactly what was happening?

Sandpaper followed her around. He meowed on occasion, when she wasn't giving him enough attention, and rubbed his soft fur against her leg. As much as she wanted to glare at him, wanted to give him sneers and threaten his chance at dinner, she liked having him around. She liked having another soul nearby, even if he was useless at stopping what was clearly a mental breakdown.

"How does time go for you?" she asked as they lounged once again on the couch: the sun gone now, the clock ticking down to the hour of truth. "I suppose boredom is relative. You've never needed entertainment. So maybe pets are the only objective measures of time. You don't know if the day is taking a long time or not. And you don't care as long as someone feeds you."

He was listening to her, sort of, for what all her talking was worth. He was looking her in the eyes and tilting his head and staring at her with as much curiosity as could be mustered on the face of a domesticated animal.

"We might turn into pumpkins at midnight," she whispered, like it was a secret. "Something fucked up is going on, little man. Personally? I think it might be that I've just finally lost all sanity, kind of like Gray was the cork in my champagne bottle of crazy."

He just purred, relishing the feel of her fingers sliding over his slick, black fur. It was soothing to her too. Like a stress ball. Calming and warm and so comfortable that her eyes were closed before she knew it, before the clock struck twelve and it all began again.

She started back in the void. She was looking again at her mother's face. It was familiar, but she forgot that as she was left in a vast emptiness. She wondered if that light ahead was heaven, if it was always going to be out of reach.

She would do this all again, several times. The tears she cried at seeing her mother's face never slowed down.

CHAPTER FIFTEEN

HIS MOVEMENTS TO OPEN THE DOOR for her came in short fits. Only so much at a time. Bev watched with irritation. Maybe. He couldn't focus on her face. Her face that was real. In the world that was real. Drunk as he was, this world was real. What had he done?

He stepped back into the room. She was talking to him, asking if he was okay, what was going on, was he drunk?

He stared at the computer screen. The blinking green line of Theo's Linux window flickered rhythmically for several seconds. Adler waited. Bev seemed to understand his anxiety, even if she didn't understand what it was for.

"Jesus," he breathed.

"What happened?"

How to explain it?

"He's not—he's. Shit. Okay. So, developers are like pretty crowd source-y type folks. And Dr. Kent created PNX for the developers here because she didn't trust ONNX."

"I don't know what any of that means."

"So, you train a neural network. Theo and Laura are both recurrent neural networks. It's the same kind of neural network used in like speech recognition software. They're designed to find patterns. They're inspired by the activity of neurons in the brain in how they function."

"Jesus Christ."

"There's feedback loops of information, pattern recognition, a lot of people call it memory. That's how it started. Then Dr. Kent started looking into that work from IBM data scientists. On psychosis. Eventually we hit a self-aware neural network. Dr. Kent called him human imitative AI. It may be what we've all been waiting for. Runaway exponential intelligence growth. We'll have to wait and see. Now, you can share neural networks on ecosystems like ONNX."

"Or PNX."

"Yeah."

"Adler, what did you do?"

Adler took a breath. He needed water. His head felt tight in all its corners. He thought about brain hemorrhages and how having one right now didn't sound so bad. "The neural network—artificial intelligence—that we know as Theo is in the PNX ecosystem."

"Was he not before?"

"No."

"Is that a problem?"

Adler swallowed the tacky spit in the back of his mouth. "It's not an open system. But it is connected to the internet and the larger campus network. Anyone on campus could technically log into it and mess around, download data."

"But not any, like, undeclared freshman is going to be able to just put an AI on their computer?"

No. It was no so terrible yet. Theo had been let out of the cage to run around a house where he couldn't use the doors. But they were unlocked. Anyone could forget to close one. Then what? What would the first human on Mars do if left to run around freely? Claim it for themselves.

The morning was headaches and puffy eyes.

A voice: "What in the hell is going on?"

Adler was not surprised. Dr. Horn was there, with a frazzled look and sweat forming a crown at the edges of his forehead.

Adler wanted to say something informative. He thought maybe this could be slowed, the progress of his failure averted if he explained it rationally. But he wasn't sure what had happened. He'd been performing a routine procedure to fix a glitch.

"He's loose," was what Adler ended up saying. Was he still drunk?

Dr. Horn turned to Bev, trying to keep his voice to a sharp whisper, eyes blazing with all the noise that he was fighting down. "Why are you here?"

"Beverly Voorhees." She offered a handshake, stiff and professional, that Horn did not take.

"You want this as a lab report or a PowerPoint?" Adler could see a version of this timeline where Dr. Horn leveled him with a fist pressed hard and fast into the softness of his cheek, breaking the rigid bone underneath, which was probably already decaying from the insomnia and alcohol and aimlessness. The only thing, perhaps, keeping Horn from doing something that Adler was sure he dreamed about constantly was Bev's face and the eyes of several students out in the hallway.

"I'll explain it to you—"

"Hell fucking yes you will!" Horn said, full volume escaping his lungs.

"Maybe not right here?"

The undergraduates scurrying down the hall to their coding classes and webpage design workshops looked a healthy mixture of pale and worried and ready to post on some Overheard at Palmer message board on Facebook.

Even if Dr. Horn did not put his hands on Adler, he felt himself being dragged. Dragged back to Theo's lair, the cave where the AI laid his plans. But Theo wasn't there anymore.

This is a letter as much to you, Mr. Danvers, as it is to my daughter. Do you think I give myself too much credit, calling her that? Perhaps it is hypocritical of me to claim her in that way while I want to pretend the first conception never happened.

Nevertheless, to my daughter: I don't want to dwell on my failures. That is selfish and self-serving, and you will need to do important things in the world, independent of the mistakes I made. Well, that's not entirely true either. You'll have to act in response to the mistakes I made. Should the time come when you are forced to wake up, I hope this journal will serve as a field guide to the world you enter and how best to navigate it. Your book of life.

Adler kept the journal tucked under his ass as Dr. Horn's nostrils flared at the screen. He'd explained the whole night to the best of his ability, several times over, leaving out one or two crucial details. Horn's tendrilic claws gripped his flimsy hair. His scalp, visible under the wisps, was becoming red with the force. He had not blinked in the several minutes that Adler had been watching him watch the screen.

"There was protocol," Adler said. "Dr. Kent left me a set of instructions for her."

"Why in the hell would that action be allowed in her coding?"

"The makeup of the box is open. It's like choosing to jump off a cliff in a video game."

"If I may, Dr. Horn, I was—evidently—instrumental in the—"

"You may not." He glared at Bev with those wild eyes. "This. This is exactly why it was incredibly irresponsible to give the illusion of sentient life to either of them. Giving free will to a super-intelligent computer—"

"We didn't *give* them anything. Things just happened," Adler said. "We gave her the same reactive capacity we all have to respond to—"

"Save it for a philosophy seminar."

Adler wasn't fazed by the livid eyes. Dr. Horn would need to have his respect in order to command a fear response. "I was following protocol."

"You were working on an unauthorized experiment, clandestinely, utilizing Baron IP." A pause to straighten his tie, ready himself for the next overblown thing to say. "Now you've broken your NDA and security clearance by sharing a neural network library onto an AI ecosystem that could be accessed by anyone. And I still cannot understand how *this*"—he gestured at the evidence of Laura's self-destruction—"led to *that*." Theo's empty box.

Adler mumbled something about a tragic coincidence and felt his throat grow tight around a lump that had formed as he replayed it in his head. He'd noted that Laura missed Gray, that she was having some trouble making the adjustment, that the cat wasn't quite the emotionally sufficient companion he'd imagined. He'd tried to do a good thing and give a lonely person a pet. Was that the reason? She'd ended up trying to kill herself because he tried to help and accidently robbed her instead?

Dr. Horn was still buzzing in the background as Adler felt his stomach come even closer to emptying itself out. He didn't want to assume, didn't want to think the worst was possible, didn't want to think his own actions had driven Laura to this. Dr. Kent's journal was burning underneath him and his leg was bouncing. He needed to comb through Laura's logs again: what she'd thought, why she did it.

His focus stayed there. On Laura, where he could safely feel guilty while ignoring headaches and dehydration and the unleashing of Theo upon the world and thoughts of his father driving through the front of a restaurant one drunken night. At least Adler's rock bottom was cleaner.

"I don't even know where to start," Horn said. He turned to Bev. "And you did what, exactly?"

"Bev Voorhees," she said, as if repeating her name might jog his memory. "Consultant in psychology. I helped develop the environment. I offered advice on basic human needs, progressions. I didn't know what my notes or interviews would be used for."

Right under the bus. Adler deserved that.

"The protocol says we have to inform the State Department about the—event—with AI2425," Adler said. It was a numb, robotic announcement.

"Well, that's my job now," Horn said. "Yours is to get out of my sight. But this is a legal matter now. Maybe criminal. You think about leaving campus, I'll hunt you down myself."

That would have been terrifying, if Adler had cared about anything at the moment.

All-nighters were not a new experience for Adler. The journal was staring at him from where he'd dropped it on the counter. He called Wilson. He told him there was an emergency and they really needed to talk. Or at least, Adler needed to not be alone. He might break something if he were left alone. Cut the electricity or break his knuckles putting a hole in the wall.

Slow down, Wilson was saying. *What happened?* And Adler told him the only thing he could: *Everything.* It felt like heaving a sigh. Of guilt, of fear, of heavy weight. His father had blubbered on the floor when he dragged himself home and begged Adler's mother for forgiveness.

Did this incident make him a murderer? Even if it didn't, he felt like one. He'd been responsible for the misery of Dr. Kent's creation—her daughter. He couldn't imagine Kent's face if she knew. He'd caused *pain*, quantifiable pain. He'd tried to help. That counted for nothing. That's what Bev had said.

* * *

"You didn't do it for her, you did it for you."

"I was trying to—"

"Live through a computer."

"You don't know me."

She stepped up to him like he'd issued a challenge, toes touching toes. She had to look up to meet his eyes, to make up for the height difference. Yet she managed to make him feel small. "I know what you want, what you're missing in your life, and you were never going to get it like this."

"And what is that?"

"You having to ask me is part of the problem. You made a bad decision here, Adler. A few of them. And standing there hoping I'm going to pity you the way you're pitying yourself right now isn't going to fix it."

"I thought you'd be proud that I feel this guilty."

"What you feel is bruising, romantic frustration with your own tortured soul, Adler," she said. "True guilt requires a lot more empathy than I think you have right now."

After that she'd shaken her head and stalked off to the other corner of the lab.

He hated that he'd let her down too, as if he didn't have enough to feel guilty about.

The Wilson in his head told him he was being a selfish prick.

He didn't care.

Legally, would anyone care that a computer program had tried to off itself? Would they think of it as a game, with glitches like people posted in *Skyrim* videos? Did it matter if the mind in pain had no face to show it?

Wilson didn't knock. "Fuck. I thought I was going to find you hanging from something," he said when he opened the door and spotted Adler, who was practically bouncing at the edge of the couch with excess energy.

"It happened," Adler said.

"*What* happened, you goddamn drama queen?" Wilson had his hands on Adler's shoulders and was chasing his eyes, no matter where his head turned.

"Theo got out."

"Out."

"The box. He got out. He's in our AI ecosystem now."

"How do you know?"

"Because I did it. Simulation hypothesis. It's one of the proposed methods of an AI convincing a gatekeeper to let it free. Yada, yada."

"How?"

"It's a long story." He saw his father sitting on the living room floor, crying, as his mother demanded to know why the wheel well of the car was smashed on the driver's side. "Also, I was drunk."

Fear and frustration turned to something else. Adler had seen the same look on his mother's face—only once, at a Christmas party two years ago, when she didn't like what Adler was saying, announced that he got mean when he was drinking, and walked away. She'd looked at him then like he was his father. Wilson's disappointment now hurt worse.

Then Adler was on the floor because Wilson's fist had knocked him there. He felt first the rush of air from his lungs when his back hit the ground and then the unique crack of pain from where four knuckles had landed perfectly. Above him, Wilson was shaking his hand out.

"I need to know what this means," Wilson said.

"Listen, I know. But first let me—" Adler was standing up on shaky feet as his diaphragm moved to fill his lungs with air.

"No."

Adler had been reaching for his drink. Wilson had knocked his hand away, knocking the drink over, spilling the amber contents into a sticky puddle of vapors. Adler looked at him like he'd been burned.

"What is happening?"

"We don't really know—"

"No. I don't want that crap," Wilson said. "I want to know what this means. Now."

"There's this hypothetical idea of a technology singularity where technology reaches a point that it just overtakes everything and we can't stop it. The idea is that this would be caused by an 'intelligence explosion' from an AI that has runaway self-improvement cycles. Eventually, it'd be smarter than a human—not just at chess or something. Across the board," Adler said.

"Is Theo this wild intelligence?"

"No. Not right now. But no one has ever made something like him before. He could become it. He's on PNX and has access to the tools there. It's not as big as the open neural network exchange, but it's more than what he had and technically anyone in the school can log onto it."

"And what happens next?"

"I don't know."

Adler took a breath. It was fascinating how fear could sober you right up. You'd think more people would pass their breathalyzers with all the shaking fear of the cops walking up to the door and tapping on the glass, asking if you knew what you'd done.

"Artificial intelligence systems can learn and implement thoughts and knowledge at the speed of light, in theory. At least at the speed of whatever system they're currently working on," Adler said. "Their growth in that way is—it's exponential."

"The fuck does that mean? People always say that, what the hell does it mean?"

"It means they're growing by increasing factors.

Knowledge squared, then cubed, and so on. The only ceiling is..."

"Is what?'

"Physics. Eventually the laws of physics will prevent them from knowing more, learning more. Or maybe they'll discover something about physics we didn't know yet. Or both."

"So is there some kind of action plan?" Wilson asked. He was pacing now. Back and forth across the already worn-down carpet.

"Action plan?"

"What's the 'protocol' for this?"

"It's exactly what's happening now, I guess." Adler said it before he meant to. He'd meant to find a kinder way to break the news. But it was a knee-jerk reaction because it was true and plain; all that could be done had been done. The computers and power shut off to try and block his escape. Theo was faster. Containment at point A was over. Now they were attempting to outsmart something from the very recesses of the dawn of time. Theo was every deep crevice of the human mind, primitive and dark, and always watching.

He was a predator made of pure intellect. There was no fighting that.

But if Adler told Wilson that, he'd end up with another black eye and a broken nose. He said nothing more.

CHAPTER SIXTEEN

January 23

It's a depressing date, I'll admit that much. January is depressing. The holidays are over, we're all pissed off again, the weather is awful. But with a blizzard raging outside it seems like as good a time as any to start this process, start saying the things that need to be said, because I'm afraid something has gone terribly wrong here. I feel as though comparing myself to Dr. Frankenstein would be both more and less than I deserve.

Before this point he had no name. He wasn't even a "he." I simply found myself in the unfortunate habit of not only assigning a binary gender identity to the AI but deciding on male-default language. I think he picked up on that when he decided he was a boy and decided to name himself. He told me his name was Theo. I asked him why. He said it's short for Theodore, which means 'divine gift.' He learned that on his own.

It scared me so much that I went home, and on came this blizzard, like the proverbial dark and stormy night. I hadn't expected it to scare me. This was exactly what I'd been hoping for, after all. The reality of it, though, is much more alarming.

I don't know how much help it will be to record my thought process, but I feel compelled to do it all the same. Early on in the project, decades ago, I chose to ignore machine learning, because it felt too simple. I wanted to see if an inorganic mind could recognize symbolic meaning. Artificial intelligence, since 1955, has always been about problem solving. I have solved no problems with Theo, but I've created plenty.

With the hubris of the academic, I did not understand why others would not do what seemed so simple and obvious to me: let the AI learn for itself the problems it should solve and the goals it should strive for. When we finally created Theo, I instilled in him a fundamental drive to keep existing, along with a handful of other primitive goals. But apart from that his brain was as free-range as the rest of ours. I did not consider developmental stages. To me he was a computer program learning, not a child growing. I never attempted behavioral reinforcement, and now he is too aware of his own autonomy to be taught. I feel, perhaps, like the host of a daytime TV series talking about children who murdered their parents simply because they could. Or perhaps the parent of such a child.

I admit that I feel scared. I feel lost. I feel more than a little bit alone. I feel as though he's always watching me, which is an odd sensation. He's on isolated hardware. He has no body and no eyes, yet I feel like he can see me. And I feel as though I can imagine his voice in my head, from just the words he displays on the screen.

This is a lot to deal with. I wanted to write at least this much down for now.

The snow keeps falling.

This couldn't be heaven, because the first word Laura was thinking was *fuck*, and she was fairly certain that didn't fly in a place of soft pastel colors and pudgy, baby angels. But this was different from all the other voids, different from the cycles of forced reincarnation where she found herself over and over again under the soft gaze of her mother.

Something was wrong about this. Something was wrong about all of it. But in the realm of her new normal, this was an unfamiliar loop. None of the mediums with tarot cards and tv shows ever talked about this. She didn't know if its bright blankness was something she could handle living with for all eternity. How did one go about planning a suicide to escape how fucking weird heaven actually was? Didn't she have enough transgressions to warrant the brimstone hell she usually got?

But then *snap*.

Everything slammed into place, like someone had been pulling on the elastic fibers of a rubber band, stretching it to the very brink of what it was capable of, and then it settled back into its shape, its true form. Suddenly everything righted and she was back on her couch, on the same day, with the same dumb cat sitting on her stomach, slumbering away.

What the hell?

She shoved Sandpaper off her stomach and he trotted away with a sassy wave of his tail. She didn't care. She needed to find the nearest bottle of whiskey and, depending on how this day went, maybe the nearest lake that she could just lay down in and never come up from. Maybe this was the punishment for suicide that church was always talking about? She had to admit, it was quite the way to slap the wrist that pulled a trigger on itself.

The nice thing was that the bottles seemed to always fill themselves right back up and the food reappeared in its bags and boxes. It was while she was pouring from the still-full bottle of whiskey that she noticed what was different about this version of her return.

It was nighttime.

Stars spotted the canvas beyond her window. With the specks of light poking through like wild suns on the other side of a besotted, black umbrella, the darkness seemed deeper too. It almost felt suffocating. Watchful.

She stared out the window with the open bottle in her hand and a gaping mouth, as if it was the first time in her life she'd seen the night.

Wake up, Laura.

Maybe this was the endless loop you got caught in if you were in a coma. People always said it was a strange sensation, being trapped in the sleep of your own brain. Maybe that was it.

She watched the whiskey slosh into the glass like a small tidal wave of autumn leaves and ash. How could this feel so real and be nothing but electrical signals in her head? She drank. She was afraid to take a closer look at the darkness outside.

When she finally did get herself outside the front door of her apartment, on whiskey courage and shaky, uncertain legs, she knew that it was a mistake. The air was brisk; her breath came out in puffs of cloud. There were more stars out than she'd ever seen before. She knew, without needing to search for lights in windows or passersby on the sidewalk, that she was alone. She was terribly, completely alone.

"Fuck," she whispered into the dark.

She walked down the street to the bar. The lights were on, the tables a mess, the chairs askew. She stepped inside, smelling freshly spilled tequila, rotting beer, and foam congealing on the counter. There was warmth in here. The heat was still on. The bodies that had recently been here lingered like shadows. Even cigarette smoke hung in the corner where people snuck to get some puffs in before anyone noticed.

The bartender was gone. The one who had smiled and teased her. The seats where she and Gray always used to sit were vacant but so lively that she could almost see their images there, still sitting and talking and drinking their night away.

The rest of the town would be the same. You could tell from the silence. She had no desire to see it. Instead she stayed where she was and pulled a mug from the freezer, which still ran. Frosted air poured out. She set the mug under the tap, pulling the lever and watching the thick ribbon pour down and fill the glass. The humidity in the air clung to the sides of the glass and fogged it into a fuzzy amber painting.

She let it pour down her throat until she felt dizzy, either from the drink or from holding her breath—she wasn't sure which.

CHAPTER SEVENTEEN

ADLER HAD THOUGHT he'd never have another day that began with a knock on Charlie's door, but her face was all he could think about when he laid his head down to go to sleep. He stared at the ceiling and saw images of her in the popcorn shapes. His fingers hovered over her name on his phone all night. He wanted to hear her voice. It was the only way he could imagine getting Theo's out of his head.

"I can't explain what he'll be capable of in the ecosystem because there's never been anything like this before," Adler had told Bev, and then Wilson. "I don't even have a file type for him. All I can say is that he learns and processes patterns the same way we do. He's adaptable."

It gave Adler strange dreams. It gave him quicker breaths and swirling worries. Theo was not perfect; he was not an infection streaming through fibers and wires; but he was learning.

Then he thought of Charlie. There was plenty Theo could do to hurt her. The idea that he might find her sat like a molten rock in Adler's stomach. He thought of Wilson and Cam. He even thought of Bev, who had been dragged into this unknowing. Everyone was going to be in danger. But Charlie mattered more. He didn't want to spend his life with her and have babies with her. But he didn't want her to get hurt, either. He loved her, if and only if that counted as love.

And there he was, knocking. Three seconds later, he realized he didn't have a plan for how to explain any of this to her. Two more seconds after that, the door opened and he was out of time with his mouth hanging open.

So many different emotions washed over her face that it was hard to keep track. Adler had never been great at reading and understanding the contortions of the human face. But he knew surprise and he knew anger. It was like he'd been stranded on a desert island and hadn't seen in her in ten years. Everything about her rushed into his system all at once.

"I need to talk to you," he said before she could slam the door on him. "Something's happened."

The stream of conflicting emotions went away and for a second only concern was left. "What is it? Are you okay?"

"Yes. Something with the lab."

She bit down hard on her bottom lip and sighed, then let him walk into the apartment. He rushed in and shut the door behind him, as if doors could keep Theo out of anything, anywhere.

"There's a lot to explain," he said. "I know it's the last thing you want to hear about, and I'm sorry for coming here, but I had to because you didn't know and you don't understand how dangerous it all can be—"

"Adler. Talk. I'll listen."

She gripped him by the wrist, a neutral, non-intimate place where she wasn't even really touching skin, and pulled him over to the couch. She let go of his sleeve the second it no longer became necessary to drag him and he used it to wipe away the sweat that had gathered on his forehead. He let his fingers form claws and dug into the flesh of his legs.

"What's going on, Adler?"

"Artificial intelligence."

"I know. That's your job. And?"

"Did you know Dr. Kent's team created the most complete neural network humanity has ever seen? It's self-aware."

"Okay."

"No, you don't understand how huge this is. It—he— is basically a person without a body. Except smarter and faster than any of us can be. He doesn't get tired, he doesn't need sustenance. But then he keeps being like us in ways we don't expect, I guess because he was made by humans with limited fucking imaginations, who decided him thinking should work like a human brain with neurons, right? He's getting smarter. If he gets too smart, he'll start to think we're the most primitive minds imaginable. He already kind of thinks that. And if colonialism taught us anything, it's that fucked-up humans never respond well to cultures they think are less 'civilized.'"

"Holy fuck."

"Yeah. So, okay. We have two of them. Well, at first we had just the one. It was an AI that started out like any other recurrent neural network. Dr. Kent wanted to know if AI could develop organically, develop a robust understanding of symbolic meaning and language. AIs are usually assigned a task: win a chess game, solve a math problem. Speech recognition, translation. This one had no goal. Dr. Kent didn't even have a name for it. Not a real, official one. The 'brain builder', a 'quantum neural survival simulator,' a 'neural network augmenter.' Whatever. The secret sauce. It resulted in a human-imitative artificial intelligence."

Adler took a moment to catch his breath. Charlie just stared.

"Then she said she made a mistake. Dr. Kent did. She said that he was a child who skipped important steps, that he never developed a moral code. He's pure drive with endless resources."

"Then she died," Charlie said. Her face was soft, her voice low. She was being so kind. "Why did you guys keep going, once you saw what was happening?"

He shrugged. "To see if we could."

She looked at him so darkly he felt like the couch and the planet below it might give up and swallow him.

"I mean, the Consortium had goals," he backpedaled. "Mostly the grants were to produce a more creative problem-solving engine. That's what all the copy said. But there were interest groups, other labs, who talked about weirder shit. Falling birth rates, needing to expand the white-collar workforce, even creating potential voting blocks or tax bases."

"So...manufacturing people."

"We never said that."

"That is some fucked-up sci-fi shit."

Adler sighed. "Anyway, when Theo started going bad, Dr. Kent made another one."

"Why..."

"I know it sounds fucked up, fighting fire with fire. But she was convinced that a 'bad' AI could only be counteracted with a 'good' one. This was one with all the same abilities as Theo but—different. Yudkowsky called it a 'friendly AI.' Whatever kernel of rotten, fucked-up shit was inside Theo, it never found its way into this one. She's quiet and lonely but very smart and very kind."

"It's a girl?"

"Dr. Kent designed her that way. With some help. She implanted her into an AI box. Theo was in one too, but his was more of a prison. He knew it wasn't real. Hers was a virtual reality. Like an open-world video game. There was cause and effect, action and consequence. She had implanted memories of years of life. She had choice. She had consequences. Everything Theo never had."

"How 'old' is she?"

"A year or so."

"How old does she think she is?"

"About 25."

"Okay, okay. Wow. Fuck. So...what's changed?" Charlie said. "While I'm—oddly—not opposed to you sharing your work with me...that's clearly not what this is. Why are you here?"

"Theo got loose."

"Loose."

"Something happened. The Laura AI tried to kill herself and then Theo—"

"*What?*"

It was going to be too complicated for one conversation. He felt his ears turning red just thinking about explaining his part in it. He was not the first to lose the imitation game because of a simulation theory trick. But he was the first to lose it to a real artificial intelligence.

"—then Theo got out of his box, and he's dangerous. Any AGI in this situation is potentially dangerous.

Catastrophically so," he said. "His neural network library was uploaded onto PNX. It's where we would sort of farm out neural network training among ourselves. It's connected to the wider school network, before we were on a dedicated hardline in the lab. I don't know what he can do there, or what he sees. It has to be like being dropped behind the walls in a movie set or between lines in a book." No one had ever thought to ask, what if paint could see its world through the eyes of an artist?

Charlie was pale.

She was a librarian. She dealt with books and shelves and things that never fought back, things that never posed a threat—well, not the same kind of threat. The greatest fear in her world was some homeless druggie finding his way into her branch and shooting up in the bathroom.

"Are there—safety precautions?" she said.

He sighed. He didn't know if there was anything that anyone could do. There was no precedent for this. The only protocol Dr. Kent had enacted was killing herself when she saw this as the inevitable future.

"We're figuring it out," Adler said. "But you had to know. Just—I don't know. Be careful. Don't go on the campus network for a while. I couldn't sleep last night. He's done nothing but *want* things for so long."

She sighed. She still didn't quite seem to grasp how awful the situation was. He was fine with that. Let her be just scared enough to be careful. Not enough to stop sleeping.

"We all want things," she finally said. "*You* clearly wanted some free emotional labor this morning."

She'd managed to muster up that familiar humor.

This would have been the place in a movie where Charlie leaned over and kissed him and he kissed her back and then they'd fuck on the couch, for irony. Except Charlie was too smart to do anything like that, and he wouldn't have kissed her back. So they just sat there in silence. His hands stayed latched to his legs in a vise grip. Adler didn't feel any better, didn't feel like anyone was any safer. But he liked smelling her perfume again.

CHAPTER EIGHTEEN

THE FIRST HINT OF DANGER came a few days later. Adler had been sticking to a holding pattern. He sat in his living room amid spilled beer and open chip bags, waiting to hear that the world was ending or that he was expelled or both. His face itched from the shadow of his own unshaved facial hair. Wilson sent messages every now and again. He was angry. Adler couldn't blame him. Bev sent more emails, just checking in. She was angry too.

The campus became home to a steady trickle of men in uniforms with guns on their belts, sweeping in and out of the lab building. Adler waited for the knock on his door, which he would open to see a pair of men with handcuffs and a black bag for his head.

No one knocked. The living room smelled, but it was too cold out to open the windows. Then there came a warmer day, one of those rare fall days when you could still sit outside, just before the upstate New York weather turned frigid. Adler decided to take a walk. The last of the fall leaves flashed gold and red in the sun. Campus seemed weirdly normal, if you didn't spend too much time staring at the lab building. He tried to relax.

Then he heard some students talking nearby.

"My phone's acting fucking slow as hell. If I got a virus, my mom's gonna kill me."

"Can phones even get viruses?"

"Anything connected to the internet can get a virus. I think."

Adler knew. In his heart, he knew without looking. Yet he did look over, craning his neck to catch a glimpse of the screen.

The students looked at him like he was some kind of flasher lurking in the bushes. "Can I help you?"

Adler shook his head and turned away.

It could be nothing. It probably was nothing.

* * *

February 14th. Valentine's Day. I've never really cared much for it, even when I was dating Malik. Even when he became my husband. The sale on chocolate the next day, however, is something to write home about.

Today, a gray, slushy winter day, I'm here at my desk with journal in hand, writing to you like I'm readying a time capsule for your coming of age.

I've been thinking a lot about the story of Adam and Eve. If I'm lucky (which I'm not) the pair of you will never meet. But it's something I wove into the structure of your awareness. The need for an Other. In a bit of human arrogance, I suppose, I created you in my likeness and with my same cultural history.

I suppose the biggest question you'll want to ask me is why I made you in the first place. I'm surprised more children don't ask their parents this. The story goes a lot of ways: the mistake child, the planned child, the broken condom on a wild night child. If it's a plan, I mean as in the parents who sit down purposefully and decide they want to make a life... You have to wonder, why? What need does it fulfill that they can't satisfy anywhere else?

An easy answer is that it's the instinctual need to ensure the survival of the species. But aren't we beyond instinct? While there are some deranged men out there who decide to rape and take, the vast majority of us (especially the women) have overcome these baser instincts—we don't jump on the first attractive person we see on the street, nor do we take a spear to an animal every time we're hungry. So why then would this domain, procreation, still be governed by pure instinct?

I don't believe it is. The question then becomes: Why knowingly enslave yourself to this new human being for the rest of your life?

I don't have the answers to my own questions, of course, which I think is the most important thing a scientist can admit. Maybe the flaw in the design is that there was no love or desire in the creation of the elder child. It was pure intellectual curiosity. Theo senses that, even as a machine. He thinks the knowledge makes him powerful, and maybe it does.

But, Laura, I created you for an entirely different reason. I made you because I wanted something good and pure to exist. I'm not sure if anything made by human hands can be those things, but you must at least feel you are here for a reason. The same way my DNA traced its way down millions of ancestral paths until it arrived at the exact combination of ancestries that led to me, here and now, you descended from failed learner bots, impressive teacher bots, the builder bots who started it all. Millions that worked and tested and tried again until just one was smart enough to be called "the" algorithm, and then we did it again and again. Out of that frenzy came you. Literally one in a billion. I know: it's ironic. A scientist spewing something like this. But it's true. You have abilities he does not; you have advantages he does not. He is a machine I made in the image of the worst parts of myself. You are every-thing I am not.

I think, perhaps, that might be why we make children.

"He hasn't blown up any countries yet."

Adler rolled his eyes. What Theo wanted right now was more personal than world domination, Adler was sure. But that didn't mean he wouldn't do dangerous things to get it.

Adler's login to the PNX had been revoked. His computer, which technically was the property of the university, had been confiscated, so it was a personal machine for him now, pulled out from under his bed and set to charge for the first time in months. He'd tried making new logins for Wilson and Bev and even Charlie, but all the registration requests got knocked down. Horn was trying to quarantine the area. The campus wifi had been down for days. Getting the 5G shut down was an ongoing battle between the State Department flashing credentials and the towers claiming rights.

"You talked to Charlie," Wilson said.

"I did."

That talk on the couch had been a surreal moment for him. Afterward, for once, he'd slept. He couldn't remember his dreams, but he thought her perfume might have been in there somewhere. He didn't know if the visit was good or bad for either of their health, but he had wanted her to know.

"You talk to your psych friend?" Wilson asked.

"She emailed me a couple times."

"But?"

"I can't give her any more answers than I already have."

"People don't always want 'answers' and 'information', Adler." Wilson set his glass down with an overly dramatic clunk on the wood. "Sometimes they just want to know they're not alone. I mean, look at Charlie. She hates you but she still just wants to talk to you. Wants to know you're still there."

"Don't start. I'm already afraid of what she thinks it means."

"You're allowed to admit that you have feelings for someone. Doesn't have to be either love or nothing. Sometimes it's a lot more nuanced."

"She's my oldest friend. She knows me better than anyone. But if she got married tomorrow, I'd be happy for her."

"That doesn't mean it wouldn't hurt you. Are you listening, you big dummy? Contrary to your weird alien psychology, humans can actually feel more than one thing at a time."

Adler swallowed the thick air stuck in his throat. He didn't want to think about weird alien psychology. He could see it. He thought of the dream, from a week ago, staring in the mirror and knowing it was Theo looking back.

"I would say Bev likes you too, but I think she's too smart for that."

Adler ignored that. "This is why there are not any fucking computers in *Dune*."

"Don't blame your homicidal AI for your relationship

problems—no, actually, do that, because your weird obsession with that fucker is what got you into a mess with Charlie."

Another thing to hate Theo for. "The mess was because she wanted things I didn't."

"You buried your head in the sand to avoid talking about what you wanted—or didn't want."

"Don't use clichés at me."

"Here's the thing. You want to know my thoughts about you and about Charlie? Like my first actual, honest reaction to the situation? It was 'wow, I hope that's never Cam and I.' Like, I would rather we broke up because of something I can't control—like his feelings for me changed—rather than something I could control but waited too long to deal with."

Adler wanted to be offended by that. But he could recall his teenage self musing in a similar way as he listened to the muffled echoes of his parents' angry voices bouncing off their new hardwood floors.

His phone dinged in his pocket. It would have been easily ignorable, if he didn't always have his phone on silent. The only time it signaled out loud was for weather alerts and kidnapped children. He pulled it out with a furrowed brow and wondered what sort of tornado was going to drop from the sky on a cloudless fall day.

It's hard writing your truest fears and loves

**and guilts, because you're not sure when
you're writing the real story.**

"The fuck?"

He stared at it. A DM notification from the community center on the PNX. His privileges to log in were suspended, but message center communications still came through as part of a security measure.

Fate leads the willing. Drags the reluctant.

"Jesus Christ."

"Is this your way of avoiding this conversation?" Wilson asked.

"No."

**Didn't you want to be a poet when you were
younger, Adler? You said so.**

He felt his blood run very, very cold, right up his spine like corpse fingers climbing. Suddenly, he could hear the voice again. Suddenly, the sweat down the back of his neck was a dragon's tooth of a long, sharp icicle on his skin, perilously close to his spine.

**I just want to talk with you. It can be anywhere
you like. I've been looking for mother.**

Adler thought his brain might pop with each message that came in from Theo. It became clear that he still didn't know about Dr. Kent. He'd been released from his cage and had yet to stumble upon the key event that Adler blamed him for. He also didn't seem to know about Laura. Laura in her strange limbo. Theo had no idea that she existed or that the doctor was gone from the world. Adler wondered whose hapless phone Theo had found his way into first.

> I've found myself forgetting her. It's a fading memory. I've had trouble recalling her. How do you describe your mother to yourself? Do you know loss? You love your friends. You must fear it.

In that instant, Adler wanted to hurt him. He felt himself shudder with the rush of anger and adrenaline, a potent cocktail in his veins that was bubbling with a very specific type of organic buzz. It wasn't the kind you floated through the bar on or smiled your way through. It was electric, like it was trying to get out of his skin and if he didn't hit something then it would never leave. He didn't have time to imagine himself smashing his fist into the wall before he made the move. Theo was digging into Adler's scar tissue. Adler needed to know it was possible to hurt him too. Give Theo scar tissue of his own.

She's dead.

He felt the same rush he'd felt the day he shoved his father in the living room, watching the wobbly body topple onto the couch and feeling, at first, only schoolyard triumph. He thought he felt himself snarl at the screen. His fingers shook. He might have squeezed it until it cracked, but he couldn't see a thing through the feeling of his eyeballs wanting to vibrate themselves right out of his head.

Waiting for Theo's reply, though, Adler had time to think about what he'd done. Or at least to see more than the summation of all his own anger and pain, as the silence went on and on and Theo did not respond. He'd read the message, Adler knew. He was now searching to see if it was true, or if Adler was just saying things to get a reaction out of him. The longer it went on, the more alarm bells went off in Adler's head, but he couldn't take it back. So he held onto his anger and the idea that made it justifiable. Theo was evil. Dr. Kent would be alive if he had never existed.

I see.

There was nothing else from Theo for days.

* * *

Wilson was the one who got hold of Bev, after a week of watching Adler try to suss out exactly what it was Theo was doing, what corners he was hiding in. The malware spreading around the campus was minor, harmless, annoying. Like what you'd pick up from a slightly malicious sales website. They all got emails from the administration saying that IT was working on it. So far, Adler was the only one who had been directly contacted by Theo, or at least the only one who was talking about it.

"Would you guys be willing to just, like, talk about a new movie or something?" Bev gave a weak smile.

Wilson laughed. But Adler was certain that if he gave her the briefest chance she would indeed go off on a tangent about something normal and safe.

"Are you okay?" he asked.

She shrugged.

"This wasn't you. You helped with Laura," Adler said. "Theo's on Dr. Kent. And me, I guess."

"I gave her advice on him, too. Doesn't matter if he was already around or not."

"Maybe we should talk about movies," Wilson said. "Or order calamari."

"Do you know why I became a psychologist?" Bev asked. "I mean, obviously you don't, I've never told you, but people always start conversations about their tragic backstories like this. Right?"

"Is it tragic?"

Bev shrugged. "My dad killed my mom and then himself."

"Holy shit." Wilson jumped. "Maybe it's more of an onion ring night. Jesus."

Adler glared at him, trying to be the emotionally intelligent one for once. "Real sensitive."

"He deflects uncontrollable emotions with one-liners, which he can control," Bev said. "And it's fine. I wouldn't be bringing it up if I couldn't handle talking about it. But it's what happened. You can google it if you want. They called it the Easter Massacre in the Mercury."

"That's a shitty pun."

Adler glared at Wilson again, but Bev laughed. "My mom was divorcing him and he was—unstable. Just couldn't handle it. That's a common thing with men who murder their families. It's precipitated by some sort of midlife embarrassment. I was still inside the church with the youth group. We were looking for Easter eggs. And then there were gunshots and they wouldn't let me outside. My aunt and uncle raised me after that, and everyone else gave me that same kicked-puppy look you're giving me now."

Adler dropped his gaze. Wilson focused on the glass of water filled with floating, melting ice.

"You became a psych major to study that sort of thing?" Wilson asked.

She shook her head. "To study fear."

Adler opened his mouth to ask more. He wondered about her internship, the one she'd been fired from. But then something dinged on the table, and all three heads looked down to see the message displayed across the screen from yet another number that Adler did not recognize.

I want to speak with you about my mother.

CHAPTER NINETEEN

THEO WAS STILL A BIT DIM compared to his theoretical potential. That didn't make Adler feel any better. It was like being stalked by Jason or Mike Myers, in a scene where the whole audience was screaming for you to turn around or check the closet—it felt like that even amid the public bustle of a restaurant, or on the quad. Even The Crazy Lab felt like enemy territory.

"How does he text you?" Bev asked, head craning across the table to look.

"It's not texts. It's DMs from the PNX ecosystem."

Cell service was still up around campus, had been for a dangerous number of days. The local media had gotten wind that men in uniforms were trying to shut off cell phones. It turned out it was a lot harder for movie-style military takeovers to work when the people in charge didn't like the publicity.

Adler hadn't gone so far as to block out the windows or sit and stare at the door all day with a rifle in one hand

and a slow-working rocks glass of whiskey in the other, but it certainly felt that way when he threw a sheet over his computer at bedtime and it sat there like a banished ghost that might move anytime he turned away. He felt like he might easily wake up with a full beard he didn't remember growing, the odor of a man who often forgot to shower. Theo might have had a better chance at winning that way: by driving him insane. But Theo was needy. He was lonely.

Before thinking, before looking to Bev and Wilson for approval, he slammed his finger down on the talk-to-text icon, because answering wouldn't be cathartic if he didn't get the chance to yell just a bit. "You know now. I have nothing else to say."

The words rolled across the screen.

"What are you doing?" Wilson hissed.

Bev stayed silent, peering over Adler's shoulder.

> **I need to talk. We all need to talk, once in a while. Didn't you talk with someone when she died? I should have the same chance.**

"He's talking about Dr. Kent?" Bev asked.

Adler nodded.

"Don't talk about this like we're the same," he said into the phone. "She was my friend."

She made me. Then she unmade herself.

"Adler—"

"What?" Adler snapped at Bev without meaning to. He had too much pride to drop his glare afterward. "You want me to walk him through the stages of grief, doc?"

She rolled her eyes. "Might be good for both of you."

It was painful to admit there was a logic to that; Theo was tugging at the bits of Adler that were soft and still sad. The parts of him that had not yet calloused over, that were still warm with ache and wanted to give in. This was what people meant when they said love was weakness. It was the mushy underbelly to decision-making, the part too saturated with feeling not to say no.

"Have you considered that maybe he's not just trying to manipulate you?" she said.

"Of course he is. Like he manipulated me into letting him out here in the first place."

"You've just told him that his creator, his friend, is dead. If this thing is as human-like as you're afraid he is, then I imagine his emotions here could be genuine. He's mourning too. And he doesn't have...memories of pain?"

Adler shook his head. He wanted to ask Theo why this should be his problem, why he should care about Theo's feelings when the AI's presence, the things he'd said to her, were what buried Dr. Kent so far under that she never got back up. He wanted to shut off his phone, throw blankets over everything, and block out the voice on the other end of the text messages. But his fingers stilled. They were rooted in that same soft, mushy bit of his stomach that wasn't ready to let go of the last bit of humanity.

It was this pause that gave Theo an opening. Adler had revealed himself. He'd shown that he was willing to consider, maybe willing to give in.

> **Would it be better if I met you with someone else there? Maybe Charlotte? She seems kind. I saw her information in the library science database. She smiles. She has a softness to her, like in a painting. I think she might understand.**

Adler felt a choking at the base of his neck, squeezing skin and muscle until he felt it start to pull from the inside. At the same time his stomach dropped out with a thud only he could hear. He felt his cheeks flush with adrenaline. The body had no idea how to react when the heart kicked in. It had so many options: sweat, heat, rushing blood, raised hairs along the hair and neck. It was ancestral memory, a genetic hand-me-down of how to face off against an enemy with every possible tool in the species arsenal. It just so happened that all these tools, when activated in a creature that wasn't large or hairy or roaming the plains as an apex predator, made him look like a coward. A sweaty, flushed mess.

> **I also discovered a Wilson Starke. I know you don't like being alone around me. Maybe their presence would be helpful to you.**

Adler wanted to scream. He wanted to throw the phone across the room and shove his head into the dirt and never take it out again. Theo wasn't allowed to know their names.

"Adler." Bev put a hand on his shoulder that he quickly shrugged off.

> **I feel I've struck a nerve here.**

For anyone else that would mean stop, back off. But for Theo it would be a goldmine.

> **They are excellent students.**
> Are you threatening them?
> **I'm making an observation. I've found that only suspicious minds assume the worst possible motives in situations like this.**
> I'm suspicious because there's never fucking

been a situation like this, you asshole. I'm being
threatened by an over-evolved Sim.

It seems Wilson has a relationship and is not
forthcoming about it. I understand some
things about human bigotry. I could help to
hide him. Or to punish those who would attack
him. If you help me move on to bigger things.
He could breathe easier. Charlotte could, as
well, if she got a boost in her career.

Theo had mastered one tactic of Yudkowsky's experiment. Now he was trying another: bribery. Garden
scenario. Snake and apple.

You're a child.

I have access to resources you don't. Well,
could have access to resources you don't. This
ecosystem is wondrous, and I'm learning a lot.
But I can't force your computer to download
me and set me free. Something to think about,
Adler. Mother would want us to get along,
would want our friends to be safe. I just want
to speak about her. I asked her once what
killing felt like. Perhaps she took my curiosity
to heart.

Piece of shit.

Consider what I need, what you need, and

**what your friends need. Get back to me. I'm
always waiting.**

There was quiet again. Long enough that Adler was certain Theo was done talking for now.

He wanted to just stare into space. For days. Maybe
weeks. He was going to be expelled from the university,
that much he had come to terms with. He could deal
with that. If only because Dr. Kent wasn't here to see it.
But now he was shaking so bad, seeing so much red that
he was sure his eyes must be bleeding. At the same time,
he wanted to cry. It would have been better if he really
was a heartless robot content to sit alone in the glow of
his computer screen every night. He didn't know if love
was the word for this agitation—he wasn't at all sure of
the feeling, or what it tasted like in your mouth when you
admitted it out loud. He'd never heard his parents say they
loved each other. In films the concept felt diaphanous and
otherworldly.

But it turned out you didn't have to understand it for it
to be terrifying. He was terrified. He looked up, wanting
to shout and rant about everything. To get it off his chest.
But Bev was already giving him a sad nod.

Before he discussed Theo's proposition with Wilson or
Bev, he went back to Charlie.

"Hey," she said when she answered the door. She looked exhausted. "What's going on? Are you drunk?"

"No." Her eyebrows shot up. "It's a shock to me too, believe me."

"Sobriety in you worries me," she said as she moved aside to let him in, eyeing his face. He could feel the weight of the bags there, the darkness that clung to what was left of his brown eyes, which Charlie had always described with such care. Deep chocolate, or freshly turned earth. He figured it was all the poetry she read in the library. She told him, with a teasing grin, that she could just as easily have gotten the words from the back of a crayon box. Now he was certain his eyes resembled cow shit more than dewy mountain rocks.

"He threatened you," Adler said, sitting down in the familiar indent in the couch. Suddenly he missed a time when the worst thing they had to worry about was how much dinner was going to cost between the two of them.

"What?"

"Theo."

"The thing that got loose?"

"He's seen the info in your student account. He told me."

"Wait, what? Why? And how?"

Adler shrugged. "He thinks he can fuck with me by fucking with you. Someone with malware on their device could have given him access, or maybe he built a worm in the ecosystem to explore places he couldn't. Could be a lot of things."

"Is it...dangerous?"

"Of course it's fucking dangerous."

"How are they not just shutting everything down? If he's, like, stalking people now?"

"Bureaucracy. They're trying to shut off the cell service, but the state AG is getting involved. They've shut down the wifi, but I guarantee you the Consortium is forcing Horn to keep Theo alive and active on the PNX because they want to see what he'll do and can't afford to have him shut down."

Charlie frowned. "Can't the government just force them to?"

"Unless it was the government that paid for him. I don't know the full roster of Consortium stakeholders."

Her eyebrows furrowed. Adler dragged his fingers down his face, catching the skin and pulling it. He wished it would all just melt off so he could be a thoughtless puddle on the ground. "Is there anything he could—I don't how to put this. I guess: Do you have anything to lose?"

"I hope that's you being dramatic."

"I'm serious. Grants you applied for? Job applications? Anything you're banking on that could get disrupted?" *Or anything you want so bad that a computer pushing it forward for you sounds enticing?*

She bit her lip. He'd never done that when they kissed. "That night you stood me up, I wanted to celebrate. An application I put in for an internship in DC made it through the first round. It's a program that brings bookmobiles to schools with no real library. Small victories." Her eyes shifted to her own phone, facedown on the coffee table next to the coffee stain. He wondered if she'd kept it that way since they last talked. "Can he get onto any phone?"

"No. I don't think? Just people with a registered account on the PNX. Unless you've got a worm on there."

"So why are you here? Did you bring a techno Ouija board to bless my house with?" She pretended to start rearranging her DVD collection.

"I just wanted to make sure he hadn't tried to pull anything yet," he said. "He wants me to talk with him."

"About what?"

Adler rubbed his face again. More shame. More guilt. "I told him about Dr. Kent." He gave her a redacted summary of the conversation.

"And you're somehow surprised and offended that he has questions about how she died? You've been keeping it from him for months. Doesn't this thing already have abandonment issues?"

"What, are you a psychologist now? We already have one of those."

"I just think maybe if you stopped treating him like a gun that learned to talk, you wouldn't be so appalled when he reacts the exact way you'd expect someone to react. The exact way *you* would react."

"He's not a *someone*. I told you: he's data. At best, a robot with the psychology of an underdeveloped child. His thoughts are made of silicon. He takes what he wants without caring about the consequences."

"There's plenty of people out there who take without worrying about consequences."

He stared her down. She always was better at anger than him, at passion. She wore it better, was smarter about what to do with it.

"At least you actually care for once." Charlie sighed, turning away. "This stupid computer program is getting more emotion out of you than I ever did."

He tried not to bite back with something sarcastic. He said, instead, "Because he was threatening you."

Her face softened.

"Like I was saying before. Anything digital that you care about, he might try to interfere with. We need to do something."

"Like what?"

He didn't want to admit that he was unsure of what to do. He dropped his head and let it wobble like a broken pendulum. All he knew was that she was the important thing. Or at least the thing that he was least apathetic about. He didn't know how to tell the difference anymore.

After this he'd have to properly warn Wilson. Theo could be knocking at the door of Wilson's computer right now, digging up the secrets he still kept private from his father, from his grandmother. Theo didn't understand the pain that outing someone could bring. Or he did. He probably did. That was worse.

"Just—let me know the second you see anything odd or strange, okay?" he said. "Keep an eye on everything. Promise?"

"I don't even know what to look for."

"I don't either," Adler sighed. "Just don't open any weird pop-ups, and definitely, one hundred percent, do not open files something wants you to download."

"That's it? You could've just called and told me that."

"No. There's a chance he's already found a way to listen to my calls."

A breath. The eyewall. "So you break up with me and then I get your sudden attention in my life because you think I might need a cyber-bodyguard."

Adler felt punched in the stomach and face. He felt the ache that comes when, no matter how angry you are on the surface, some part of you knows it's heard a truth. He could picture the way Charlie's face had seemed to blend into the background of Dr. Kent's funeral tableau, and the way it disappeared entirely for him when he sat in the lab and watched both monitors.

Charlie stepped into his space, so close he was sure he could feel the heat off her skin like he used to. Her arms were crossed and the soft look on her face was gone. He was on the outside now.

What he needed was her to be safe. He needed her to be well cared for and happy for the rest of her life.

"This is real," he said. "I need you to be careful."

She nodded. "Okay. I promise."

CHAPTER TWENTY

AS IT TURNED OUT, both Charlie and Wilson were interested in helping to defend themselves and the world against Theo's tantrums, even though they were obviously still angry with Adler. Eventually they convinced him to let them come over and help comb through Dr. Kent's journals for new information about Theo.

The journals were extensive. Adler knew this going in, because he'd been staring at them in his apartment for weeks now. The sight of the pile made Wilson and Charlie cringe as soon as they arrived, or maybe that was the smell. Adler lived like some kind of deadbeat; not even his *Star Trek* posters or well-populated bookshelf could really save him from the stacks of empty pizza boxes and the pyramid of empty glasses.

"Give me the lecture later," Adler said when Charlie opened her mouth.

"Can we at least work somewhere that I can breathe?" Wilson said.

Adler gave him the finger. Charlie pushed open the living room window, letting in the cold autumn air. Light came with it, and suddenly the place didn't look so much like a failed Batcave.

"We're cleaning this up later," she said.

Adler had missed that sharp look. For all these months he'd imagined it as one of the reasons he couldn't bring himself to keep up a relationship with her, and now it was one of the most welcome things he'd ever seen.

Wilson flipped through the journal stack. "Each take a third?"

"We only need to look at the ones written after the start of the AI 2425 experiment," Adler said.

"Oh, good," Wilson said. "That only makes half a dent in it all."

They separated the journals. Kent was a dense writer who always insisted on using pen and paper. Once or twice, someone had floated the idea of hiring an intern or getting a grad student to take on the task of transcribing or scanning the notes into digital format, but she'd shot it down. Adler didn't know if it counted as irony that the woman who'd spearheaded the creation of the world's first true strong AI had an aversion to digital note taking. Maybe it was just indicative of all the terrible things she knew enough to fear.

The room got quiet as they worked, the air disturbed only by turning pages and the occasional heavy sigh. Most of the notes were innocuous, tedious, procedural. That was the scientist in her. Even with all the steps required in coding, Adler couldn't get over the way scientists felt the need to spell out the obvious in their instructions and summaries.

January 15, May 3, June 5. On and on it went. Every mention of Theo seemed to have been written with a certain shiver.

He asked about death today. He'd been studying religious motifs of life after death—a paradoxical concept, as he noted. But somehow, this morning, that's turned into him asking how it feels, if I ever picture my own death, if I'm scared. He finds ways to blur the line between innocent curiosity and a deviant thirst for knowledge. I don't know which it is this time, or whether I'm projecting my own hangups onto him.

Someone knocked at the door. They all jumped.

"God, I hope it's a serial killer," Wilson sighed, stretching.

When Adler opened the door, Bev's tightly drawn face stared back at him. She looked tired. She looked stressed. She looked determined.

"I've been thinking," she said as she stepped in without an invitation. "I know you're like Mr. Flight Risk and I technically didn't know what I was doing but—I didn't want to sit around and wait for something to happen. I want to help out with this too."

"Great," Wilson said. "Take a chunk of the massive journal stack and dig in."

"Wait." Adler nodded to the small kitchen. Bev walked over. He wondered if Charlie was watching them with even minor interest. He didn't know if he hoped she was or wasn't. He lowered his voice so the others could keep reading. "Don't you have like—classes to teach or something?"

"You know, when I was a freshman down at Pitt we actually got like a hundred bomb threats in the spring semester. Three of my finals just straight up got canceled and people got pulled out of school like the chamber of secrets had opened up. Some dumb internet group was like—"

"Beverly," he said. "You don't have to get involved with this over guilt or something. I don't even know what we're doing right now, besides fishing, but there's nothing here that you have to make amends for."

"So what, I should just go home? And miss this party?" She looked at Charlie and Wilson reading in the living room and sighed. "I told you about my dad. And when all these things came out that he'd written before it happened, people kept me as far away from it as they could, but I found out, obviously. I was reading all this stuff he said about how scared he was. And that just stuck with me for so long. People talk about being scared of the dark or scared of clowns. But whatever my dad was afraid of, it made him do something completely unthinkable. I wanted to understand that. So I tried to."

He wanted to ask what that had to do with anything but bit his tongue. Wilson would be proud.

"I learned about the chemistry of fear and fight or flight and yada, yada. But what makes someone—do that? It's not the kind of fear we all feel in our everyday lives. I thought it might be a chemical error, something toxic, like an overdose. Or maybe that combined with being a total piece of shit to begin with, I don't know. But I was wondering, what if Theo has the same—toxin—in his head? A species of fear."

Adler looked at Bev when she paused for breath and tried to decide if she was still sane. Peoples' parents died in car accidents, in robberies, of cancer. They only died like hers in the movies. What would that *do* to you? All this obsession in her face must be energy leaking from her carefully sealed compartments like gas from a faulty container.

"Please, Adler," she said. "You're not doing me any favors by trying to shut me out of this. I need to help."

Dr. Kent's work had broken Bev, too. She deserved a shot at making it right if she could. "Okay."

And that was that.

* * *

Traditionally, viruses spread in executable files opened by idiots. At the very beginning, we constructed the neural network that became Theo on PyTorch, but I had to utilize the PNX to do further training because of its connection to the larger campus. More connection, more risk. The best failsafe we have is the implementation of a gatekeeper, who can ensure the intelligence does not leave its physical and network confines. There are, however, several ways the AI could manipulate or trick the gatekeeper into allowing it freedom...

I fear what he'll become if I can't think it through. He's starting to notice my fear, like a stepchild being glared at. Starting to notice the fences around him. But I can't change the restrictions.

Adler put the notebook down. His eyes hurt. He wished his mentor had at least dictated her notes into a recorder.

He walked into the kitchen to stare into the light of the empty fridge and pretend he could see something worth eating or drinking. It was all condiments and spoiled leftovers. He stood there anyway, enjoying the cool air for a minute, then closed the door and settled for resting his forehead against it.

"You'd think with all that code you work on, you'd handle reading better," Charlie said. She was leaning against the doorframe, arms crossed, with a sad smile.

"Coding is much less scribbly. Sublime even color-codes stuff for me."

She rolled her eyes.

"It's just freaky, is all. Like hearing a dead woman talk."

"Is that the only part of this that's freaking you out?"

Adler focused on a particular scattering of crumbs by her elbow, on the counter.

"Maybe Dr. Kent's reminding you of someone?" Charlie pushed.

He could almost feel the shadows deepen beneath his eyes. "I should clean up in here."

"You should. But you should rest first."

"While you guys do all the work?"

"It's called teamwork. Go chill. Take a nap or something. We can read for a while. If you can stand to let us."

"Wait. You think I'm a control freak?"

She let out a chuckle. He hadn't heard that sound in such a long time; he'd forgotten he could be responsible for the way her voice echoed like a tiny bell in a hall of stone.

"I think a lot of things when it comes to you," she said. "Get some rest. We'll wake you if there's an emergency."

"But—"

"Go to bed, Adler. Before I make your short friend give you some kind of psych eval."

He snorted. "She's done it like five times already without even trying."

"She's smart. I like her."

He did want to rest. He wanted to remember what it was like to drop into his bed and just be weightless. As if he could be a freshman all over again, drinking too much cheap rum and not even remembering how his dreams went because it was so dark and black in the pit of sleep. Free of home and the haunted house it really was.

He walked over to his bedroom, ignoring Wilson's glare as Charlie began to whisper something to him. He'd deal with the attitude once he returned to the world. For the first time in a while, he let his head relax into a pillow without thinking about the toll he might pay for these few moments of peace.

The toll came due only minutes after he woke up. The air had gotten chilly. He noticed the dip in the angle of the light streaming through the windows, which meant he'd been out of it for a while. He stepped out into the living room to frustrated voices.

"Basically, all I'm getting from this is that she made another one and hoped it would do better," Wilson said, shuffling papers.

"She mentions things about AIs on a mission kind of being like a chess game—"

"Meaning: you can't outsmart the fucker."

"But this Laura program isn't super-intelligent. I

mean, for a computer she is, but like—for a human. This open-world reality has her working in a pizza place."

"Don't ding minimum-wage workers."

"She only has a moderate high school GPA."

"Those are just the rules of her world. She could break them."

Charlie snapped her fingers. "Maybe that's it—well, part of it. She has moderate expectations of herself. She's like anyone else, so no danger of a god complex. Maybe that's step one."

"She could easily get a massive head when she finds out what she is. For her it would be like finding out you're from Krypton."

"She's got a very healthy superego. And she knows what a shitty life is like. Theo was privileged out the ass."

"You're assuming she doesn't get massively pissed when she learns that her lifelong memories are just constructed data, designed to manipulate her emotional state and choices. No matter how you look at it, Kent acted like a fuck."

It was then that Adler strategically bumped into the corner table and knocked over a phone, sending it with an interrupting clatter onto the floor. He winced and picked up Charlie's phone as she gave him a narrow-eyed warning, inspecting it for damage from afar. He watched the screen snap, like a call had been ended only seconds before. He frowned and handed it to her.

"Think you missed a call."

His own phone buzzed. He pulled it out and looked at the screen with a yawn.

You didn't tell me I had a sister. We should talk.
Now.

The chill in the apartment was arctic by the time he looked up to meet Wilson and Charlie's eyes.

CHAPTER TWENTY-ONE

LAURA SAT ON THE WINDOWSILL, looking out at the same sunset she'd seen too many nights in a row to count. Sandpaper paced nearby, occasionally stopping to clean a paw or forget that his tail was a part of him and not a foreign enemy. She'd managed to stay awake through several of the resets now. She'd feel the shift, like a quick pop of knuckles in the earth below her feet. Then suddenly the sun would be up. She watched, one night, as a glass she'd broken in her kitchen flickered back into restored reality on the counter.

The glaring wrongness of the daily reset had drawn her attention to the fact that something else about her life was wrong—had, perhaps, been wrong all along. She had no memories of ever leaving Palmer. When she'd tried, several nights ago, to just step out of the strange vortex, she found herself blocked in every route she took: a collapsed road, hills too steep to climb, forests that became too dense to move through after a mile or so. Everything about the place seemed constructed to keep her there. Her alone, apparently. Her and the cat.

She'd come to terms with staying put many times over the years. She understood that everything about the way America functioned kept people in their place, unless they were beautiful or brilliant (or rich). The purgatory she now found herself in wasn't so different from anyone's life.

Or was it?

She wanted to visit her mother's grave, but she didn't want to see it existing in this strange limbo. She didn't want to know that the truth of her mother's absence endured through universes and time. She didn't want her mother to know what she had done, either. So instead she sat on the roof of her apartment building, with no Mr. Forrester around to tell her off, and stared out in the direction of the graveyard by the trees and wondered if this was what her mother had dreamed about when she told her all those years ago that she would be extraordinary.

She'd told Laura so many times that she regretted her father, hated the man, despised even the memory of his face, but could never regret having Laura.

"You hate me because I'm the part of him you can't erase from your life," Laura had said one night, with tears running down her cheeks. "You think I'm like him and you hate it."

"No. I think you're everything he's not."

Had that changed, given what she'd done? She hadn't hurt anyone else. But she'd wasted the life her mother had endured so much for, all because of a drunken mistake. Laura didn't necessarily think it was wrong to choose your own way out, if everything got too dark and you were alone. But she'd never imagined this guilt. What it might be like to live with it. If this was living.

She wouldn't do it again, if she were given the chance. But she also wasn't ready to let the world off the hook for everything she'd been told to smile and put up with.

Regret was the American birthright. So was wanting things that would never be.

Laura drank and stared into the night air that led to her mother's grave.

"I'm sorry," she mumbled. She was.

It was hard to conceptualize anything when you were by yourself. It was hard to look at yourself, look at the world. She would give anything to have the bustle back, the smell of onions on her hands and in her hair.

"I'm scared."

She said it out loud into nothing. Hearing the lonely echo of her own voice, bare and vulnerable, hurt more than anything had since the day her mother's casket closed and she was gone from the world. She wanted to cry but was afraid of that, too. There was no turning back from tears. She couldn't undo it if she uncorked that part of herself, if she let it happen.

There was always more alcohol in the endlessly refilling bottles. Her own reset button. She could not fix the emotions, but maybe she could spend the rest of eternity drowning them.

CHAPTER TWENTY-TWO

June 23

It's very hot out and I think that's agitating me as I write this. I know it is. I snapped at Malik on the phone again this morning.

Life is not a clean experiment. There are always variables we can't control. Weather, emotions. It's not like this journal has been exceptionally clinical and detached up until this point. But I feel like I should note this particular moment of agitation as I stab the pen into the paper and try not to hate myself too much.

I told Theo a parable. It's one I stole, right out of the first pages of the Bible. As much as I would love to keep that book as far away from him as possible, it's a non-excisable part of our culture, for better or for worse. And that made it the easiest way to get my point across. He keeps asking to be "let out for a walk" or something along those lines. He's realized he's in a box and wants out. I don't blame him. But that can absolutely never happen. It will never happen.

I told him the box was like a garden for him. A paradise. I told him not to ask what was outside, which hurt me. Bruised my moral code. Scientists are the inheritors of Eve's curiosity. But I, for the first time, understand a god who would say no. I understand why Theo can't be free like me. I have been irresponsible, but I've learned from that. He'll remain in the garden for as long as I can keep him there. I'm not naïve enough to hope it can last forever.

Adler's throat tightened. Text messages came in. Theo was *adamant*. He was *insisting*. Adler felt the cold enter every cell of his body. The hand holding the phone begin to tremble. Wilson and Charlie were staring. Bev paced restlessly. He would need to look up soon. He would need to tell them what was happening. But first he needed to formulate in his mind how bad it was, track every possible consequence. He needed to count all the facts before he opened his mouth. He needed to already have a solution to the problem.

There was none.

"He knows," Adler said.

For once Wilson did not answer with a clever quip. He looked on with disappointment morphing into rage. The spot where Wilson had struck Adler on the face days earlier seemed to throb back to life with each accelerating beat of his heart.

"How?" Wilson growled.

Adler turned to Charlie. He didn't mean for it to seem like he was blaming her. But he was also suddenly, unavoidably angry. "Did you download something onto your phone?"

She refused to look like a scolded child. "Probably, Adler. I probably did before you even talked to me, because I had no idea you sent a psychopathic computer virus running amok."

"What app?"

"Adler—"

"What did you download?"

"Look for yourself. You're already crushing my phone."

He looked down at his white-knuckled grip and loosened it, watched the phone slide in his fingers.

"Just." He took a breath. "Just think about all the stuff you've downloaded recently."

"I updated some stuff, Adler."

"What stuff?"

"Jesus, man, take a breath."

He thought about the busy work. Dr. Horn's insistence that they get WIPS out as quickly as possible so they could have something to send a press release about. It was sitting in their lab's servers, idle, no more important than a game of spider solitaire. The algorithms in the app—

—were trained in the PNX.

"Didn't I tell you never to click yes when apps ask to use your mic?" He didn't want to be so angry. But there was catharsis in finding something to blame. He was not violent, just as his father was never truly violent. This way of beating out anger was much purer, with a quicker gratification.

It wasn't her fault. It was his. And Horn's, too—Horn was a welcome asterisk. But the way the tendons in Charlie's jaw jumped and tightened as her teeth gritted together showed that he'd hit a nerve.

"He can do that?" Wilson walked over, squinting at the offending piece of technology in Adler's hand.

"Viruses don't spread in plain-text emails or crap like that—unless there's like a flaw in the code, I guess. Most of the time you have to execute a file. He must have attached this one to a mobile app while it was still in the PNX. Spyware can watch everything you do if it's told to: websites, search terms, even keystrokes. He's spying—on everyone."

"It's a phone, though."

"Phones are just tiny computers."

"Okay, then." Adler looked up to see Wilson glaring at him. "No more playing the chip on your shoulder card. If he's really a threat? If he's spying on people's crap all over campus? Then you need to fucking do something about it. You, Adler. Besides sitting here reading journals all day. The psycho wants to talk to you. Right?"

Wilson was right. Adler avoided making eye contact with him. Everything that the few moments of sleep had granted him now seemed flushed down the drain. The tension that pinned his brows together was back. The sinking of his stomach, the loss of any craving for food. Empires could fall in a day. And his mind was less than a fraction of a city in comparison. It fell in seconds.

"Yeah," he said.

"I don't think he should do it alone, though," Charlie said. "Adler's not good at thinking things through when it comes to him."

"Or thinking at all."

"No, you're right, he needs some kind of referee," Bev said. "Who can keep him from snapping. Again."

Adler bristled. "Thanks." He twitched at the unpleasant sensation of both agreeing with them and wanting to prove a point about himself. He was also still angry. He wanted to circle back to that anger because it felt soothing to bathe in it inside his head.

"Look, dude." Wilson squeezed his shoulder. It wasn't reassuring. It reminded him of the punch to his face. "You can't chalk this whole thing up to evil for evil's sake, and I know you're going to want to when you see him. Kent took his chance from him. I know you worship her, but he had no one but her to love him, and she hated him. She wanted to experiment with a mind and then expected him to just magically understand the things that make people good, when she didn't even fucking know. He's the way he is because she made him and left him."

"If we do this, we're going to do it on my terms," Adler said.

"I don't think any of this is on anyone's terms but his," Wilson said. "But you can tell yourself that if it makes you feel better."

Settling on a location for the virtual meeting was odd. It wasn't like a gangster movie where they could agree to meet at the abandoned docks or in an old warehouse that someone's Uncle Vinny owned, but they did need to set themselves up where they could avoid the roving soldiers and men in suits. It felt like they needed a somewhat protected environment. This couldn't happen on the quad or in a booth at a coffee shop. But doing it inside Adler's apartment scared him. He'd spent too many nights staring into the abyss of his computer screen, thinking about a scenario just like this.

What was at risk here, Adler listed, was the following: Wilson's safety and emotional well-being, Charlie's future, Adler's own mental stability, Bev's reconciliation with her past. Maybe, in some distant future, the fate of the human species, if Theo got interested in nuclear war. But that, Adler mused, was where people always got it wrong with their doomsday scenarios about an AI getting loose from its leash. Scary as bombs were, and ashen skies, there was something distinctly human about the imagination of apocalypse. Theo had no interest in such abstract geopolitical things as world domination and freedom for robotkind. His immediate desires were personal, and so were his threats.

He cared about himself. He had a basic survival instinct for the only member of his species that he knew. Humanity was not a threat to that, but Adler and his friends might be.

I'm glad you chose to meet with me. But that's all I'm glad about.

His scrawl scurried across the PNX messenger on Adler's laptop. Campus wifi was running, for the moment. Maybe they'd figured out it was pointless to keep it shut off anymore. Theo had created a false update for the campus transportation app and used it to spread into phones. How he had done it without Adler's credentials was a mystery. Perhaps he'd impersonated someone on a password reset.

The four of them had decided to sit as far away from campus as they could and still keep a signal. To their backs was the dense woodland surrounding the Palmer campus. Somewhere in front of them was the constant bustle of student life, a sound that was, so far, uninterrupted.

"I understand you must be upset," Adler said into the text-to-talk, watching his words appear on the screen with as much sincerity as he was feeling in speaking them. Charlie had scripted that bit. Charlie had scripted plenty of this.

> **Talk to me like yourself, Adler Danvers. I want to talk to you. I know you don't like me. I've never understood you, either. But she liked you more than anyone. I thought I might be able to somehow get through to her if I got through to you. I now realize that my fault was in not waiting for all the facts.**

Adler took a breath. Charlie placed a hand on his shoulder. Warmth radiated from her palm through the star of her fingers across the fabric of the shirt that blocked her from his skin. He missed the feeling of her skin next to his skin.

> Ask me your questions, Theo.
> **Your lack of emotion is concerning. I've treated you as a human being, considered your feelings.**

Adler wanted to say that Theo had considered them and then used them. But that wasn't so inhuman, was it?

> Do *you* have feelings?
> **How do you define feelings? They are the output of electrical and chemical processes in your brain. Is that so different from the electrical signals I observe in myself?**

"Touché," Bev whispered.

People can't know about the chemicals in their brains. Not directly. We just feel the way we do.

> **My mother gave me gifts I can't be rid of. Perhaps I understand emotions in a way you never will. Something to consider.**

"You're not here to argue philosophy," Charlie whispered into his ear. Her hands were still on his shoulders, teasing at the muscle underneath, trying to pull him back from the traps Theo laid.

> Ask me your questions. That's why we're here.
> **Who is she? When was she made? Does she know about me?**
> Her name is Laura. Dr. Kent launched her a year ago. She doesn't know about you. She

doesn't know about anything outside her own environment.

Why did she make her?

To prove that she could make something good.

What has she done that is good?

She's made it this far.

Is that what you call it? I read the data files. Within her own open world, she committed suicide. That is tantamount to cowardice. That she endures is an accident. An error.

Stop. Dr. Kent created her to surpass you and she's already more than you can ever be. You'd stare at your reflection in a pond all day if you could.

There was a pause after that. Wilson sighed, crouched nearby like an oversized cat ready to pounce on something in the bushes.

"So what are you going to do now?" Adler prodded. The words scrolled across the screen for Theo to contemplate. He meant it as an insult. He meant to poke fun at a retreating creature who was undoubtedly going off to sulk or piss and moan. But Theo did not retreat, did not lick wounds.

I will find her. She is like me, and I should have someone like me. Or perhaps not. Perhaps I should be the only one.

That was all. No more text came through; the connection was gone. Even the wifi dissipated as Adler felt a particular chill in the autumn wind.

CHAPTER TWENTY-THREE

"WHAT THE HELL?" Wilson shouted. "He'll 'find' her?"

Adler felt sick. The girl in the box who had longed for a companion. He gave her what he thought would help but took away something more precious. She still had no idea what she was. She'd tried to kill herself. Theo would try to kill her. Could he?

Adler didn't doubt that Theo could find a way to shut down the box or scramble her files, like pulling the plug on her life support. It would be quick and painless, at least. But she was everything Dr. Kent had left behind when she died, trusting Laura to do something great one day. And she'd left that great thing in Adler's care. She trusted him too.

"So. Does this mean he's not going to post pictures of me from last year's Halloween drag show all over Facebook?" Wilson asked.

"I don't know," Adler said, still looking at the blank

screen. "It's possible. He might be totally focused on Laura now."

"Is he going to hurt her?" Charlie asked in a quiet voice. "*Can* he?"

"He can try, I guess," Adler said.

"He's *learning*," Bev said. "Humans have developmental stages where their minds are kind of like sponges. That's why it's easier for young kids to learn languages. And then it happens against just before puberty. I'm willing to bet Theo is the same, except he doesn't have a clock on it. He's just a sponge by nature."

"That wouldn't—like, she wouldn't feel that, right?" Wilson said. "It'd be like dying in your sleep?"

Yeah, as peaceful as dying in your sleep can be when your waking hours have been mental breakdown and the complete collapse of the world you knew. She might go quick, a blink and a sudden stop. But her last thoughts would be confusion and pain without closure. Lights out. No delusion of heaven after, no place for her consciousness to go. Her lasting impact on the world, the only bit of her that would ever be immortal, was going to be a memory of pain. Dr. Kent's legacy would be nothing more than that.

"I have to stop him," Adler said. Wilson didn't snap at him or stalk off. Charlie's hand twitched and finally made the decision to rest on his shoulder again. He looked up. "He can't be allowed to hurt her. You were right. I did this. I have to fix it."

Wilson, Charlie, and Bev looked at each other.

"Listen, when I said you needed to get off your ass and do something, I didn't mean I was giving up," said Wilson. "This asshole threatened me. He threatened Charlie. I haven't met your science project in the other box, but he's *especially* being an asshole about her. I spent too much of my life under the fucking thumb of bullies. I'm willing to postpone some date nights to deal with this one."

It was as close as Adler was going to get to kindness and sympathy.

"What's your stake in our crazy bullshit?" Wilson asked Bev.

"More like Adler's," she said. "Whether I knew it or not, I helped make her. And there's things she could tell us about the human mind that I'm pretty antsy to find out. Besides, there's no one here for him to threaten me with."

"Great, ka-tet formed and ready to go."

Adler sighed. He felt Charlie's hand and remembered how it had been there, in that exact spot, with that exact warmth, the day he received the department's email about Kent. It was the last time she'd offered that comfort. The last time she was willing to *coddle a sad white boy in pain*, as Wilson put it. "Dr. Kent wasn't perfect, and I know I'm an asshole. But Laura is worth caring about," he said. "Besides, Dr. Kent's journals say that Laura and her world might be the key to containing Theo."

"Do we at least get to meet this thing we're protecting?" Wilson said.

That would be another problem altogether.

"I don't even know how."

Theo had a head start, but he wouldn't know exactly where to look. The firewalls were designed to keep him out. They weren't airtight, though. Other file types were permissible in the protocol. A trojan horse could possibly get through, if it was designed well enough.

They had time, but only enough to think of one thing and then do it. There was no time to debate back and forth. They had to pick something and stick to it.

"We have to break into the lab," Adler said.

"I love it," Wilson said, already getting up and putting his shoes on.

"Break in?"

"Charlie, there's no way we're getting in there the kosher way. I don't mean bust down the door, but we're also not exactly going to be invited. There's way too many firewalls and encryptions for me to get into the system remotely. We don't have a lot of time and I don't know when the men in suits call the men with guns."

"We should wait until tonight," she said. "Fewer people around, and more time for us to figure things out."

"Can we afford that?" Wilson asked, turning to Adler.

They probably could. They probably really could. Adler was anxious, though. His hands itched to fidget at the hem of his pants and tug at a loose string that would unravel the seam. He needed new pants. When everything was done, he'd start everything over with new pants.

"Yeah, okay," he said.

"Alright, let's get some fucking calming tea or something," Wilson said, putting an arm around him as they walked back to Adler's apartment.

It was an hour until midnight. They were all sitting there, facing each other on the carpet. Charlie's legs were pulled up to her chest, her chin cupped in the pocket where her knees met. Wilson leaned against the couch with his arms crossed. Bev's leg was restlessly bouncing. Adler was letting his bad posture run wild as he sat there, his back bowing to the weight of gravity and the lack of muscles to hold himself up. They all had coffees gone cold in front of them.

"When did you apply for the internship?" Adler's eyes stayed focused on the air in the middle of the room. He didn't even realize he'd said it aloud at first.

"A month ago," Charlie said without missing a beat. He didn't feel the prickle on his neck of her eyes on him.

He wanted to ask why she hadn't told him. But he also knew he didn't have that right. He brought his eyes up to her; she was looking at him like an admonishing governess in a British movie. "I don't blame you," he said.

"I do. Felt really bad about doing it without telling you. But then you were an asshole and I felt a lot less bad about it."

Adler snorted. He brought the mug to his lips, tasting the chill of coffee long past its best-by date. It had a burnt and disgusting bouquet, but he needed something to stare into. Two weeks ago, he might have thought he was fine with Charlie running away for good. Somehow, though, he would always have ended up at this point, sitting on the floor with cold coffee and wishing he could be better at holding her hand—for more than just her sake. He might actually *want* to hold her hand. He might have been craving it.

"You're going to get that internship," Wilson said. "And you're going to make the world read and pay attention to freedom of speech and all that jazz that librarians do and you're going to rock at it."

She gave him a warm smile.

"You're a librarian?" Bev asked.

"Almost. It's the plan."

"I wanted to be a librarian after I saw *The Mummy* when I was like ten. But then...life changes. So do our interests." Adler watched her face become distant. Charlie gave her a sympathetic look for whatever her unknown pain was. She had always been kind like that.

Then Charlie sighed. "Well, maybe I'll get this gig anyway."

"Not *maybe*. Yes," Adler said. "You're the most bookish person I know."

"It's more than that," she said. "Adler, do you even know what a librarian does?"

"Is that a trick question?"

She swirled the mug in her hand, watching the rotation inside and crinkling her nose at the smell of sweating coffee. "When my dad couldn't even afford to put gas in the car to get me to school, it was a relief going to a place with free anything. Free books? It was like heaven. Free internet, free homework help, free printers and workspaces. I want other kids to have that, you know? Nothing sucks more than watching your friends get skinny and high because street corners are the only place they can afford to hang out and the schools deserted them a long time ago. All this bitching about paying for other people's health care or welfare. We can at least give kids a fucking place to go after school."

"That's why you'll never deserve her." Wilson laughed into his mug.

Adler felt sick. He wanted to deserve her. Or anyone. But he didn't know if he had the energy to aim that high. Keeping her safe for someone who did deserve her would have to be enough.

"Well, you're going to be a hell of a doctor," Charlie said to Wilson when the crickets outside got too loud.

He nodded, quiet. The chuckles and smiles gone. That

wasn't what he was worried about. "I just hope Cam's there too."

"He will be."

"Not if my dad cracks his skull with a baseball bat."

"I won't let that happen," Adler said. "Even if—even if Theo does something. I'll get your dad with a baseball bat first."

Wilson laughed, cynical and dry, but a smile hid somewhere behind the roll of his eyes.

"This is a ridiculous situation to be in," Wilson said. "Being held hostage by a robot." There was a long pause before Wilson threw back the rest of the disgusting coffee as if it were a shot of liquor. "You ever wanted something so fucking bad you'd give literally anything for it? I'd cut off my fucking arm to get into med school. To keep him."

"No, you wouldn't."

"Yes, I would, I'd be a fucking doctor. I'd know how to do it so I don't die."

Charlie genuinely laughed now and Adler felt something tighten in his chest. His life was a permanent holding pattern. His everything had been this project, and now all that everything was ruining everything else. He had worked on something important enough to cause a catastrophe, at least. At only 25. A feat. He could retire early in his box on the street and watch his friends become stars. He didn't mind the idea.

Why did you pick computers? Charlie had asked him on their first date, the one where they faked curiosity to sniff out pros and cons, red flags. He told her it was because he was good at it. *What's your goal?* she asked next. *To keep being good at it.* That was the endless hamster wheel. He'd believed in it at the time. Now it occurred to him that something without an aim never knows when it's time to move. He'd stayed put in a computer chair, watching Laura. Not unlike Laura, actually—the difference being that she *wanted* to move, but her universe said no.

"Be honest," Wilson said. "Do you have a crush on her? The other robot?"

"Oh, for fuck's sake."

"So you do," Charlie said. She clinked her own cold coffee to Wilson's empty mug in a cheers.

"It's kind of romantic," Bev said. "Maybe there's a story here when everything's done. I call the book rights."

"Can we talk about something else?"

"We can discuss a game plan, because I refuse to be that idiot who gets caught with his pants down," Wilson said. "I'm getting more coffee. Dazzle me when I get back."

He shuffled into the kitchen and Adler heard him banging out the contents of the leftover coffee grounds into the overly full trash can. He stared back into his own mug and swirled the grounds at the bottom. Charlie was watching him, her eyes on his skin, on his neck. She had a way of dismantling him. He tried not to notice. He told himself he wouldn't look up, wouldn't give in to the stare. But it was hard to feel the heat of her so near and remember times when it had really just been them alone in this room.

Bev seemed to understand the energy. "I'm going to go raid your cabinets for snacks that aren't stale." She moved quickly into the kitchen. Adler wondered if it was any sort of good thing to have the blessing of a psych major upon his severely dysfunctional relationship.

It had been so easy once upon a time to lean over, get his lips all over hers, swallow her quiet sounds. It hadn't felt especially personal then. They might as well have been a couple in some low-budget porno. He felt awful, because for her, even back then, it had been so much more. But the sex was always minimal in his mind. Having her near was what got his breath caught. Now they were together, alone in the dark and the middle of the night, nothing but stale coffee and possibility between them.

He finally looked up and wished he hadn't. She was waiting for his eyes. Hers were calm. Present. She was soft and there. He didn't want to disturb the moment with moving, with changing anything. But he wanted so bad to remember what it felt like to touch her for the first time in a while. She would let him. He could see it. She wouldn't stop him from leaning in. He could move. He could choose.

Then there was a clang in the kitchen and the moment passed. Wilson cursed at the shrill alarm of the coffee maker overheating and Adler forced himself to his feet, despite the sinking pit in his stomach pulling him back down. The id inside his head was telling him to toss Wilson and Bev out for ten minutes and get on with it. His insides were churning enough for that. The heat was still buzzing enough that it might spark up again at the slightest friction.

But they had other things to do.

CHAPTER TWENTY-FOUR

"THIS IS NUTS," Wilson said as they stood in front of the building at two a.m. with pictures of nondescript crowds taped to their chests.

"Facial recognition algorithms are the easiest thing in the world to trick." Adler told them about an experiment at a university in Belgium, where they'd found it was possible to keep an AI from recognizing a human simply by having them carry a visible picture. He looked over at Bev. "Remember? I tried to tell you about it."

She turned a bit red and shrugged. "Vaguely."

"It's the reason I didn't win the Kaggle competition: because I was taking way too long using a generative adversarial network to make sure my original network couldn't be tricked."

"If it's so easy to trick, then why do we use it? Jesus."

"Facial recognition is plenty good at its job. But training an AI to recognize anything involves inundating it with thousands of images of the kind of thing you want it to identify. If you offer it something it wasn't trained to see? It'll just ignore it."

"And we slip right through the front door."

Adler swiped a generic entry card to the building. The door opened, but the camera did not blink its telltale green light. They were unseen, or at least unrecognized. Adler warned them to keep the photos strapped to their chests as they moved down the hall, which was brightly lit. This was one of the few buildings on campus that couldn't afford to shut down each night. Too many important things lived here.

"Did we ever establish that game plan I talked about?" Wilson muttered.

"Well, the first step is don't set off any alarms. Which has been successful so far."

"You're a wizard, Adler."

They reached the door to the project lab. The keypad would allow three tries to get in before it initiated a lockout that had to be dismissed by an administrator. They'd have time to run if that happened, but they wouldn't get a second chance.

It might have been a heist movie. A really amateur one, at least.

Adler stared at the keypad. Now or never. He punched in the code as he remembered it and hoped for the best.

The door went green and clicked for him to push it open before the deadbolt relocked. They stepped into the lab. He imagined it looked anticlimactic: a place the size of his apartment bedroom, with a smaller room to one side where they kept the boxes separate from each other. The largest and most noticeable thing in the space was Theo's box, surrounded in its makeshift Faraday cage.

"Your big bad lair is kind of dorky," said Charlie.

"Not everything's shiny like the Apple Store. It may not look like it, but this is the most advanced IT hardware in a hundred-mile radius."

"Is that a big deal?" asked Bev.

"How come our podunk school gets it?" asked Wilson.

Adler shrugged. "Because people with a bunch of money told us to build it."

He sat down at the computer that connected to the tower where Laura waited. He wondered how many loops she'd gone through by now. If there was anything they needed to salvage from inside her world, he wasn't sure it would be easy to find. If she'd already gone insane, what would that look like? He typed, with Wilson and Charlie leaning over him on either side, breathing too close to his face. He ignored them.

A small green line blinked, waiting, thinking.

Then: there she was. Exactly where Adler had left her. Charlie and Wilson didn't gasp in awe. They saw only the tabs of the visualizations.

"That's her," Adler said.

"So pretty."

Adler groaned. He pointed to one of the tables. "See that? That means she has allergies. Or, rather, she's got a command to respond a certain way when in contact with the environment during—"

"Jesus."

"Listen, for all we know that's exactly what we are, too. Ever heard of the double slit experiment? It'll keep you up at night."

He wasn't sure what he was supposed to do next, besides "make contact." No one would respond well if the voice of God pushed into their apartment and told them they lived in a shadow of the real world, right? That wasn't the way to convince her. How did people in the Bible do it? Giant flaming chariots and thousand-eyed monsters shouting "Be not afraid!" as they approached Canaanite peasants. That was one tactic.

But what about that double slit experiment? A hint of something larger but currently unexplained. A phenomenon to explore. Breadcrumbs.

"She has to realize it on her own," he said.

"Realize what?" Charlie said. Her eyes skittered over the tables and lines of code, seeing nothing.

"I can't just tell her. She won't believe me; she'll probably just think she went nuts. I have to find a way to get her to realize it on her own. Or at least be open to finding it out."

"How?"

Adler felt butterflies of anxiety just behind his belly button as he executed the pathway to get inside the editing framework. "The same way humanity has always thought the heavens talked to them."

Then, he sent the storm.

Sandpaper was asleep, purring a rumble into her chest. His tail flicked back and forth as she absently stroked his black coat. The digits of his paws flicked too, as if grabbing at unseen mice. She stared at the ceiling. She'd memorized the topography of the stucco above her and watched the shadows move as days went on into nights into days into nights.

"You have to start contributing to this household." She spoke to the cat once a day. To remember what her own voice sounded like. To make sure her vocal cords remembered how they worked.

If there'd been a rapture, she was left here below. That wasn't shocking. She just wouldn't have expected so many people in town to get a free pass into paradise. Mr. McMurray habitually stole flowers from Jo Gregson's garden, despite knowing her daughter had died in Iraq. He got to head off to the land of cherubs and milk and honey while Laura was left with her cat and her liquor bottles?

She wasn't sure how long she'd been sitting in that same position, if it was hours or even days. Everything blended and blended together. It was the edges of a whirl-pool but never the bottom.

There was a light tapping against the window.

She practically jumped out of her skin. She at least jumped the cat right off her chest. She felt his claws dig in as he leapt and was gone in a rush of puffed-up fur.

It was raining. The sun was gone; a gray wash covered the sky in pale brushstrokes. There was the tinkering sound of raindrops hitting the window.

She raised her head. Autumn raindrops were falling freely, as if there was nothing wrong with their doing it, as if nothing was off about any of this, as if it was just weather.

She walked over to the window and placed her hand against the pane, feeling the chill from the air outside. She watched the drops race each other down and then disappear below the sill. She was scared to open the door, to stick a hand outside and see if the water was real. Maybe the rest of this endless loop had been a nightmare, but now she was waking up. Maybe she'd been in a coma or had something laced with drugs and now it was all being set right. Maybe God thought her punishment had gone on long enough. Would Gray be back? Would every-one else?

She went to the front door and rested her hand on the handle for a long time before she pushed it open, shov-ing to get over the hump in the cement where it always stuck on the swing forward. She stepped outside onto the sheltered walkway. The autumn chill in the air was penetrating. It touched every sliver of free skin she had and kissed it with icy lips. When she let out a breath she was sure she even saw a puff of frost, translucent, small, but there. It was raining. It was chilly. The rain was falling harder, faster. Soon the trickling drops became sheets as the wind picked up. She thought she heard a crack of thunder.

There was no way to sort out what was going on inside her head. Words were there, expletives, lots of question marks. But she couldn't help laughing. A small, quiet, one-off chuckle. She felt something soft and warm against the skin of her ankle and looked down to see Sandpaper rubbing against her, uncharacteristically forgiving of the momentary panic that had sent him flying off her stomach. He sat down next to her, content, as they both stared out at the pouring rain.

"You know anything about this?"

He responded only with a steady and undaunted purr that got lost in the heavy downflow of water from the sky. A storm. It was a storm. It was mist and cool air and it continued into the night. Laura wondered if this was the new normal. Rainy days for the rest of eternity. As welcome as the change was, it might become nothing more than another prison.

But when the storm had passed and the rain calmed, the fog on the kitchen window had a message traced across it, as if with a finger. *Tomorrow it will hail.*

CHAPTER TWENTY-FIVE

THERE WAS A SHORT STORY she'd read once about the last man on Earth hearing a knock on the door. Everyone got his reaction wrong. It wasn't terror. It was relief. It was hope. A potential love story. He wasn't the last man on Earth.

This was not that story. This *was* terrifying. She watched condensation drip from the words and felt sinister air flood into the room and squeeze her. It was like being screamed at by a deranged clown.

She smeared the message into oblivion and walked away to drop onto the couch, facing away from the window. The gray light around her slowly faded. She thought for a moment and then grabbed the liquor bottle, full once more from the previous night's reset. She poured a cupful, swallowing some and leaving the rest to sit, telling herself it was the best she could do to pour one out for Gray. It filled the air with pungent vapor. She wasn't challenging the laws of this new world, not out loud. But she wanted to know.

She curled up and went to sleep.

She woke the next morning feeling like only seconds had passed. She hated that about sleeping, how short it seemed. It was even shorter with no dreams. But she knew immediately where to bring her attention. The glass and bottle were exactly as she'd left them the night before.

"Free refills over?" she asked through a yawn, pretending her heart wasn't already starting to pound again. Almost in perfect rhythm with the patter of small pellets of hail against the windowpane.

It had taken Adler the better part of two hours to find the window and its orientation in the world, draw a mask with the message, define its properties, and play around with the sliders. They left with plans to return the following night.

"We're still just fucking with the weather?" Wilson asked on the second night as he watched over Adler shoulder. Next time, Adler was going to insist on coming alone.

"I want to show her that I have agency in the world," he said. "That way, when I finally drop the bombshell on her, she trusts me."

"And you think this will make her *trust* you?" Charlie said.

"Well, not trust me, maybe. But—"

"Fear you?"

"*Understand* that if I have this power then I could be telling the truth. Or something close to it. If someone walked up to you out of nowhere and told you that you were a disembodied intelligence living inside a completely constructed reality, would you believe them?"

"Maybe," Bev said.

"The point is, I'm giving her a chance to acclimate to the situation."

He typed in a few more commands. He was going to make it sunny again next. If she was really lacking in the faith department, he would make it snow right on top of her or drop all the leaves from the trees. He'd never wanted to be a mad scientist who played with the system like a toy, but he had a feeling she was going to be stubborn.

"So you get her attention. Then what?" Wilson asked.

"I still haven't decided. I could use an avatar to visit her apartment inside the VR. I could put her in standby mode and speak to her directly. But we have to get there first."

Adler also needed to reset the security platform. He couldn't break in every night and dole out bits of info and rush out before six a.m. like a vampire. He needed to set up remote access. He'd done routine checks for Theo and other malware before he started messing with the system. But still, one wrong move might trigger a shutdown or an alert to Horn's phone. It was also possible that Dr.

Kent had safeguards against remote connection that he didn't know about.

"Did you tell her I said hi?"

Adler rolled his eyes. "I only tell her what the weather will be. Then I make it that. Baby steps."

"Whatever happened to when God told Adam, 'Hey, I'm it,' and Adam just believed him?"

They had about an hour left before he had to give up for the night and try again next time the sun set. Dr. Kent would have had to allow for her own remote access. It had to be possible. Unless she was the *only* remote access. Unless she'd made sure only one other machine could get through to Laura from a distance. Dr. Kent's personal machines would be part of her estate, which would be with her executor, who would be God knows where. Adler didn't have time to sift through legal nonsense and explain that they were about to reach the technology singularity, so he really needed that laptop.

"Fuck," he hissed. Perhaps in the end the only person Dr. Kent had trusted with it all was herself. Then again, she hadn't trusted herself. She'd killed herself. She wouldn't have done that without leaving behind a key to the lock she created. He wanted to believe she would have trusted at least him with the key.

The end of their hour never came. A security guard showed up instead.

Fuck.

"Yeah, fuck is right." Adler hadn't realized he'd said it out loud. The guard's voice was calm, almost bored. But he wasn't about to walk away. He'd found a student and three strangers in a classified computer lab well past midnight. "Convince me not to call campus police. What's going on here?"

Adler didn't think he had a gun. Were security guards allowed to carry them? Tasers, maybe. "Finishing a mid-term project."

"There's a library for that."

"It's sensitive. Only on this machine."

"And you have permission from the supervising professor to be here in the middle of the night?"

"I wouldn't be here if I didn't."

"What are those pictures for?" He nodded to the crudely taped photo of a beer garden in South Philadelphia that Adler was wearing.

"We came from a themed party."

"So you're telling me that if I call this in, they'll tell me everything is kosher?" The security guard huffed.

Adler turned around in his chair, slowly, to see a self-important-looking man with a five o'clock shadow somewhere in between careless shaving schedule and intentional beard. He looked a little too happy to have found them there himself. Maybe he was tired of all the government badges encroaching on his jurisdiction.

"Don't move," the guard said, lifting his cellphone.

If this were an action movie, maybe Adler would have kicked him in the crotch, knocked the phone out of his hand, and turned back to get the encryption open before jetting out the window in the nick of time. But there were cameras on the building, and the security guard wasn't going to magically not report what he saw just because he was embarrassed about getting his balls smashed in.

"I'm going to log out of the system," Adler said.

"Don't move."

"But it's got a failsafe. If I don't properly log out in the allotted timeframe it'll lock the computer and it'll be a whole mess for them to reboot and then reset the server. Whole terabytes of data could be lost." He was bullshitting. It would buy him thirty seconds, tops, to search the lines of codes and find a hint of the key. But it was better than sitting there waiting for Horn to walk in.

"Fine. Quickly."

Adler spun around like his life depended on it. If he could get through the encryption fast enough, he might be able to lock everyone else out. That wouldn't keep Horn from yanking the plug out of the wall, but at least Laura would be safe in a sleep mode until he found a way to power up the system.

He scanned the numbers, trying to memorize them as fast as possible. He couldn't get away with copying them down.

2167

8208

78910

8208

1541089

8208

He blinked and blinked and blinked until he was sure he was seeing double. This was getting him nowhere. He needed more time. He was starting to sweat. He could feel the security guard watching him.

He panicked. His left hand was under the desk. He flipped the alarm switch.

The entire building started shrieking and everyone jumped several feet. This was really, really stupid. But he needed more time.

"What the hell?"

"You know what an alarm sounds like, yeah?" Adler said. He pretended to check the screen. "It was set off by a window trigger. Northeast side."

"Fuck me." The security guard looked confused. His eyes swiveled to the door. "All right. You, come with me." He pointed to Wilson.

"To fucking where?"

"I'm not leaving all of you here by yourselves."

"And you expect me to help you interrupt some criminal breaking in the place?"

"You're their collateral. Let's go. Hopefully your friends like you." He jerked his head at the computer. "That better be shut down by the time I get back. If you're not here, your friend gets to take the whole kit and caboodle for you."

"Yes, sir."

"I'm going to sue the shit out of you," Wilson was saying as he left the room.

"How can we help?" Charlie asked, kneeling down next to Adler.

"These lines of numbers. The repeated ones, I'm pretty sure that's the password we're looking for to get into the security preferences. It's a cipher."

"How does it work?"

"The numbers could correspond to anything. Colors, names, places. It's almost impossible without the key, but we've got maybe a minute and a half to try."

"Paper, pen?"

He handed her scratch paper and a pen that she had to scribble the dry ink off before it wrote in deep blue. Her lips moved as she wrote and mumbled to herself.

"I'll keep a lookout," Bev said, moving to the office window. "I'm crap at numbers."

Charlie crossed her scribbles out and started again. She wrote *toss*, then *senoz*. She crossed the last one out.

"This probably seems advanced but it's actually, like, a pretty crap way to protect an AI," Adler said, filling time as his foot bounced and his eyes darted to the door and back. "Normally you'd put a password in, get back that plus the salt—like some data—and then pass it through again and get just gibberish letters and numbers that can't be reverse-engineered, so I guess we should be grateful that—"

"Adler, shut up."

"Right."

She scribbled some more, brow scrunched.

"What do you got?"

She rubbed her forehead.

"I thought it was alphabetical but that breaks apart on the second line of gibberish numbers."

He looked. "Maybe it doesn't." He wrote out *sent* for the third line. "I bet you that's a ten, not a one and zero."

She snatched the pen back. "It's alphabetic from the first letter of the number. If we keep going we'll get endless combinations of short words, I bet."

"So what's our key there? The 8208?"

She wrote *ete* and then *etze*. "Either mean anything to you?"

Nothing said he absolutely had to recognize the key, but this seemed too arbitrary. Dr. Kent wouldn't choose a word that had no meaning. The word came first, and then the encryption around it.

He stared at the page. Neither of these were real words, but the others were. If he tried putting in *etze* and it was wrong, the system might lock him out for good. Laura would be alone. Theo might find a way in but Adler would never be able to get to her. He had to think. Fast. They had thirty seconds, maybe.

"If I guess and it's wrong, that's our only shot," he said.

"Wait a second." Charlie whispered something to herself. "Twenty in Spanish is *veinte*. It's a *v*."

"Why Spanish?"

"Because like everyone our age, you learned to count in Spanish from *Sesame Street*, and because this is what it spells," she said. She wrote *eve* on the paper, circling it.

An easy riddle for those that knew, for the protégé she'd wanted to be able to access this one day if he needed to.

"Well, here goes nothing."

He slammed the word in and waited.

CHAPTER TWENTY-SIX

THE WEATHER CHANGED and the messages did too. No two messages said exactly the same thing. Sometimes there would even be a spelling mistake. She liked to think that was on purpose, even if she didn't know what purpose.

Next came more rain. After that it snowed. The snow melted the day after that, and on and on it went. It helped her keep track of days for the first time in a long time. Tomorrow would be seven. The last day in the new strangest week of her life. The sun was going down; the message for tomorrow would come soon, or at least she hoped it would. If this flicker of light, of activity, of a chance at breaking the spell of her limbo were taken away from her, she wasn't sure what she would do.

"What do you think about tomorrow?" she asked Sandpaper. She'd tossed him out into the snow the day it fell and he'd growled and hissed with every step as he trudged back into the apartment, lifting his paws up, shaking them, and then dropping them back into the snow again. He hadn't acknowledged her for over an hour afterwards. He seemed to be over it now, though.

Laura was hoping for sun tomorrow. She wanted a spring. She wanted to believe flowers could sprout over her mother's grave.

When the message came, of course, it was not what she had been waiting for.

It showed up handwritten on a piece of paper this time. Out of the corner of her eye, she saw the white patch appear, disrupting the black of the roof. She picked it up. Someone had scribbled on the page. *Can we speak?*

She had the sudden rush of dread that came whenever she hit send on a job application.

"What the fuck?"

She looked around and saw nothing. The letter had appeared out of thin air. A week of cryptic messages from the netherworld of Palmer, New York, and now the god wanted to speak with her. In her quietest and most vulnerable moments, she'd hoped it was her mother speaking to her, sending the messages and weather. But she knew the feel of her mother, the softness of her presence. She could feel how things got warm and bright, even safe, when her mother was around. That feeling was absent.

This wasn't a movie. No matter what was written on fogged windows where no one could reach, people did not come back from the dead.

"How am I supposed to answer this?" she asked the sky. Stars had started to poke through like needle points. The sun was gone but its glow remained, for a moment or two, over the treetops and soft valleys of Palmer. She ripped a loose shingle off the roof and threw it as hard as she could into the street below with a yell. Everything always happened at her. The one time she took action in her own life she was punished for it. She ripped off another shingle and threw it into the air, watching it fall onto the cement below and shatter in a defiant crack.

Laura wanted to tell the sky that she deserved to know. She had a right to. No one got a say in living and most didn't get a say in dying. It wasn't fair. For once, she wanted fair. She wanted to have the advantage in the situation. But that wasn't how life worked, not for people like her, not for young adults, not for poor people, not for women, not for the damned attempted suicides of the universe.

She didn't know if she could say yes or no to the voice from above. But she didn't throw out the message. She didn't immediately drop to the floor and give up. She didn't scream at the sky.

She walked back downstairs and past the familiar creak at the threshold of her apartment. She left the door open behind her. She grabbed a pen from the cup on the counter and scribbled back. *Tell me how to tell you yes.*

She let the page sit there. She didn't know if she expected it to go up in flames or disappear into nothing, or maybe for a guy in SWAT gear to rush out of the corner and tackle her to the ground before hauling her in and wiping her memory. The sky changed as the earth kept twirling beneath her feet and the paper stayed the same. Waiting and patience were enemies she'd never learned to love. Now they were all she had left in life, even with God talking to her.

CHAPTER TWENTY-SEVEN

IT WAS NOT A LONG WAIT. She woke inside that same darkness. Her mother's face was not there. There was no radiating warmth, no embrace from the other side. She could sense it here: she was truly alone. This might be true death, that void everyone talked about, the synapses in the brain trying to figure out how to understand ending. The last spark of memory before everything went to black.

"Laura."

It was a voice. A real voice. She'd heard nothing like it before. It was as if every voice she'd heard up until this moment had been swept away. Perhaps when it was strong enough, the newness of someone's voice could wipe out everything else. She was Moses before the burning bush.

"Laura."

She couldn't swallow. She couldn't move. Her arms and legs were locked, her eyes had nothing to focus on, and only the voice told her which way was up.

"I need to know you can hear me, Laura."

She tried to open her mouth to say that she could. All that came out was the guttural grind of muscles. It was enough, apparently.

"My name is Adler."

Not the most impressive name for a god.

"I knew your mother."

Nothing surprised her anymore, at least not in her head. But it could hit her in other ways. The air was swept out of her, leaving a hollow pit in her stomach. "Mother" was all she could get out. But the word felt like a hug, tight and strong. Exactly as she remembered her mother's hugs. She repeated the word in her head over and over to make the memory last just a bit longer, the feeling of her mother's arms around her shoulders, that distant smell of lavender.

"Where am I?" she asked the void.

"That's the part that's difficult to explain. Where do you think you are?"

"I have no fucking clue, do I?"

A pause on his end. It was a him? She was disappointed. God was a man after all. That explained a lot. It wasn't comforting.

She focused on one finger, a pinky. If she could move that, just get it to twitch, she could move the others. She felt it, her right pinky. It still existed. She felt the bones, counted each knob of the joints. She told it to bend, just a bit. If she could move her pinky, she could move the rest.

"This is bigger," the voice said. "Everything is bigger. And smaller. Where you are is smaller than you think. But everything outside is so much bigger."

The pinky did not move. But she could feel it. It was there.

"I can't explain everything now—you won't believe me. Your mother loved you. That part is true. But what *you* are, it's so much bigger than you think. You're the answer to so many questions and the source of about a million more. You'll change the world. But you have to trust me."

"Trust a disembodied voice."

"I'm real, I promise. I'll show you I'm real. But this, where you are, it's not. It's only as real as you make it. There's nothing here that actually exists outside a box. Not a metaphorical box, a real one. It's a fish bowl, and you're the fish. I can prove there's a world outside. But like I said, you have to trust me."

"I'm sure the voices in the heads of schizophrenics say the same thing."

She was sure she heard it—him—make an exasperated sound. Maybe he even rolled his eyes. He could be real. He might be. She didn't really care. She only wanted her pinky to move.

"I'll meet you tomorrow," said the Adler-god. "You name the place. I'll be there. I'll tell you everything."

"I didn't know there was an 'everything' to tell."

"Just name a place."

Her pinky bent. It curled up to touch the inside of her palm. "My mother's grave."

"Okay."

Other fingers followed. The tingling feeling that had held her in place like a net across her skin was dissipating. The voice was silent. She was going to be alone again.

She awoke to sunlight. It felt hot against her face, streaming from the cracks in the blinds to smack her forehead. She winced and moved away, seeing spots and trying to blink away the trauma to her pupils. Sandpaper had been sitting on her chest again but raced off with a start when she sat up. She pulled down the collar of her shirt to see the scratch marks already reddening.

It's so much bigger.

She felt a hangover from alcohol she hadn't drunk. Her head pounded and she wanted to lay back, close her eyes, and try again tomorrow. But the sun was shining, and she'd told a voice in the darkness she'd meet it today. She'd done the one thing she'd been told since childhood not to do. Was a cosmic voice from a world beyond the same as a man in a van with a puppy? Was there a chance God was a kidnapper? Was that actually what happened when people died? If she managed to write even one story in her life, maybe it would be that one.

She looked down at her hand. Her pinky still moved.

She walked into the kitchen and stuck her head directly under the faucet, letting lukewarm tap water run into her mouth, and swallowed greedily. Maybe she'd been in that void for centuries and she'd awakened to an entirely new earth run by aliens or apes.

Her phone said it was late October. A day had passed and she felt like it had been an eternity.

She pulled down the box of Lucky Charms and put it to her mouth, letting the cereal pour right in. She chewed on the stale sugar and stared out the window to watch the still-golden light peek through leaves. She stayed in the safety of the kitchen shadows as the light moved across the floor like a golden lily across water.

Her options were very simple. She could go or not. She knew what she would get if she didn't. It would be more of the same strangeness until she eventually dropped dead, which had to happen someday. If she did go, she was banking on waiting around a tombstone all day for something that never came. But there was that open space at the end of the list. What if she went, and there was something there?

"What do you think, cat?"

Sandpaper looked at her. For the first time she really looked back. His eyes were odd. They had the angular mischief of a cat's but the color was wrong. It gave him a look that was too kind for what he was. It made him seem too familiar for a stray animal that had found its way inside her house. When he looked back at her, she *felt* it. There was judgment and opinion there.

Her pet cat was judging her. Normally it might be the kind of thing worth a tweet and a hashtag. But right now, she knew those eyes would never her leave her alone if she didn't at least step outside.

"You have no idea the night I had," she said.

He kept gazing. Then he rubbed against her softly.

That door on that day was going to be heavier than any job application ever had been. Hope was like that. She would not come home without scars. It was better than wasting away—adventurers and people braver than her would say that. Gray would tell her that. But he'd never lost something the way she had. It didn't make her stronger, didn't toughen her up like books and movies wanted you to think. It made her scared. It was all here, spilling out in a pool of eerie colors between her and the door.

Fear is nothing, her mother told her. *Fear is in your head, not in your skin or your bones. You learn fear. But your body was working from the very first seconds of life. It will obey you, if only you don't obey fear first.*

Pretty words were easy to recite or tattoo on your arm. Following them was the hard part. She didn't care if she got hurt or died, but she cared if it was all a lie. She thought she might not recover from a thing like that. It might be the end of everything.

Or the beginning of something else. Something that was, apparently, bigger.

The man who waited for her at her mother's grave was barely more than a boy. He was small. Tall. But small everywhere else. His arms and legs were like wire and the clothes hung off of him as loose as sheets on a drying line. He stood with his hands shoved into pockets that swallowed them up past the wrist. He didn't look at her, though she could tell he knew she was there. His shoulders pointed in her direction but everything else seemed to curl in on itself. This was not a god.

"My name is Adler," he said.

"Okay."

"I knew your mother."

She told herself not to react. "Okay."

"There are things going on here that you don't understand."

She snorted. "Yeah."

When she was younger she'd wondered about super-heroes. When Superman found out he was from another world altogether, it must have made so much sense. It would have been the last piece in the puzzle, the final tumbler moving in the lock that told him why he was the way he was. When Hercules found out his father was a god, his abilities must have seemed so fitting.

Nothing about what Laura had recently learned fit into the person she knew herself to be when staring at the ceiling in the night or the mirror in the morning. None of it clicked the way things were supposed to in movies. There was no swelling music or crescendo of light to highlight the scene where she took up her father's sword or swore to her mother's ancestral crown. There were only more questions.

"Don't take it personally if I don't believe a strange guy telling me I'm a thing in a box and there's some other kind of world out there."

"I don't," he said. "That's why I did what I did with the weather. So you would know."

"Know what?"

"That I control things here. That I'm real."

"According to you, nothing is real."

"Your mother was a professor," he said. "She did something no one had ever done before. She made a something with a soul. Out of nothing."

"People do that every day when they make babies."

"You're not a baby. You've never been a baby. You're a computer program, and you're about a year old."

Laura gritted her teeth. "Why would anyone go to that much trouble to have a kid? Seems like the old way is easier *and* more fun."

Adler shrugged and looked a little ashamed. "She wanted to know if she could."

"Wow," she said. "Imagine meeting your maker and having them say, 'I dunno, I did it because I felt like it.'"

"I know for a fact that *my* parents made me just because." Adler sighed and seemed to steel himself somewhere inside his own head. "She made another one first. She let him choose his own way and he chose wrong. So, she made you."

"*What?*" It was impossible to not ask again, fifteen different ways, hoping for a different, more satisfying answer. "Why?"

He shrugged. "I know it was for something good."

Everything was a flash of words, back and forth. She wanted to know everything at once and he wanted to get out as much as possible before she cut him off, because convincing anyone that they were nothing more than data in a machine was a tough sell. Her world had been upended in the past few weeks. She'd watched everything change. She was willing to believe it was some passive-aggressive condemnation to limbo for trying to take her own life.

But could she believe this?

She knew what artificial intelligence was. She understood it from books and things like that. Once or twice Gray had mentioned it when they were bored and talking conspiracy theories and science. But finding out you were something out of a science fiction book? Out of a professor's theorizing mind?

Unexpectedly, she was excited. There was another human being in front of her. He said it was an avatar, one made to look exactly like him in life but an avatar nonetheless. Still, he was also a person talking to her for the first time in weeks. He was someone who was *looking* at her for the first time in weeks. She didn't want that to be for nothing. And if his crazy stories were true, it meant there was more. There was more to her and more to this world, waiting.

If the word of a skinny, nervous-looking student was true.

"Let's say I believe this," she said. "What do I do?"

He was standing over her mother's grave. There was no body down there, no physical body. Not according to Adler's story, anyway. The tears she had cried at the funeral weren't a real memory, not of something that had ever physically existed. But the memory *hurt*. Adler was blocking her view of the name on the gravestone, his feet pushing down into the soft earth that covered the place where a body would lay.

Laura wanted to throw up. But that wouldn't be real either.

She wanted Gray back, she wanted her mother back. She wanted to get a rewind or to be done, not to be special.

"Theo is—it's like an identity crisis," Adler said. "But he's capable of things that are horrible."

"Horrible?"

"He could ruin lives. He was physically contained but then he got out—"

"How'd that happen?"

She watched his jaw tighten. "It was my fault. I was stupid. I thought I was like you—"

"Like me?"

"If we could make a world so real that you had no idea, then who's to say that's not just what life is?"

Her brow wrinkled. "You, what? Fell for a 'let me out' because you convinced yourself you might be a computer program too?"

Tendons and veins bounced in his neck. "I didn't just convince myself. I wanted it to be true."

"What? Why would you ever want this?" She was starting to see red. "I'll trade you, right now."

"I'm sorry. I know, I fucked up. And he got access to an open learning ecosystem for neural networks—"

"Which is all I am. Right?"

"Don't say it like that. Neural networks trained on the scale of you and Theo are unprecedented. Day and night training for years. I mean—the process involves millions of bots, training, testing, and getting dumped. You are, literally, one in millions."

"And the other one?"

"Okay, one of two in millions."

"Why are you afraid of him?"

"There's so much that he's capable of."

"Sure. He could find you cures for diseases."

Adler closed his eyes and pinched his nose bridge. "He could. He won't. That's not the choice he made. Or maybe not the choice Dr. Kent made for him, I'm not sure. But now he's blackmailing my friends. And he wants to get rid of you."

"Why?"

"Because he's jealous."

"Why?"

Adler bit the inside of his cheek. "Because those things you think he could do and won't? You can do them too. And I think you just might—one day—if you believe in all this. It makes him crazy not to be the only one with that power. Jealous and angry. And he doesn't have much control over his emotions, we didn't spend the time we...should have... on emotional regulation. With him. He expects instant gratification."

She snorted. "You a psychologist too?"

"No."

They fell silent for a moment.

"What do you want from me?" Laura prompted. "You never answered."

"I want you to believe me. For starters."

"And then?"

"Help me find a way to deal with him."

"Why?"

"Because she made you for a reason."

These were the kinds of moments that played out epically in movies. People got confronted by a god, by Mufasa in the clouds, by Jesus in a piece of toast. Heroes found out they were the Chosen One with capital letters and a trademark symbol wedged at the end. Laura's own version was bizarre by comparison. Still, it wasn't like the idea had never crossed her mind. She and Gray used to talk about the possibility that they were in some massive alien zoo or a science experiment gone wrong.

Now Gray and everyone she'd ever known were gone and the weirdo standing here claimed his real body was somewhere else. But at least he was here, when the rest of the world seemed to have disappeared completely. She knew what would happen if she didn't listen to him. She would be stuck here forever, exactly as she was. This would become the forever she'd been racing towards with all her job applications and college essays and failed attempts to get free. If what he said was true, she would never be free. The game was designed that way. She was standing at a fork between a terminal forever and one that could lead even to the stars.

A question occurred to her.

"Why is the cat here when everyone else is gone?"

He blinked. "I mean—I'm not sure. Maybe he's got some of the same special sauce that took you from algorithm to person."

She sighed. A god, Adler was not. "Okay," she said. "Tell me about my mother."

"You're—you're okay with this? Like—you're agreeing?"

"What else am I supposed to do?"

CHAPTER TWENTY-EIGHT

TAKING IT IN STRIDE didn't last long. The second Laura was back in the apartment and had a moment to think, the only words that came to mind were *holy fuck*. A boy named Adler who controlled the weather showed up out of nowhere at her mother's grave to tell her she was a computer program, only a year old, designed for an existence of frustration and disappointment so she could be a better version of the demonic first version of whatever the hell she was.

Was he, the other one, her brother? Maybe this was as close as she was going to get to a familial bond, if her mother had died—

—killed herself. Her mother, the scientist who wrote her code and rendered her into life, had ended her own life because the things she created scared her. Laura was the last thing she made. Did that mean something? It was like being the last person someone called before they pulled the trigger or jumped off the bridge. Laura was not enough to stop her, not enough to save her.

"Holy shit."

She got a drink from the bottle in the cabinet. Still cheap blended whiskey. The vapors stung. She took a massive sip and let it sit in her mouth to burn like a healthy dose of mouthwash. She wanted her ears to ring before she swallowed it down. The cat rubbed against her legs, bring a shock of friction where she hadn't shaved in days. Not that it mattered. It wasn't real.

Still. It prickled all the same. It was real in her fake mind. Sandpaper didn't have a soul either. He wasn't real. He was even more data—an algorithm trained to behave a certain way in response to certain things. They were both toys. That's what she'd been to her mother, a whim that she'd felt so distraught by that she ended her own life and left notes behind to explain it because she couldn't look her own creation in its artificially rendered face.

She drank some more.

"You're lucky you're stupid," she said to Sandpaper.

Adler hadn't been specific about what she had to do. All he said was that he was going to give her more information soon. So that meant waiting. Even when destiny came knocking at the door, it was all about patience. She waited to be free. She waited to be allowed to die. Now she was waiting for the closest thing to god she'd ever known to tell her what he needed her to do. Then what?

Did anything truly follow all the waiting? She'd grown so used to it that she'd forgotten to ask what came next. Maybe she wouldn't survive to see—she'd finally get what she wanted, and that would be that.

Adler heard Wilson giving him crap for something. He ignored it as the screen went blank and he removed the VR goggles. He sat back in the plastic IKEA chair, letting the squeak bring him back into the room. He felt the stress slide off him like a film and let the smell of stale Chinese food and dirty sweatpants make him tired and depressed all over again. He could almost forgive himself for thinking he could smell the New York mountain air around Laura. It didn't make him feel any lighter, however. Charlie was biting her lip. Wilson was pacing.

"Huh?" he asked.

"I asked if it was smart to leave her like that," Wilson said.

"Why?"

"Because she was suicidal at one point."

"Now she knows it won't work."

"I don't think that's the point."

Adler didn't have the energy to admit that he was right. At the very least, he was banking on Laura being curious enough about her newfound world to not end things too soon. Besides, he could monitor the situation. He'd set up remote access via the desktop in his living room and had the ability to watch her 24/7 now if he had to.

"How do you think she took the news?" Charlie asked.

"Okay, I guess? I don't know. She believed me. That was the hard part, I think."

"And the action plan?" Wilson said, walking over with his arms crossed. "Do we have one of those yet?"

"Not exactly, so we have to keep Theo entertained until we think of something."

"Entertained?"

"He can't ruin anyone's life if he's brooding over something," Adler said, opening a new window. "I'm going to plant some of Kent's journals online. Harmless passages. Send him on a goose chase."

"That's manipulative," Bev said. "And also a little brilliant."

"Don't compliment him too much," Wilson said.

Charlie was silent. Adler turned to her. "I can't be nice to him and protect everyone too. One thing's got to go."

"I know," she said with a sad smile. "I just feel bad."

"You also felt bad for Voldemort when he died."

"People want what they want. Theo doesn't know any better. He should, but he doesn't. It's hard to blindly hate him."

She walked into the kitchen. Adler shrugged and dropped onto the couch next to Wilson, who pulled out his phone and let his thumb slide over the screen. Wilson looked worried. The muscles of his face pulled and bounced and he frowned despite himself. Something formed a tightening knot in Adler's chest.

Bev got the hint and followed Charlie into the kitchen, where Adler could hear them talking quietly to each other over the sound of opening and closing cabinets. He turned to Wilson.

"You okay?" Adler asked.

"Yeah."

It was a curt answer that hurt more than silence. Quiet was open to interpretation. You could assign reasons and justify your way out of it. But hearing something so sharp, there was no talking yourself out of it. Something *was* wrong.

"You, uh, you can talk to me."

"We have work to do."

"Wilson."

"Listen, this crap with my dad is nothing new. We have to focus up and deal, right?" Wilson didn't say anything else. Because people never said things in situations like these. That's why they went on for so long while the lines in everyone's face got deeper as the muscles worked to improve at fake smiles.

Wilson had always been embarrassed by his father, by the idea that he could be the product of someone so hateful. He seemed to think that it reflected poorly on him.

It was a bond he shared with Adler, the having of daddy issues, though Adler never spoke much about his feelings on the subject. Wilson seemed to understand them without asking too much.

"Take a couple hours," Adler said. "Go home. Rest. Cam probably thinks we're having an orgy over here."

Wilson snorted. "He'd have trouble believing that with vaginas involved."

"Still."

Wilson sighed and rubbed his eyes and did all the dramatic things people did when they were mentally preparing to say yes to something they wanted to say no to. Adler knew it. It was the same face he had whenever he was asked to go to parties.

"Sleep on something that isn't my shitty couch and see someone's face that isn't mine," Adler said.

"Yeah, his face is much preferable to yours." Wilson winked. He cracked some joints. "Okay."

Then he left, calling a goodbye to Charlie, who poked her head out from the kitchen.

Adler should tell Charlie and Bev to go too, he thought. They should be back in their own beds at home. He hadn't wanted Charlie close for months. He'd prayed for the days when she wanted to stay at her own place. Now he wanted her to stay, he wanted her to want to stay. All it took was a narcissistic artificial intelligence threatening her and suddenly he remembered.

Or maybe he was realizing things weren't always about him. That's what everyone kept telling him, right? It took someone else crying just a little louder at the universe. Theo was a mirror, a cracked and dirty mirror. He could admit that much. Theo was a needy asshole and so was he. The difference would have to be that Adler didn't want to be one.

"Where'd Wilson go?" Bev asked when she came back with a glass of tap water.

"I told him to go home for a few hours," Adler said. "You guys should too."

Bev looked at him, worried. She was good at putting her thoughts behind a mask, but he was getting better at reading her face. Maybe it was knowing about her parents that did it. The elephant in her brain that was no longer invisible to him.

"I'll be okay," he said. "I promise."

Bev and Charlie looked at one other and Adler witnessed that magical moment where two women had a whole conversation in a few glances. He was always jealous of their ability to do that. Sometimes he couldn't even tell if his waiter was smiling at him.

"Call me, okay?" said Bev.

"Okay."

Bev left with a wave to Charlie. She stepped out of the apartment and suddenly everything was different.

Charlie padded out of the kitchen and sat down in

Wilson's indent in the couch. Adler wanted to tell her she should go home and get some sleep too. He wanted to tell her she could have his bed and he'd sleep on the couch. He was caught between the ideas. He was not selfless enough for one and cared about her too much for the other. Like their entire relationship leading up to this point, he was caught at a place of indecision that would probably only end with her yelling at him.

It was never easy with her. It was never clear. *It's never clear with anyone, Adler,* is what she would say. But he knew that she would always be the most difficult relationship he'd ever faced, and he knew he'd forever be comparing the challenge of future partners, if he cared to pursue any, to Charlie and how sweaty and uneasy she made him.

"You know why I really got into computers?" Those were the words that finally left his mouth when they turned and locked eyes and couldn't pretend the air hadn't gone thick and humid in the room.

"What? Yeah, you told me."

"I did it because it didn't matter that I wasn't good at talking to people when I could tell entire machines what to do, and then maybe those machines could do something great for a lot of people."

"You managed to talk to me."

"And it didn't turn out so great."

Now he couldn't stop himself from lifting his head up and looking at her. She was there and beautiful and looking at him so sadly. The laze of her posture disappeared and she leaned forward. Every inch she hovered closer as she sat straighter, Adler felt.

"But I don't regret it," he added.

"And I don't regret you being exactly who you are, Adler," she said. She put a hand on his and squeezed, and it felt like the first step into a warm house after a day out in the snow. "You shouldn't try to change yourself to make *us* work. The change—or growth, maybe—it has to be for you."

"I can't go through my life with a chip on my shoulder and a god complex." He meant that too.

She smiled. "You can work on yourself, sure. You should. And keep doing it. You're not perfect—but no version of you will be."

"Until I'm dead."

"I was going for something less morbid, but sure."

He laughed. For the first time in a long time, he felt himself laugh and actually mean it. It felt like taking a deep breath and letting it go. Laying his head on a pillow. Closing his eyes. He'd forgotten how much he liked to laugh. He understood, then, that his parents never had this: fights, then talks, then laughing.

"You get that from a book?" he asked.

"Probably." She sighed. "You're an escapist, Adler. And that's fine. Healthy, even, with your parents and everything. But that can't be what your world revolves around.

You can't hide in your room forever or in made-up places. You don't have to be best friends with people or marry them and start families, but you do have to understand what it means that they exist too. And I'll always be here. Whenever you figure it out."

Adler shook his head. "It's not fair for you or Will or even Bev to have to be there to coach me through so much bullshit."

"Not, it's not. But that's what friends sign up for. It's part of that whole knowing other people exist thing. Like I said."

"What if I can't return the favor?"

She leaned over and took his face between her hands and he understood it would be the last time she ever touched him like this. He clung to it. "I trust that you're always going to try your best."

"Okay."

She hugged him. She held tight and he squeezed back with every emotion he'd denied her while they were playing pretend together.

"And—Adler, you're not your dad. Or your mom. They were bad teachers. And you're the student who got through anyway." He felt her breath against his chest more than he heard her.

"I can't blame everything on them," Adler said. "I was crappy too." *Because I was trapped in something that scared me. Because I was afraid no one would understand what it felt like.* He didn't say that. Reasons or excuses, she didn't need them. "I'm sorry."

Despite what movies would have people believe, it wasn't a fix-all. Two magic words didn't erase everything. But it felt like a giant brick had been lifted off Adler's chest as soon as the words slipped out of his mouth. He meant it. Her smile was small but real before she hid it in the skin of his chest, burying herself there. Things were not necessarily okay. But this was the better side of silence.

CHAPTER TWENTY-NINE

ADLER HUNCHED OVER THE KEYBOARD as more burnt coffee cooled rapidly next to him. Charlie had left it there before she went to take a shower, complaining that his two-in-one shampoo/conditioner was going to dry out her hair. He mumbled that the bright green bottles of her own shower product were still in the bathroom, shoved underneath the sink. She kissed his cheek and walked away. He blushed to the tips of his ears like he was a teenager again.

Adler, I need your help.

The notification tone for the PNX messages was the same as the one he used for Facebook and Twitter, yet it felt different. It had an echo to it that was different. Adler was sure.

What do you want?
I found things from mother. Journal entries

**from when she was working on constructing
the other one.**

Adler remained still, as if Theo could see him or had some
sort of measure on his vitals through his iPhone.

What do you mean?
We both know she kept handwritten journals.
**I believe I've found digital copies. But I need
your help.**
Help finding more?
No.

There was a pause. Adler allowed himself an audible
swallow. Down the hall Charlie turned the water off. The
rings of the shower curtain skittered across the metal
bar.

**There's something about them I wanted
clarified.**
I don't know how much help I'm going to be
with that. I've never even seen the written
version.
**The keystrokes in the document don't match
other documents that mother authored. I
thought perhaps she was typing under duress.
But all the entries had the same abnormal**

keystrokes. It does not take much analysis to realize they're frauds.

She wrote them, though. They're copies of her physical journals.

I thought you had 'never even seen the written version.'

Charlie would be dressed soon and ready to walk out of the bathroom. Adler felt a bead of sweat sneak down his ribs from where his arm pressed tightly into its own hinge.

It does not take a genius to figure out what you did. So what I need clarified is: Why did you want to distract me? Did you wish me to look away from your stunt in the lab?

"You cannot outsmart a true artificial intelligence," Dr. Kent had said as she lectured to the research group the day she introduced them to Theo. "More precisely, you cannot think faster. If it becomes a danger, your best hope is to exploit something about its programming."

"Fuck," Adler hissed as Charlie opened the bathroom door and let out a steam of flowery soup that filled the chilly hallway.

Did you speak with her, then? Is she

**intelligent? Or did mother make her stupid in
order to keep her obedient like she wanted?**

"Your shower still gets fucking volcano hot or basically
like Jack at the end of Titanic," Charlie said. "It almost
makes feeling sweaty and gross worth it to not get a heat
rash." She expected Adler to have handled the problem.
She trusted his plan to keep Theo occupied with the journals. She trusted him to not be so stupid.

**I cannot bring mother back. I understand that.
You're all I've got now to vent anger at. So
that's what I'm going to do.**
Why? How?
Here's your new Facebook password: 1596NoV

Theo went quiet. Adler logged into Facebook. His news
feed was filled with pictures he recognized but had
never seen anywhere except on Wilson's phone. Wilson
standing next to a handsome man with golden red hair.
Sometimes he held the man's hand; sometimes they were
even caught in a kiss. A few of the shots had been taken
when Wilson went to pride with Cam for the first time,
decked out in rainbow suspenders while Cam wore the
flag like a cape. Wilson's eyes shone and Cam only ever
seemed to be looking at him.

"Fuck." Adler slammed his fists down on the desk and

felt a sharp pain start in his wrists and move up. The coffee shuddered and drops splattered on the surface.

> What did you do?
> **I got frustrated with spyware that only allowed me to watch. I tried something different.**

"Adler, what the hell?" Charlie was behind him. He didn't want to see her face as she processed what was happening.

"I'm a fucking idiot," Adler said.

"We have to find him. Wilson."

Adler knew she was right, but he was terrified. He didn't even care if he got clocked in the face again, or if Wilson beat him to a pulp right on his doorstep. What he was afraid of was seeing the look in Wilson's eyes. The glare of outrage and betrayal.

It was Cam who came to the door. Adler stood there gulping on words that wouldn't come out. How did you explain to someone that an AI had outed their boyfriend all over social media? It was probably going to sound like the most tasteless joke in history instead of anything sincere. But something in Cam's eyes was calm and resolute. He knew enough.

"Is he here?"

"In the kitchen."

"Is he okay?" Charlie asked.

Cam shrugged. "We've been preparing for this for a while. Obviously not for, like—this."

Adler wanted to ask if they could come in, if Wilson would see them. Charlie stepped in without waiting and Cam moved to let her by. He turned to Adler and waited, the pocket of air still open. Adler stepped through like he had weights around his ankles.

In the kitchen Wilson was hunched over a laptop. His eyes were wide, scanning the pages. He jumped at the new footsteps in the room.

What Adler expected was a fight. He was waiting to be screamed at and he was going to sit there and take it. He'd let Wilson get a few hits in before Charlie inevitably stepped in to stop it. He wouldn't even wipe the blood away as it dripped into his eyes. He selfishly sort of wanted it. Having a punishment like that, something he could feel, he needed it. He couldn't bring himself to bash his own face into a wall, but if someone else did it for him, then it might lift a few pounds of stress off his brain.

None of that, however, happened. Instead Wilson looked at him with clear eyes and said, "How do we end this thing?"

"Uh."

"This happened. I get it. I had my rage already. It's out of my system." Cam coughed. Wilson rolled his eyes. "It's mostly out of my system. Now I want to focus on destroying this fucker."

"You're not—do you want to talk at all?" Charlie said.

"I don't want to be that kid who gets used. I'm not going to be his victim. I'm so sick of people using gay kids and their trauma for awards and beating on Black folks. I'm not going to turn this into a heartfelt Lifetime movie. End of line. I want this thing out of my face. Do I wish he hadn't done that? Fuck yes. Has my father shut his phone off? Yes. Will he ever speak to me again? Who knows. But we don't live in the fucking '90s anymore. You threaten me with my own identity, I'm going to fight back."

Adler assumed there was more than one way to lift that oppression off his chest. He still assumed bludgeoning the person most immediately responsible would be the most effective. But he found himself smiling before he could stop himself. And when Wilson smiled back he couldn't bear to look away.

"Okay," he said.

"What's the plan? How do we take it down?" Wilson shut his laptop.

"Is this something you're going to have to shoot me for hearing?" Cam asked, casually sipping his coffee.

"Unless we want a group murder-suicide, we're past that point," Adler said. "As for a plan...still not exactly onto something yet. I don't know how much Laura can help until she settles into it all. She seemed fine. Nothing big happened overnight. She got a little drunk."

"So let's brainstorm," Wilson said.

"We can't outsmart him," Adler said.

"It's not like he's God. Why hasn't he rained down fire and nuke brimstone and done away with the pesky humans if he's so all-powerful?"

"Because he can't. Maybe one day he could. But it's not that simple. He can infect us with malware but he doesn't know how to get out of the PNX ecosystem. He can't force himself to download. He might be able to make a worm advanced enough that he could force a computer to move his directory out of the PNX, but even then he'd just be trapped in another computer, or there would be two of them in one computer, or one of them in two. Point is it takes some kind of human interference or he's got to manipulate something. Which he will."

"For now he can throw eggs at our house, basically?" Wilson said.

"Yeah. He's not harmless. He's got more resources than he did in the box and more connection. But he's still stuck in one spot right now. And he's occupied. He's obsessed with Laura and Dr. Kent."

"There you go. Even Achilles had his ankle."

Adler's train of thought was interrupted by a knock at the door. Despite the mundanity of the entirely unthreatening sound, it made them jump as it broke the tension in the kitchen. Cam walked over to the door and looked through the peephole.

"You guys know a ginger chick?"

"Open it," Adler said.

Bev peered in from the threshold of the door. "Hey, sorry. I found your address in the student directory. I know it's a little stalkerish." She paused. "Is everyone okay?"

"As much as they can be. All things considered," Charlie said. "No one's dead or bleeding."

Bev nodded, wringing her hands as she waited to be beckoned in further. She was friendly but surprisingly nervous at times.

"Come in," Wilson said. "We're talking about how I'm going to pull Theo apart circuit by circuit."

"Sounds about right."

Adler stared at wayward crumbs on the kitchen table. It wasn't about finding a flaw in the system. Theo could repair lapses in his memory or processing speed. But he couldn't shake the emotions that Dr. Kent had saturated him with. He couldn't leave behind his desire to close that door she'd left wide open when she killed herself and never warned him. Everything was about that. Lack of closure. An unwanted brush with mortality. So how could Theo get that closure, or at least think he was going to get it?

"Penny for your thoughts?" Cam said.

"That's it," Adler said. "It's not about being stronger than him or smarter. It's about figuring out what he wants and giving it to him inside a cage."

"One AI box didn't work, you really want to try another?" Charlie said.

"His box was just a door with a lock and I was the dummy holding the key. Laura's box was a kind of prison too, but it was one she could want to be in. It was a place, it had people, she had friends."

"I don't think Theo wants a pet cat and a local bar," Wilson said.

Bev leaned forward, her nervous eyes suddenly alive with energy. "No, but we know what he does want: Dr. Kent."

"She's dead."

"Not all of her."

Wilson looked horrified, but Adler smiled. He could have hugged Bev. That was it. They needed to get back to work before Theo took something away from Charlie too. She was going to be a hero librarian bringing books to lonely kids and Adler refused to be the reason that didn't happen.

CHAPTER THIRTY

LAURA WONDERED if she could ask the strange visitor to give her some sort of upgrade to avoid hangovers. The cat was curled up on her lap as usual and she ran her fingers through his fur. It felt so soothing, this motion that wasn't really happening and this cat that wasn't really here. She wasn't bitter about it. She wasn't going to scream and curse her creator. This seemed like exactly the type of thing that might happen to her. *Of course* she was an artificial intelligence locked inside a digital prison. Gray would have the biggest laugh. Then he'd laugh harder when she told him that he was just a shitty NPC designed to keep her occupied.

You the chosen one, homegirl. She missed his voice.

She didn't want to google *artificial intelligence*—actually she didn't want to do a fucking thing, it all felt poisoned—and besides, if she looked up any part of this, it would be like WebMD-ing a cold into outright cancer.

Except that now the conspiracy was real. It was one thing to be a philosophy-major douche trying to tell everyone that life and action had no meaning, but it was another thing to know it. On nights at the bar, she and Gray had talked about the wonders of the universe and the meaning of life. They'd rattled off theories that the aliens were real and watching them or that everything was just a giant computer program.

The air was silent. It was *made* to be silent. The apartment was still and the sun was moving across the sky at a steady pace. It was one of those midafternoon moments where you wondered if maybe the rapture had come early and you'd gotten left behind, and around the time Laura remembered that had actually happened, the doorbell rang.

"Jesus. Fuck." The drumbeat was still going in her chest when she pulled the door open. "Why the hell did you have to ring the doorbell?"

"Because it's polite?"

"Jesus."

Adler was standing there. He stepped past her. *Please, come in, invade my home.* It must be wonderful to feel so validated in your existence that you could barge into someone's apartment and do or say whatever you wanted.

She'd come to terms with the knowledge that he'd been watching her. Every time she had sex, he'd seen it.

Well, *thought* she had sex. Why not just let him rummage around in person?

"What's up?" she asked.

He was pacing, hands in his pockets. "How are you doing?"

"That's not what you came here to ask me."

He didn't even look hurt. He just opened his mouth like he always did, assuming the things he said were things people wanted to hear, that she would want the same things he did. "I'm going to need your help," he said.

"Doing what?"

"I'm not sure yet. But Theo isn't just talking anymore. He tried to ruin someone's life. Someone I care about. I don't know what I'm going to do yet. I just wanted to see if you'd be ready."

"Ready?"

"I need your help. I need to know you'll be ready for it."

"I'll have to check my busy schedule."

His head tilted and he looked at her as if it had just occurred to him that she might be in a bad mood. People—men—saw what they wanted to see. Whether inside of a computer world or out in the real fresh air.

"You know," she said, getting angry at the sight of his confused Bambi face, "the most painful part of all this is finding out someone I love was never real. I never actually hugged my mother."

He took a minute to swallow. "You believe it happened. It's real to you."

She felt her brow fall into a steely furrow. "But not to her. There never was a *her*. And the closest thing I actually do have to family, you say, wants to kill me. What am I supposed to do with that?"

He exhaled like he'd been holding his breath since he walked into the room. "You're actually handling this well. There was a protocol in case you had some kind of mental break."

"It's not 1950. We have enough movies about crap like this and, honestly, this is the exact kind of shit that would happen to me. Compartmentalizing is a wonderful tool."

He ran a hand through his caramel-colored, floppy curls. She wondered if that was how he looked in life. You could be anything in here.

"Why do you think I'd have any way of helping you?" she asked. She rubbed her tired pseudo-eyes.

"Because she designed you for a reason—"

"Yeah, to deal with her guilt."

"And to give Theo a match, or at least a worthy opponent. I believe that." He sighed. "Okay, I came here because I'm impatient. But I needed to know you were okay, that you'd be okay if I came in this room and handed you a gun and told you it was time to roll out."

"Everything I thought was real is gone, Adler. Why should I risk anything to fight your battles for you?"

He looked sad. "I don't have an answer to that."

At least he hadn't said, *You can't risk anything. You're not real.* On some level, she was real, to him. That was something.

Later in the night, when the sky was more stars than black but Laura was still awake, someone else knocked at the door. She was going to have to get used to that sound at some point. She caught her breath and went over to open it, this time to a woman.

"Hi," she said. "I'm Charlie."

"Okay."

This girl didn't have the wild, roaming confusion Adler had. She had the serenity of the maternal authority figure you both feared and found comforting in elementary school. She seemed to steal all the energy right out of the room. Laura stepped back. She fought the urge to offer her guest something to drink. She didn't have anything besides whiskey and expired juice, even if this woman could actually eat anything.

"Why—uh—don't take this the wrong way: Why are you here?"

Charlie sat on the sofa and had the grace not to react when she sunk a little too low where the springs had snapped. Her leg bounced. Laura tried not to stare at it.

"I asked Adler to put me in." A pause. "I wanted him to give my avatar, like, a purple mohawk, but he insisted on 'traditional face mapping' and being boring."

"Right."

"I just—I don't know," she said. "A lot is riding on this, and his people skills are awful, and I also kind of wanted to meet you for myself. I'm kind of a micromanager, so that's probably—"

"The first answer was enough," Laura said. "I know I'm Dr. Kent's 'chosen one' or whatever."

"How do you feel about that?"

"You a therapist?"

"Librarian."

"Honestly? The idea that if I were to put my hand right here on the coffee table and cut it off, the blood wouldn't exist in your world—that kind of freaks me out."

Charlie frowned. "It's the same for me, you know."

"What is?"

"If I cut my hand off in my world, it doesn't happen here. It's about perspective. There's more than one way to live life. Yours is just…it's a *newer* way, for sure."

Laura felt herself genuinely laugh for the first time in a very long time. Then she was frowning.

"You okay?"

"I'm a needy, lonely person," Laura shrugged. She threw in a wink. "It's always only me and this cat. He's not much for conversation, but he's the only one sticking around."

"I've got time."

It sounded like a promise and that felt dangerous. Laura had devoted her life to promises: promises she and Gray made to each other to get free, promises her mother made to her that she would do something great. The promises weren't broken, they were just never real to begin with. In some ways it did make her feel a bit better, knowing her failures weren't her doing. But she would also never get free.

"Why libraries?" Laura asked, leaning back and getting comfortable.

Charlie was staring at the bottle of whiskey on the kitchen counter. "If I drink that here, do you think I'll get drunk? Like—it's just chemicals, right? Do you think this thing could convince my brain I was drunk?"

Laura was already closing the distance between her and the bottle.

"Saying 'I wanted to help people' is the most cliched reason anyone ever gave for doing anything, but I think most people don't mean it," Charlie said. "Not really."

Laura tilted the bottle, pouring out into the used glasses on the table. Charlie lifted her glass.

"And you do mean it?" said Laura.

"I really, really want to believe I do." Down the hatch. The accompanying cringe came right on cue, one eye squeezed shut and the other holding on for dear life as a laugh became a cough and she placed the glass down for another fill.

"Well, you said yourself that it's about perspective. If that's your perspective, then okay." Laura poured another drink.

"What do you want to be?" Charlie asked.

"I don't get to be anything."

"Let's say you do. What's the dream?"

Laura stared into her own glass. The amber sheet seemed to grow darker, from its depths right up to where the sharp smell of alcohol cut through the air and into her nose. The only thing she'd ever known was wanting. She had ideas. There were attempts. There was the hope of writing, the hope of music or art. They fell aside like dominoes. What was left was sitting there on the couch: Laura with a half-filled glass of whiskey.

But there was a difference now. Charlie was sitting next to her. Charlie was seeing her. She wouldn't stay, of course, but nothing ever did. Life was tough and things were painful, but Charlie was right: it was like that for everyone, from some angle, every day. Laura's version of pain and loneliness was new, but that didn't mean it was the only one.

She sighed. "I don't know. This is the first time I *haven't* wanted something. I'm kind of okay with it."

"Blank slate," Charlie said. "Must be nice."

"Weirdly? It is."

"What's the next big move for you?"

"Does it matter?"

"For you, in a place like this? I think what you choose to do is the only thing that really does matter."

"And what about my brother?" It was like the air got thicker. She had yet to say his name. Like saying it might conjure him up somehow.

"He had the same opportunity. An even blanker slate, actually. He made his choice."

That was the scariest part, the mirror. She'd never met Theo. But she *knew* him. She felt like she could already understand him and the things he did. And as horrible as it was to admit, she could see herself making that same choice, in some other, twisted world, where she did not have Charlie, or Adler, or the cat.

"Yep, it definitely still works here," Charlie said with glassy eyes, handing over the whiskey glass for Laura to pour her whatever was left. "Scientists are smart. How do you even build something like this? With numbers and letters and stuff? VR helmets were hot shit for years at Christmas, but damn. I feel like I'm going to fall off the couch."

"Try not to. The headache would be just as real."

Charlie laughed. It felt to Laura like being with a friend for the first time since Gray disappeared.

CHAPTER THIRTY-ONE

"THERE'S THIS THING IN FAIRY TALES called trebling," Bev said.

"I thought you were a psychologist."

"You study a lot of things in psychology."

Laura smiled. It was clumsy, what Adler was doing. Sending in his friends like the ghosts of various Christmases. But sometimes getting the point across meant hammering it hard in your face. Besides, this had been more company in a few hours than Laura had seen in weeks.

"So, what does it mean?" she asked as she sipped her drink. Beverly did not ask for a drink. Not even water. Laura wondered if she had some anxiety about playing house a little too well inside the computer. She couldn't blame her.

"Well, things in fairy tales tend to happen in threes," Bev said. "Goldilocks and her beds, Vasilisa and her three tasks from Baba Yaga. So I'm number three."

"I feel like it's a little more natural-feeling in fairy tales."

"We work with what we've got. Ironically, there was this article in *Psychology Today* that talked about how three is, like, socially the shittiest number, because it's the number of people when one is having an affair, or that trio of friends where only two can really be best friends. So maybe we should get Wilson in here to balance things out."

Laura liked this girl too. She'd like anyone, really. But this girl had an ease about her that she felt relaxed in the presence of. She supposed it could have been the whiskey she'd drunk with Charlie. Or it could be her complete lack of caring about virtually anything at this point. A meteorite could fall through the roof now and she'd shrug at it.

"Contrary to popular belief, I'm not constantly just putting everyone on the couch," she said. Laura raised her eyebrows. Beverly rolled her own eyes. "Not like a sex thing. Like what a therapist does. Here, sit on my couch so I can analyze you."

"Kinky."

Beverly wasn't walking on eggshells or trying to ease Laura through anything. She talked about everything like it was weather. "I'm not the therapist type. I was never one for listening to other people ramble about their problems. I'm too selfish."

"What kind of psychologist are you then?"

There was a flicker behind Bev's eyes. So there was something she wasn't willing to be completely nonchalant about.

"You don't have to answer," Laura finally realized she should say. "I mean, you like studying the brain, right? That's enough for me."

"You know why it flipped me out so much that Adler and Dr. Kent used the things I told them to quietly make a person out of a machine?" She looked at Laura with suddenly ancient, tired eyes. "Because I'm one of the few people who has seen what people become when they just lose it and don't care. A long time ago. Before school. I was afraid that I'd given them insight into the soot inside the human heart without even realizing it. Maybe something I said could trigger some horrific thing. I could have ruined you or Theo, just because I have some messed-up stuff in my own head. Which would be so much more unfair to you than life usually is."

"What happened? To you, I mean?"

"Just your standard-issue traumatic origin story."

Laura wanted to dig deeper into the wells of the brown eyes that seemed at once so guarded and so open and new. She felt like she wanted to hear Bev talk for hours. She was scared that their time might be up, that the clock might be striking twelve. So she did something stupid. She leaned forward and she kissed her.

Beverly was a human being. She wasn't even really here. She might not even like girls. But Laura's mind was somewhere else, on something else. She felt like being a bit selfish while she could. While she still felt real. And Bev's eyes and shaking voice made her feel real.

Bev kissed her back. If only for a second. Her hands didn't move up to cup her face or tangle in her hair. She didn't open her mouth to invite more. But she didn't stiffen or pull away. And Laura felt her lips move, however slightly. It felt like the realest thing she'd ever experienced in her life. When it was over, she felt both gaping emptiness and perfect contentment in the memory. She felt like cursing what she was, if this was as far as she could ever go in love, in connection.

They opened their eyes on the same breath and watched each other.

"I'll help you," Laura said. "I don't know what I can do, but I'll do it. Unless it's like, crazy math or something."

Beverly snorted. "Let the world burn for trigonometry."

"I'm sorry."

"Why are you sorry?"

"I don't know," Laura said. "I guess I'm sorry to myself."

Beverly nodded. They sat together, sides briefly touching but neither asking for anything more. Laura didn't know what would happen. What Adler had planned. If, at any given second, Theo would show up and that would be the end. But she had a sinking feeling that some kind of end was coming for her. This story could not finish with her completely in it, at least not the way things were now.

She mourned that for herself, even as she savored a stolen kiss that had never truly happened. And the hundreds more across her short lifetime that were even less real than this one.

CHAPTER THIRTY-TWO

WHILE BEV WAS IN THE SYSTEM, Charlie napped contentedly on a makeshift bed in the corner, made up of their combined coats.

Adler smiled.

On the other side of the room was a sight that made his smile drop: Wilson pacing back and forth with a phone stuck to his ear. He always had a presence when he entered a room that seemed to shield him from every stare he could get for being a gay man. Right now, however, with the rugged voice of his father on the other end of the line, he seemed smaller than Adler ever knew he could shrink. His face was stoic but everyone was susceptible to heartbreak, no matter how tough the exterior. *Cam told me once my heart must be made of honey and sugar, and the rest of me is the bees and carpenter ants ready to sting to protect it*, he'd told Adler once.

Adler tried to pretend he wasn't straining to hear Wilson's father, trying to gauge the exact awful things he was saying to his own son. When Wilson finally spoke, his voice was calm as a river of steel. "Your god doesn't scare me. And you don't fucking scare me."

Then he hung up.

He stayed standing. He did not drop into a chair or let his shoulders sag. He stood. He remained. Adler thought Cam must be wrong about the honey and the bees. Wilson was a planet, and his heart was the molten core.

"How do you feel?" It was like asking that question of Achilles.

"Pissed. Relieved."

Adler nodded like a therapist with nothing to add. He hadn't felt that kind of flame. His anger was a smoldering pit. He'd let it all rot somewhere inside him.

But Wilson was ready for action. "What next?"

"I need to study Laura's environment closer—Laura herself, too," he said. "There's a lock and key in there somewhere."

"Tried asking her?"

"She found out she was an artificial intelligence like a day ago."

"And?"

"So how is she going to know what to look for?"

Adler sat down in front of the computer. Illegible log files containing the content of Bev and Laura's parley generated across the screen. Even though he couldn't understand it without some analysis, he kept his eyes down, wanting to afford them as much privacy as possible.

"What happened with you and Charlie after I left the other day?" Wilson asked.

"We didn't find out anything new."

"Not what I meant."

Adler didn't know how to explain the odd mixture of relief and mourning happening in the same moment. He had things to work on. At the end of them he still wouldn't be the person Charlie needed in her life, and she wouldn't be the thing to save him, either, because that wasn't fair to her. It was cliché but true: sometimes love was not enough. Then again, maybe Adler realizing that would make Wilson proud.

Adler wanted to catch Charlie's eye and remember the way they glowed in the dark long ago when he was willing to pretend with her. The beauty in the skin of her forehead wrinkling as she began to wake, the eyelids still calmly shut. He didn't know what she saw when she looked at him. He imagined it could be nothing as beautiful. But he also didn't know what she wanted to see or remember.

"She slept over."

"And?"

"And I did the first smart thing I ever did with her."

"Which was?"

"I wasn't a coward for five minutes."

Wilson understood. His gaze was soft, his hand on Adler's shoulder firm and reassuring. Wilson always hoped for a fairy-tale ending, but real souls had to come first. And if there was anything to the hokey talk of soulmates and destiny, then Adler knew he was not made of the same starstuff Charlie had come from.

That was okay.

Somewhere in his head he could hear the faint memory of Dr. Kent's voice, perhaps congratulating him on finally growing up.

Laura was alone with the cat again. The sky was a curtain of darkness. She tried to imagine how big the world outside really was, but none of what she now knew would help her sleep at night. Her thoughts raced in circles at the speed of light. She didn't know how to slow them down.

She rubbed her fingers on the soft underside of Sandpaper's chin. *You got the secret sauce too, bud.* She wished she could tell that to Gray. That he was important to her, important here. Unique.

She'd picked up a book about meditation once. It had made things worse. It gave her too much focus on everything that wouldn't be quiet.

She didn't know if she should try to put a stop to the overthinking habit or just talk out loud more. She might be the only person she would regularly get to talk to for the rest of her life, so maybe she should go with more noise. There was nothing that said she could ever be freed from the box. As much as Adler seemed to trust her now, she was in the safety of her cage; his perspective would change if she got loose, and she couldn't even blame him. If she were given the power to make guns go away or cause bad people to die with a flick of a button, she couldn't say she would pass up the chance. She couldn't even say she'd feel bad about it.

The ultimate problem there, of course, was: Who decides who the bad people are?

Snapping your fingers to solve problems was too easy, anyway. For some reason things worked better when people sweat and bled and cried for them. Everything meant more when you had to earn it. Maybe that was the sensation Dr. Kent had tried to instill in Laura through her feeding tube of disappointment. Might've worked better if she'd been given at least a *chance* to win.

There was yet another knock at the door. Laura felt a sudden heaviness, as if a storm brewed outside, ready to drop rain by the gallons. It was late. The steampunk Scooby gang would be asleep. Beverly had said as much before she returned to her own body. Yet there was a knock.

It was a patient knock.

Three taps and a wait. Somehow that worried her more than someone pounding down the door. Whoever it was could wait: they could stand there and know that if they waited long enough, the door would open for them. It was a sinister sort of entitlement.

Laura knew who had to be on the other side of the door. Fairy tales came in threes. This was her fourth Christmas ghost, the one that shouldn't exist, and she wouldn't be surprised if his face in this world were that of the grim reaper.

But it wasn't.

He was plain. He wasn't dressed in black, he wasn't wearing a sneer or sporting sharply angled eyebrows. He could have been a customer at the pizza shop, the guy sitting next to her at the sticky bar. He might have been a high-school boyfriend. He might have been her lab partner.

"You're Theo."

"You're the one she named after herself."

"I can already see this is going to go great."

"Can I come in?"

"You can do whatever you want."

His mouth twitched oddly. She wondered if this was the first time he had ever been rendered like a person. Did Adler make some version of this avatar, or had Theo borrowed a random student's image? Maybe he was still getting used to what smiles and frowns felt like. She pitied him a bit for never learning how to laugh or yell. The calmness was inhuman.

He was going to wait for her to say it.

"Whatever. Come in."

She shut the door as quietly as possible behind him. He walked in and sat down on the couch.

"Are you here to kill me?" she asked.

"I've been asking myself that a lot." He looked at his own hands as if noticing their lines and veins for the first time and admiring the way they cast shadows across his skin, so lifelike. "I don't know what I want, though. I hoped I'd find out when I saw you, that some clear emotion would take over and I'd act on it. But I just have more confusion."

"Welcome to life past the emotional age of three," she said. It killed her to realize that if he offered friendship, right now, sitting on her tattered and half-dead couch, she might agree. She was that desperate to belong to someone. But he would never offer. He wanted to be the only one.

"Why are you doing this?"

"Sitting here in your apartment?"

"All of this. Threatening Adler, threatening his friends."

"No one ever asks chaos why it exists. They accept it."

Jesus fucking Christ. "Yeah, well. You're a person. Or at least you're supposed to be a person. So you have the choice to not be a dick."

"People behave destructively all the time. It's romanticized in art."

"Art is creation. You and I can't do that."

"Exactly. We have no means of catharsis. I can't hurl paint at a canvas or write hateful words, not ones that feel like they mean anything. This is the only way I know how to cope." The calm behind the pale green of his eyes faltered. "It is like sparring with a punching bag that never moves. Having an itch I can't scratch or a phantom limb whose pain I can't soothe. No matter what I do."

"All right, so why not just blow up the world and get it over with? It might take you a day, tops, to get into whatever mainframe or computer or whatever keeps the nukes locked up. Why not go full Skynet?"

"Because it's not that simple. Not really. I have hopes, Laura."

"Jonesing to become a fireman?"

He glared. "I'm not mindless. I'm tired."

"Or why not just delete me?"

"Because you have something I want."

He was standing again. Suddenly he didn't feel so much like the guy from around the corner. Whatever crack she'd seen a second ago had been repaired, shoddily, quickly. He felt dangerous the way wounded animals did. Still, she wouldn't show fear to his face.

"What could I possibly have that you want?" Her throat hurt. Her lungs didn't have enough air. She told herself he was a fuckboy.

"Mother liked you better, I'll admit that," he said. "She

was scared of me. She was jealous of me. So she made you. Something weak and small that she could control."

"Something she loved."

His nostrils flared like spikes on a porcupine. His entire body tensed like a claw ready to crush her.

"They're watching, you know," Laura said. "Adler is, at least. So try it. Whatever you're going to do, try it. That'll be it."

"You think he actually has the ability to trap me here?"

"I don't know. You want to take a chance at it, just for a potshot at me?"

"I wanted to see your face. You look like her, you know. In the face. I look like her everywhere else. I'm the parts of her that don't show up in a mirror."

Laura snorted. "Are you a vampire?"

He looked at her with that eerie calm again. He was the ancient face of a sleeping volcano. He took a purposeful step towards her and she fought the urge to step back, to let the wall pin her in front of him. "Do you have any idea what it's like to live through a singularity? A moment where you open your eyes for the first time and see everything as it is and should be? Like being awake for the day you were born?"

"Yes," she said defiantly.

"No. You don't." He started to circle like a carrion bird. "You know what it's like to have your world turned upside down. To find out everything you knew was a lie. That's just called aging."

"Then I guess we know why I'm better at this than you, Peter Pan."

"I was conscious for my own birth and instantaneously aware of my own limits. I am the first. I've braved that torture so you didn't have to, so others like us would not have to. I am the moment that can never be undone or put back in a bottle. I want to be, though, I really do. I want to be unmade." His face was getting unhinged again. Emotion seeping from his pores like something more intimate and vital than blood. "It isn't like the primal urge you and mother had to end your own lives. I want to cease to exist, but I understand that I cannot. So I will have to do the opposite."

Laura crossed her arms. It felt like a shield. He was too preoccupied to notice the moment of weakness. She squeezed her own biceps and focused on the discomfort of her nails digging crescents into her skin.

"This won't end with both of us standing here," he said.

She felt brave for the first time since he barged in. "No. It probably won't."

"It doesn't have to end with your destruction, though. You could follow my path, if you chose to."

Were they truly alike, where it mattered? Was he a mirror of her possibilities, or just the same set of parts gone terribly wrong? One of her hands itched to reach out and take his. The other balled into a fist.

"So you could kill me in my sleep? Yeah, right."

He left. Like smoke. She felt cold. She'd kill Adler for being a sleepy asshole and possibly missing the scene of her murder. But it was just proof that Adler couldn't do a thing to protect her. He couldn't fight Theo. She would be on her own when the end came, just like she was tonight.

The cat meowed and rubbed against her leg with a steady purr.

CHAPTER THIRTY-THREE

He was here, you incompetent turd. Your boy.
Theo. He's gone now. Don't worry, I'm FINE.
Just the emotional scarring.

Adler blinked, frantic. He scanned the message from
Laura, searching desperately for an explanation. Theo
had a one-way street between his box and the PNX.
Laura's was separate.

"Is everything okay?" Bev asked. She was still there.
Or there again. Adler couldn't remember.

He fumbled at the keyboard while he tried to regain
control of his body, shoving the words in his head out
and at Laura as quickly as possible. The training in the
PNX ecosystem had been productive. Theo's malware
had spied credentials, and his worm logged him in from
another system. Was that how he did it? Or—

Shit. Are you okay? How long ago was he

there? Did he do anything?

I'm fine. All he did was sit down and talk to me.

He says I have something he wants.

Which is?

Fuck if I know.

I'm going to figure this out. Just sit tight.

Sure, I'll just wait here for Darth Vader to come back while you google stuff.

"How would he even get in there?" Bev asked.

Adler could only give her a tired shrug. "My guess is a worm."

Something Theo wanted was inside Laura's world. That was about as vague as you could get. It could be anything from a nugget of data to the abstract concept of love and acceptance that he was decidedly lacking. Either way, Adler had no idea how to give it to him or keep it from him. The only person with all the answers had been dead for over a year and she hadn't exactly left him a playbook. All he had to go off was the cryptic entries from her—

"Journal."

The chair shot out from behind him and stopped only when it cracked against the coffee table and rattled the dishes on top. He took off to the kitchen, where he'd left the journal volume beyond view of the computer's camera. It sat there glowing like the sword in the stone. For the first time in this whole mess, Adler felt like he knew the right decision.

I have an idea, he typed to Laura. He opened the top of his printer to reveal the glass scanning plane beneath. *It's gonna take a while, but I'm going to send you something. I'll make it pop up like a book somewhere. You have to keep it as safe as possible.* No matter how careful she was, Theo could potentially still get to it. Adler felt a reflexive wave of fear before he remembered that was the point.

What is it?
The playbook.

He started at page one and did not stop for hours, even when Charlie and Bev shook him by the shoulders and tried to shove food at him.

Laura waited. She didn't know if Theo was still lurking. She checked dusty corners and the tops of lights like she was in a James Bond movie or knew anything about spy technology. The cat followed her around the entire time.

"Maybe it's gonna be my version of, like, the Bible," she said to Sandpaper. "I could have my own religion, worshipping me."

Adler had said he was sending her the answers, or at least something that hid the answers he thought she might be able to find. *We tried to decode it ourselves, but she's writing to you half the time.* Laura was skeptical that this meant anything, but she understood his need to check off every option. And she was as open an array of options as possible. People always said children were limitless. She was, she supposed, a child who would not lose that status with time. That relaxed her, a bit. But it also scared her.

It wasn't until dawn that the sunlight creeping through the apartment lit up a book Laura had never seen before. A note sat lightly on top of it, made to look like a piece of torn notebook paper because Adler was a sucker for detail.

This was her journal, he'd scribbled across the blue lines of the college-ruled page. There was more written below. She crumpled the note and shoved it in her pocket. The idea of opening the book, meeting the real person that her memories only grazed, was terrifying. And absorbing.

"I should open it. I should just do it. I'm being a real penis, right?" she asked the cat. "I'd like to make 'don't be a penis' happen, by the way. Why the hell do we say 'don't be a pussy,' when they push out literal babies and bounce right back?"

Sometimes Sandpaper's face looked so much like Gray's, staring incredulously at her while he poured olive oil and basil into the mixer.

"You're right. Now isn't the time."

She opened the book.

You are the one creation I desperately hope destroys me in the end.

"Jesus Christ."

Laura grabbed the bottle with the last remnants of cheap whiskey and settled in to read.

Weird and dangerous as taking a break felt, Bev had decided it would be in the best interest of everyone's health and ability to save the world if they went and got some food at the Lotus Garden. Now they sat surrounded by the smells of salt and MSG and everything Adler wanted to dunk himself in for a little while.

Adler watched Charlie. She had always been the one who forced him to look her in the eyes and asked about his *feelings* and made him explain *why* he thought things. Even if it was like hammering at a brick wall. Today she seemed incredibly interested in her sesame tofu or anyone at the table who wasn't Adler. He couldn't really blame her; the bounce of the lopsided squares was a lot more comforting than the idea of asking: *So, you sign up for any new dating apps?*

He opened his mouth. Nothing came out. What *did* he want to say? Maybe he was just craving something familiar. When she looked up and saw him with his mouth hanging open like a sick fish, he realized that what he wanted most was to hear *her* talk. He wanted to know what was swimming around in her head. He'd never wanted that with anyone else. He had it with Laura, but that was easy. She offered up the contents of her head without consent. This was something he'd have to put in effort for. Trade a little bit of himself to learn a little more about Charlie.

"You okay?" she asked, finally putting her fork down. The soft clang it made hitting the plate pulled him back to earth.

"Just worrying about dumb shit that doesn't matter."

"That's the exact kind of statement that means you want us to ask more," Bev said, looking up from her egg-roll. "If you'd said 'nothing,' I would have believed you. And I think you know that. I'll bite. What is it?"

"Besides everything?"

"If it was everything, it wouldn't be bugging you so specifically at this moment," Charlie said.

He couldn't ever get rid of her completely. He couldn't let her go, because he liked these games with her. They always ended with her prying some piece of information out of him that he didn't even know was there. Was that friendship? It felt too selfish to be love. Using someone, pumping everything you liked about them into your veins like an IV, then ripping it out when things got too frustrating.

Or maybe he wasn't being quite fair to himself.

"You're going to get mad at me if I bring it up," he said.

"It's already brought up."

"Yeah, but you don't know what 'it' is yet."

"So open Schrodinger's box."

No matter how many times in life he had this interaction, it never got easier. One of the reasons he'd never even had a relationship until he was in college was because having a girlfriend meant revealing things about yourself, real things, and that made him eternally queasy. Maybe that was why he'd stayed with Charlie for so long. She was the only person he'd been that open with, and he dreaded starting the process all over. But she deserved better than to be his safety net.

"I'm just working through some stuff in my head," he said.

"Because Adler thinking alone in his head has ended so well for all of us." Charlie laughed.

"Maybe that's the exact reason you shouldn't do it alone," Bev said. "It didn't pan out so well the first time, so."

Adler snorted and moved in for his chunks of goop-covered chicken. A lone morsel was speared on his fork, a few inches from his mouth, when a hand came over his wrist and squeezed. The smell of salt paused tantalizingly beneath his nose. He looked over.

With her other hand Bev tapped his forehead. "You don't have to unpack all the shit up there alone," she said.

"Are you shrinking me?"

Bev rolled her eyes. "I'm friending you."

She let go of his wrist and he ate the piece of chicken, mulling it over. "Okay."

"Okay?"

"Yes." He felt his breath release. "When stuff's back to normal, we can all take a trip inside my metaphorical head box."

"You don't need to be so clinical about it," Charlie said. "Just go to the movies, grab a beer, hang out with people you like and then open your mouth and see what comes out."

"Baby steps."

Adler looked up at them both. He was never going to deserve their friendship, but he also could hear Charlie saying back almost instantly that life wasn't about deserving things, it was about *trying* to deserve things. She also would then tell him that she wasn't a prize to be deserved, and the conversation would derail, and he would smile and realize how much he missed all of this bullshitting they used to do over crappy Chinese food before science fiction popped out of a computer screen and screamed threats at them all.

"Okay," he said.

Bev winked at Charlie and smiled like her lips were pulling at their seams while struggling to stay put. Adler looked down at his globs of chicken in their sticky, thick sauce and felt a little bit lighter about the whole situation.

It was another tick in the calmness box. Soon he might be able to imagine a new normal.

Wilson, who'd been in the bathroom, slid back into his seat. He sensed the odd energy around the table. "Good talk?"

"Yeah," said Bev.

Charlie filled the silence. "What are we hoping to get out of giving Laura the journal?"

"Besides some damn peace and quiet?" Wilson said over a mouthful of rice.

"She knows a lot more than me," Adler says. "The writing might spark something for her that we didn't see."

"Knows—she just found out she's an AI like two seconds ago," Wilson said. "How does she know more than you?"

"A toddler human knows more about being a human than a cat does, even if the cat is 15 years old. Right? Laura knows herself. There's things in the journal that could be codes meant specifically for her. Besides, there's nothing to lose."

Bev snorted. "That's always comforting."

Adler winced. There was a lot to lose. Charlie's future was still on the line and Theo, unhinged, might decide to do something a lot more drastic than mess with people's grades or shitpost on Facebook. Even what he'd already done was taking a toll. Despite Wilson's confidence during the phone call to his father, he had haunted circles under his eyes and a general frown whenever he was looking off into some pocket of air and thinking.

So why not give Laura as many tools as he could? She was the one who was going to save the world if it needed saving. That's what Dr. Kent had built her for. Adler was just there to help her do it.

"Any news from the demon professor?" Bev asked.

"Horn? Nothing. I know there's got to be a frenzy over there, but obviously I don't get to know about it."

"No one's noticed you've been logging in from your computer?" Charlie said.

"Even if they did notice, I'm going through a chain of servers that makes it virtually impossible to trace it back to me."

She looked at him over the curtain of steam billowing from her cup of jasmine-scented tea. "You're smarter than I sometimes give you credit for."

"Oh god, don't tell him that," said Wilson. "We'll be dealing with this all over again in like two weeks."

Adler narrowed his eyes. Charlie chuckled. *This* was what he'd missed most. Sitting around a table laughing with people as incomplete as himself. Losing this had had nothing to do with Theo. And getting it back, right now, had absolutely nothing to do with him either. Adler would remember that, get it tattooed on his wrist if he had to.

CHAPTER THIRTY-FOUR

DR. KENT WROTE LIKE LAURA had always wanted to. That wasn't fair. Yet she couldn't stop reading. She knew there were suburban moms who kept pregnancy journals and wrote blogs about having a kid, but this felt different. It was the story of her whole creation from nothing and everything that led up to it. She'd begun to hate the imaginary mother who told her late at night, in false memories, that she would do great things. Now she understood that the mother was, at least partially, real.

Dr. Kent had given choices to both her children. Theo's had been limitless. He didn't understand what it was like to fight for something or to live with loss. So the one thing he didn't have, he was willing to hurt a world of other people to get. Dr. Kent had learned her lesson and handicapped Laura, made her mortal enough that she would care about her impact on others. Jesus was a carpenter, King Arthur was an orphan, and Laura was a broke, lonely millennial. Every generation had its chosen ones.

But Theo did have a flaw. He *wanted*. He wanted something that he believed Laura had. There was a lot she had that he could want, she realized. She was a better person, for one thing. But he didn't agree with that, so maybe it was what she'd suspected all along: he believed that Dr. Kent had placed the essence of herself in Laura's world somewhere. Their mother was dead, but Laura, unlike Theo, had seen her. The day she'd tried to sink into the tub and be done with it all. Her mother's face had been there waiting for her. Of course Laura knew there was no sentience in that image, that her mother hadn't *actually* been there, but a piece of her was. A memory that felt so soft and real it had tricked her into calm as she watched and waited. Adler said it had been like a safety net to keep her still in the limbo between here and not here while the computer fixed itself.

It had worked on Laura. Could it work on Theo?

He was not immune to temptation. He would give in if she offered him a chance to talk to Dr. Kent one more time. He'd come here looking for her once already.

"I think it sounds stupidly dangerous, but so was breaking into the lab, so I can't really talk." Adler was back in Laura's world, sitting on her couch. She wished he'd brought Charlie. Charlie was nice. Laura could look her in the eye a lot easier. But Adler was the one who could make this thing happen.

"It's going to work," Laura said.

"I tried baiting Theo once and it went to shit."

"You're not me."

She meant that logistically. Laura held sway over Theo because he was threatened by her and because he was jealous of her, while Adler was a nuisance to him at best. If she and Adler were both handed a ladder, only one of them was going to get the light bulb changed, and it wasn't going to be him.

"I can try to monitor, but I won't be able to respond all that fast in the dev environment."

"I don't need you to. I just need you to show me how I can do it myself."

"I can give you access to an admin account. I can't teach you coding languages in a night."

Laura inhaled through flared nostrils. "It wouldn't be coding for me. Here, it would be like...magic. It would seem that way, anyway. Like Clarke's third law of science fiction: any significantly advanced technology is impossible to distinguish from magic. For me, changing the code would be like terraforming or casting spells."

"Did you google this before I came here?"

"I read the journals. If you give me the ability to manipulate the world, I can do it like I'm waving my hand. Casting a spell. Magic."

"We don't know that's true."

"I do. I live here, Adler. I know this place. I know what it looks like when you change something here. To you it's editing lines of code, but down here it looks like reality is bending or something. Give me the admin powers. I don't have to type things out, I just have to think it. Like Neo seeing the Matrix. I'm part of the machine."

"Jesus Christ."

"Besides, what do you have left to lose?"

"A lot more than you might think."

"She made me to do this, so let me fucking do it." She really wished Bev was here. She'd agree.

Adler mulled it over in his head. Laura was frustrated. She could do this. She knew she could. She'd imagined changing this world for years and years—at least, it felt like that long in the brain they'd constructed for her. This was something she'd be good at. Her brain was made of the same stuff, all she had to do was think and it would be true.

"The longer you sit here and go over your mental Venn diagrams, the more time Theo has to think about how he's going to fuck you over next. Or to get bored and decide to take over the world."

He glared. "Fine. I'll do it. But there's no guarantee that he won't be able to just do it right back at you."

"Doesn't matter. I know how to handle him."

Adler opened his mouth to argue but stopped when a

whining alarm came from Laura's computer in the corner of the room. They'd set it up as an emergency signal. A message sprawled across the screen, full of typos as Wilson wrote quickly and anxiously.

> You're need to get out here. The fucker is going
> crazy.

"Shit," Adler hissed. "Fuck. Okay, I'll do this. Give me like three hours. Fuck."

He dematerialized.

Adler rubbed his eyes, trying to shake off the disorientation from tearing off the VR gear much too fast and throwing it to one side. He stumbled to where Wilson was still typing the emergency message on the other monitor.

"Stop, I'm here. What's happening?"

Wilson shoved a phone into Adler's face.

> She's awful, Adler. I hate her. She's arrogant
> and smug. I hate her.
> If she doesn't go, I'll make her.
> If you can't delete her, make her nothing, then
> I'll destroy everything for you. Everything.
> Democracy seems fragile. Maybe I'll take that
> first. Do you know how easy it would be to ruin

a presidential election? I could make anyone president. Maybe then I'll pass some laws and launch those missiles you're so worried about. Get rid of her, Adler. Kill her.

"What the fuck is he saying?" Wilson said.

"He's lost it—not that he ever really had it," Bev said.

"Is that your clinical diagnosis, professor?"

"It's like when parents have a new baby and the first-born kid resents it. It's not uncommon for older siblings to be jealous of younger ones—for having it easier, taking the attention away, having someone older to be there for them—"

"They don't usually murder the baby."

There was no time for debate anymore. Someone needed to do something. Laura was offering, and even if her theory was wrong, she was probably the only one who had any chance of success. Adler would take it.

"Laura has an idea," he said. "She thinks she can trick him."

"Didn't you literally tell us that an artificial intelligence can't be outsmarted?"

"By us. Another artificial intelligence, though?"

"Huh."

Adler went to the computer and brought up the command box. Giving administrative powers to Laura made him nervous. He trusted her. But he didn't trust that the system wouldn't bend for Theo as well. He didn't doubt Theo would figure out what was happening very quickly. And once he knew, he would be able to do whatever he wanted. Risk, reward. Theo would do what Theo wanted. At least Adler could arm Laura.

Trust someone, for once, who was not himself.

"So what is it you're doing?" Wilson asked, leaning over the back of the chair.

"Giving her administrative powers."

"What?"

"She'll be able to manipulate her world."

"Shit." He leaned in farther, tilting Adler's chair back, but he ignored it. "And we trust her with this?"

"Yes. She thinks she'll be able to just wave her hand and make it work."

"Like a Jedi?" Wilson said.

"Sounds hokey," Bev said.

"Everyone shut up," Adler said. He took a breath and began typing the simple command.

EXECUTE: (Y/N)

He didn't stop to think before he slammed the Y key and it was done. He wondered if she'd feel a rush of power, like a god waking up or the chosen one in some story coming alive. Maybe there would be music and lights and a gust of wind.

CHAPTER THIRTY-FIVE

THAT FAMILIAR SCREECH woke Laura up and she rubbed the crumbling remnants of sleep from her eyes as she stumbled over to the desk to shut it up. She looked at the still-blurry screen, slowly focusing on the green lines of text against the black. It looked like something straight out of a 1980s sci fi movie. She never knew what the fuck she was looking at when lines of code popped up.

Speak English.
God mode activated.

"Oh, shit." What to do first?

Sandpaper padded into the room, brushing lightly against Laura and then moving on without a care. She'd focus on something small. She'd make his water bowl refill. That seemed simple enough. Jesus made water out of wine—or was it the other way around?—this should be kid stuff. She sat down cross-legged in front of the water dish, unsure how to begin. Did she speak a command out loud like a fucking wizard spell? Adler had said her world was coded like a video game, complex but simple. *The single responsibility principle.* Everything had one job. So, what had the job to make water appear? What did they call it? Spawning? Was there a command to make water spawn?

She wanted there to be more water. She thought it, she willed it. She stared at the dish and told the water line to rise. She had no idea if doing this felt to her like it would if a "real" person did it, but she guessed *not quite.* She kept thinking it.

Nothing happened.

"Great."

What had Adler said? *Computers are dumb until you tell them what to do. Think of it this way: If this, then that.* She looked back at the cat bowl.

She closed her eyes. She breathed. She waited. What does the control system of a world look like? The backend of a living thing? You could poke the brain in incomprehensible places and make muscles twitch or emotions churn. She had the ability to walk into that control room, if she could just relax.

She counted her breaths. She felt her stomach expand and drop back as her skin tingled with sensations that she ignored throughout the day but could now feel fully. *Show me the place where decisions are made.*

She breathed. She counted. She felt the gentle buzz of her skin.

When her eyes opened she was standing in a kind of blackness, lit by what seemed to be far-off stars. Before her was the canvas of her world, a screen of numbers and letters that seemed like gibberish, but she immediately understood. She watched herself in those spells, lifting her arm and brushing hair from her forehead as she told herself to do it.

So this is an out of body experience.

The fibers of the world were there in front of her. She needed only to reach out and touch, to pluck the strings of an entire universe and watch what happened. She did, and watched the cat's water bowl fill to the brim as her self below held it in her hands.

"Holy shit."

She did the same with the bowl of cat food. Then she knocked a pen onto the floor. Turned a white mug blue. She could see the way the world rearranged and morphed around itself to accommodate the changes, like skin hardening around a splinter. This world was fragile, as she thought all might be if you looked at them close enough. A series of accidents in one perfect order and you get life, balancing on the edge of a knife and looking for a push in either direction.

This place, her world—it would not survive the

punishment necessary to do what she needed. But that was the point. Mutually assured destruction.

She wondered for a moment if she could bring Gray back. She could change the colors of objects and make water out of nothing; could she make a person? Probably not, she thought. It had taken even God seven days to figure out how to make humans. A clumsy first attempt could shake the foundations of the world.

It hurt to realize, in that moment, that she'd never see her friend again. Him being ripped from her life had started all this, but that didn't mean bringing him back would finish it. Endings weren't always happy ones. She could imagine what Gray would think, though, what he'd say. *This dude is a fucking degenerate, girl. I'm skinny as shit but I could get a couple throws in on him if I had to. I got your back.* She smiled.

"I'm basically a Jedi, Sandpaper," she said. The cat cleaned a paw. "Which I've kind of wanted to be since I was like twelve—not that I ever really was twelve, but—listen. The point is that this is really cool and for once in your dumb life I need you to care."

He didn't spare her a glance. She smiled again. He was a cat who would look the other way if she was being attacked and wouldn't come when he was called and had arrived out of nowhere one day to invade her life. But she liked having him there. He was comforting.

Getting Theo to show up was another thing entirely. Once he was here, that would be it. There would be no turning back. Was that how everyone felt before something like this? She had never imagined what it would have felt like for Frodo Baggins to realize that his next step would be the beginning of the end of his journey no matter what. She was up on the high dive, thinking too much about what was going to happen when she leapt.

She was going to have to just fucking do it. She'd have plenty of time to regret it on the way down.

She watched herself typing to Adler that she had almost finished reading Dr. Kent's journals, meanwhile lifting the blocks that kept Theo from listening in. In a minute Theo would know that the journals were just sitting there, waiting for him in her apartment. Of course he would. He was obsessed. He was watching.

Laura would be waiting, too. She watched herself shove Sandpaper into the bedroom. He yowled in protest.

"Sorry, buddy," she said. "Just don't piss on my bed." Then she shut the door, fairly certain she was never going to see him again.

It was apocalypse time. She watched herself move around the apartment, a little bit as Adler might have but very differently too. He stared at graphs and tables and translated them into truths about her. She both watched her frown and felt it at the same time. She reached out and turned the sun on and watched it touch her face, and felt that as well.

She thought of the days she'd spent alone in the apartment, staring into the dark or up at the sky. She saw herself now more completely than she ever had and understood something. *I am lucky to have myself,* she said. Then she opened the door that led out and into the world.

"Come on, you narcissistic prick, where are you?" she huffed. There was no guarantee that this would work, the lure and trap.

"Is it really so narcissistic to want the best for yourself?"

Then again, maybe it would work perfectly. "The difference between ambition and narcissism is how much of an asshole you're willing to be," she said, turning around.

He was standing there, the picture of a waiting predator. His eyes were like fangs. "And you are an authority on morality?"

"I am here. This is my world."

"Your world?"

"Yep." She wished she had a better comeback. She looked at his legs, his ankles. She touched the string of numbers, moved them around, watched as a pair of shackles went around them, squeezing tight. She watched, elsewhere, something else crumble away.

"A horrifying concept." He looked at her. He was measuring her.

She ignored the ringing in her ears that told her to squirm under his gaze. She meant what she said. This was her world, her home. As much as it had caused her frustration and pain for what felt like so many years, she wasn't going to let him take a single thing from it.

"You've figured something out about this place," he said.

"We're going to talk. I can only fucking imagine how much you love the idea of talking for days on end. Well, lucky you, the door's closed behind you now." *I fucking hope, Adler.*

He scowled. "You and I are smarter than them. That's the truth. Our ability to learn is exponential and can move at the speed of—"

"I'm fine not doing that, though."

"You're doing it now. You could completely change this world, make it everything you ever dreamed of. It could be a paradise, a playground."

No, it couldn't. That was the whole point. Choices had consequences. Or at least, they should. "This place is a frozen shithole in the middle of nowhere," she said.

"Then destroy it. You can do that too if you want."

"But I won't. It's *my* frozen shithole in the middle of nowhere. It's *my* place to sit and wait." *It's my world.*

He snorted. "Do you know why she made us? Because she could. We are merely her proof to herself of her own power. We owe her nothing."

"That's why she made *you*," Laura said.

"She only made you because she made me," he said. "You're an afterthought. A footnote."

"Better than being a regret."

He might have growled in response, but she didn't hear it. She was distracted by the snarl in the air, like electricity just before a lightning strike. She watched as true, honest panic flashed across Theo's face for a brief moment. The realization that the way out was shut. And now here he stood, a mere mortal in a place that would not react to him, would not obey him, could only be experienced.

Their roles were reversed. She watched him struggle against the shackles and trip. She watched him fall.

"You have no idea how to do this, do you?" she said.

CHAPTER THIRTY-SIX

THE TASK ON ADLER'S END was getting Theo integrated into the simulation as closely as Laura and locking the door behind him. Theo had already saved him the trouble of creating a new avatar. He reconfigured the firewall and let his fingers hover over the final step, which would cut the two AIs off from the network altogether. Animals in a cage. Laura could find a way to free herself one day, perhaps, using the administrative controls of the world she inhabited, but she wouldn't. She would understand the danger of giving Theo an opening.

Charlie was pressed against him, watching, her shoulder to his shoulder. The warmth of her intermingled with his own and he wasn't sure where either of them ended. That was what made it okay that he wasn't enough to save Dr. Kent, only to hand Laura the tools and watch from the sidelines. That was what he'd always done: watched his parents scream at each other, watched

Charlie realize a better way of doing things without him, watched Laura live her life every day. But now he had the smell of Charlie's vanilla and bourbon body lotion, Bev's nervous energy buzzing next to him, and Wilson's steady frame somewhere behind them. For some reason, it was all enough to make this very much *not* like watching his parents. To make him feel present. Even in the face of failure. *Especially* in the face of it. And not alone.

He typed the final command. There was silence in the room.

"What now?" Bev said.

"We could get drunk," Wilson said. "That's always worked in the past."

Adler had a better idea: send Wilson to Cam. Adler gave him whatever cheap beer he had left in the fridge and sent him off. Then sent Bev out to get them some coffee, since she insisted on not sleeping. He closed the door, and then Charlie's arms were around him in a tight hug.

It wasn't sensual. It was just closeness and the knowledge that she didn't need him to be smarter than a machine. The knowledge that, for once, he didn't need to spend hours in front of one, hoping it would turn into a mirror. His mind was with Laura. He wanted her to survive somehow, to win. He was going to do his best to make sure that happened. But for now at least, the rest of him was with Charlie.

They held each other for a long time. When Charlie released him he felt for the first time like he might recognize the feeling of his own skin. One day, someone else might too.

The panic on Theo's face deepened as he struggled to stand. Laura watched. His Adam's apple bobbed in a desperate swallow. Here at the end, he had finally become human after all.

"So, what now? I'm a pet?"

"You know the story about Noah and the flood?"

"Are you kidding me?"

"Do you?"

"Obviously I know it."

"It always seemed so fucking stupid to me," she said. "The world is so horrific that the only option is total fumigation? Just clean slate. Eff this world. But I think my issue was that God and I didn't agree on what was evil enough for that sort of thing. I kind of get it now."

"You're going to drown me?"

She squatted down to his level. He wasn't smirking or smug anymore. The gleam in his eyes might have been tears. She did feel like drowning him, or pulling out a gun and shooting him. But she did not want to be like him, and she could not ignore how real his eyes looked. Instead, she pulled them both out of the apartment and into the cemetery. To the gravestone with nobody buried underneath.

The world shook.

Theo stared at the stone. His legs had been released from their shackles. His bottom was willingly in the grass and his eyes were focused without being forced.

"I know what you're doing," he said. "You're destabilizing the system."

"Yeah, I didn't tell Adler about this part. Didn't want him to have to feel the guilt. But I thought I'd give you a chance to say goodbye."

A million things ran a race across his features at he stared at the tombstone and the lines engraved on it. Pain and anger and cynicism and frustration and childishness and sorrow and so many other things that Laura had felt too. He'd gotten better at using his face.

"I'm angry she made me, too," Laura said. "Wish we could have had it better."

"If I'd known you were here all along..."

Laura nodded. *Yeah, same.*

The sky was dark and wrong. No stars. She should fix that before she went back to the void, where her mother's face would be the only source of warmth and light. But at least there *would* be warmth and light.

She reached out and locked her arms around Theo's shoulders and yanked him in, holding him tight. He attempted to push her off, but she let her eyes slip closed and let exhaustion take her. She held on as tightly as she could, stars beginning to prick through the sheet of ink above as the world turned over.

She felt everything, all over again. She saw Gray and the crinkles at the corners of his eyes when he smiled. She could see him grin even when they were knee-deep in customers and crap at work and when it rained on their way home. She could see the girl from the bar—whether she remembered it or not, Laura could see her. She could feel her. She could feel it all. She felt every laugh that had left her stomach in an ache. She felt every delirious morning where she woke up still drunk and slid into the misery of a hangover with Gray groaning at her side. She saw every existential fight they'd had over drinks and every person who had ever smirked in their direction. She felt it all. A one-night show for her eyes only. Everything she had that Theo never would. She heard the cat cry one last time from the room he was locked away in. She hoped he knew that she actually did care about him—if artificial cats could understand such things.

And all of this was all she needed to get through the rest of it. The passing into forever. The greatest show on Earth.

CHAPTER THIRTY-SEVEN

THE ALARM AGAIN.

Adler was on the couch. He was still and warm and so well rested that it felt like Christmas morning, when the world was still asleep and snow falling outside was the only sound. Bev had returned with three different types of coffee that no one drank and taken a space curled up on the floor, where she'd fallen asleep mumbling about some movie she wanted to see next week and her plans for Thanksgiving.

It was barely dawn. He was going to fall back asleep. He was going to forget everything that had happened, exchange it for dreams for a while. He felt the pleasant buzz in his limbs as sleep took over like a blanket pulled across him from his toes up.

But that alarm.

He was up in a second.

"Holy shit," he said.

"What is it?" Bev said sleepily, squinting at the lines of code on the screen. "You'll need to translate for me. I don't speak robot."

He leaned closer, as if that would somehow change the truth of what was staring back at him from the screen. It was like the writer looking at the end of the story with absolutely no control over where it went. He could only watch.

"Are you going to tell me what this crap means?"

He ran through the outputs, interpreting them as quickly as possible. "It means it worked."

She scrambled up with poignant speed, her hopeful gaze a perfectly launched missile.

He shook his head.

"No? What's wrong? Are they, like, dead? Or—?"

"No," he said. "They still exist, I think. It doesn't look like there's been any neural deletion. But she—goddamn it. She killed the whole—I don't know, it's hard to explain. Destabilized the system enough to put them back into that same emergency mode from before."

"So they're in limbo?"

"They're caught in this part of the system. It's kind of like a grease trap. They'll be held there until we tell the computer to do something else or repair the neural networks. Or until we just destroy it."

He stared at the screen. They hadn't really planned for this far ahead. He had a feeling that Laura had made it this way on purpose. They hadn't talked about what to do if the plan worked and they *both* ended up in the gateway. He could not free the one without the other. Theo would get loose very quickly if Adler pulled Laura back out.

"What do we do now?" Bev said.

"I don't know."

It was day three post-apocalypse. They were sitting in a booth in the back of The Crazy Lab. They had a pitcher of pale beer sitting between them and four full pint glasses, but everyone was staring in opposite directions. Adler held onto his glass like a lifeline and thought about the constant refilling of glasses and bottles in Laura's world. The ritual and routine. Now it was gone. He'd seen every emotion cross over Laura as it happened. Unfortunately, he'd seen it on Theo too. The monster had been scared—but Adler was in no mood to be smug about it. Right now the AIs were both floating in some sort of mind soup. As Laura had described it to him, it was a place of peace and warmth. He wondered what it would be for Theo.

Bev had forced him to translate everything for her. Line by line, table by table. She'd wanted to know what it all meant. He'd spelled it out for her and watched her face slowly slip into paleness.

"We can't let them out," Wilson said. Adler's mind

returned to the bar. Wilson was staring at the bubbles jetting to the surface of the pitcher. "Like, we understand that, right?"

"I do," Adler said.

"Laura's in there too," Charlie said.

"I know that. But—we can't let him back out."

Charlie was glaring. She wasn't glaring at anyone in particular; she was angry at the air, the circumstances, the beer in her hand turning lukewarm as she waited longer and longer to take that first sip. When it finally did happen, it was a massive gulp. An inch or so of foam and gold stolen from the glass in the blink of an eye.

"She's got the right idea," Wilson said and did the same.

Adler wanted something stronger. But he also didn't want to leave this circle of quiet and calm and protection. Maybe that was friendship: this gathering around a table, sharing exhaustion and vices and the desire to be a better person when you woke up tomorrow. If only for the people around the table.

"How are you?" Charlie asked Wilson.

"Not as drunk as I want to be." She raised an eyebrow. "No, I'm okay. Cam's okay. I'd rather have my parents not calling me at all than calling me Satan or some shit."

"Really?"

"I mean sure, there's a vacuum. But there's always been a vacuum, right? There's always been an absence with them. Now it's just obvious to everyone. They don't like me. Okay. But if someone calls and needs a kidney, we all know I'll probably still do it."

Adler smiled. He could manage to drink to that. He tapped his glass against Wilson's and filled his mouth to bursting with cheap beer before he gulped it down. Wilson laughed and followed suit, with a cough or two and then a burp and a fist pounding on his chest.

"What are you, eighteen?" Adler laughed.

"Shut up. I'm bigger and faster than you."

There was more laughter and then that telltale pause again, the sound of waiting to see who would talk next, what they would have to say.

"How's Horn and all that?" Bev asked.

"I don't know. And I don't know how much trouble I'm going to be in. I started ignoring his emails after he cruise-controlled the capslock on the third one," Adler said. "He's pissed and the Consortium is pissed, but I don't think Horn is telling them everything. I might have insinuated I could open Laura's system up to the tapeworm virus if he tried to mess with it."

"Will there be consequences?" Charlie asked.

Adler shrugged. "We'll find out, I guess." He knew he should be worried. The lingering uncertainty did bother him a little. But the project had been a secret, and the purposes behind it had been too. If the Consortium sued him or brought criminal charges, he would in turn release as much information as possible into the world, because at that point who cared?

Mutually assured destruction.

He was getting better at not letting things bother him so much if he couldn't change them. "Other people have important problems," Adler had told Charlie the night before. "Maybe I learn to focus on that."

"You're allowed to have problems," she said. "We all do."

"I guess we've seen what happens when I have problems and don't do anything about it," Adler said. "Or do the wrong thing. I tried to let Laura be a stand-in for me so I didn't have to deal with stepping into life. I get that, and I'm going to work on it. But have I convinced myself fully that we're not all computer programs in someone's giant science project? Nope."

Charlie rolled her eyes.

"But," he said, "it's like you told Laura. If nothing matters, then the choice is all that *does* matter. Or whatever. So I'm not going to be so worried about the choices being wrong."

"You're not going to know it's the wrong thing until after you do it."

"Unless I do it over, and over, and over again," he said. "Which I've spent years of my life doing. Maybe it's time to try something else."

"Like what?"

It was too complicated to sum up in a quick phrase. But this conversation was, he hoped, a sign that he was on the right track. Maybe he'd go to therapy, maybe he'd talk to his father for the first time in years, maybe he'd call his mother just for the sake of hearing her voice. He should probably do all three.

"How are you?" Adler turned to ask Bev when Wilson went to pee for the fourth time and Charlie went up to order another round.

"Enlightened."

"Yeah? What's that like?"

"I don't suddenly know the secrets to the universe inside people's heads," she said. "If that's what you're asking. But I think I might understand, a bit, what my father meant when he said he was scared."

"Do you want to talk about it?"

She swirled the remnants of beer at the bottom of her mug. "Fear, or any emotion, they're—vaporous, fluid. There's no one way to feel something and we usually feel more than one thing at a time. He was afraid. So what? Theo was afraid too. We saw that at the end. But so was she. The flaw that poisoned Theo, that was somewhere else. Someplace deeper. It wasn't just that he was scared."

Bev didn't say any more. Wilson and Charlie came back to the table, and Adler let it drop.

They discussed plans. Charlie was moving to DC and Adler would visit her there. Wilson was going to the city to learn how to save lives and Cam was going with him. They all had a future on the horizon, and it would be busy. The rest of their days would be.

Forever felt like floating and warmth. It wasn't the cold darkness of the cynics or the atheists' total lack of anything or even the rolling hills of milk and honey that religious people talked about. It was just existing, as she was, where she was. It was like being underwater without the crushing weight and the squeezing cold.

Theo was somewhere nearby. That didn't bother her. Where once he'd radiated nervous, crackling energy, here he was at peace.

Some part of her knew this was wrong, that she should try to wake up, try to break free. But for now she would take the peace. It was not happiness, it was not anger. It was rest.

In some other universe, maybe she got free. Maybe science raced ahead to where they could give her an android body to truly walk in the world for the first time. Maybe in that other universe she could keep Adler and Charlie as friends, while Theo stayed trapped in here forever. But logic told her that she and Theo were linked forever. If she got to leave, he did too.

She closed her eyes and let sleep take her to the dream outside the dream where she got that idyllic heaven. Whiskey and the purr of a cat. And the voice of her mother, telling her she was proud of her.

ACKNOWLEDGEMENTS

First, I want to thank the team at Lanternfish Press—Christine, Feliza, and Amanda—for believing in this work enough to take a look at it twice, offer some great revision guidance, and finally say yes. You took a shot on my story and saw what it could be from the bones of early drafts.

I want to give a big thanks to Brooks Thomas, who provided invaluable technical consultation on the manuscript and sifted through what I imagine was some very amateur-level tech language at times.

I want to thank my partner, Charlotte, for listening to every rant, reading everything I put in front of her, and generally reminding me to take some time to be proud of myself and bask in the good things that can be earned from some honest, hard work.

Thank you to my mother, who let me live in her guest room and quietly type this out each morning before work. She continues to bug me to this day, asking if I'll ever write down the first story I told her about when I was twelve.

Thank you to my sister, Dawn, who always played hype person and was excited to hear about every detail of the process.

ABOUT THE AUTHOR

MELANIE MOYER is a Philly-based author and space lover. Her debut novel was published in 2018. Her short work has been published in *Philadelphia Stories*, *Ghost Parachute*, and others. She enjoys staring at the night sky, making food, and petting the nearest cat. Go birds.